MW00700567

BURN SO BRIGHT

···

JENNIFER BERNARD

Copyright © 2017 by Jennifer Bernard.

All rights reserved. No part of this publication may be reproduced, distributed or transmitted in any form or by any means, including photocopying, recording, or other electronic or mechanical methods, without the prior written permission of the publisher, except in the case of brief quotations embodied in critical reviews and certain other noncommercial uses permitted by copyright law.

Publisher's Note: This is a work of fiction. Names, characters, places, and incidents are a product of the author's imagination. Locales and public names are sometimes used for atmospheric purposes. Any resemblance to actual people, living or dead, or to businesses, companies, events, institutions, or locales is completely coincidental.

Book Layout ©2017 BookDesignTemplates.com

Burn So Bright/ Jennifer Bernard. -- 1st ed.
ISBN 978-1-945944-05-5

For my family.

CHAPTER 1

Suzanne Finnegan always had a plan. And a backup plan—sometimes several. In her opinion, planning was essential for a happy life and for success in anything. Take the Y's Outdoor Education fundraiser she'd spent the past few weeks planning, and which was now drawing raves from the guests. Words like "spectacular," "sensational," and "fabulous" were wafting through the well-dressed crowd gathered on the grounds of the Jupiter Point Observatory. Every detail, from the damask tablecloths to the pink champagne flutes, was exactly how she'd imagined it.

Every detail except one. Logan, her fiancé, was once again missing in action.

She fixed her gaze on a red balloon, part of the bunch that marked the entrance to the kids' area. Not only was Logan missing, but he'd dropped a bombshell on her right before the start of the party. She'd had to shove it aside so she could focus on her job. But now that everything was underway, his shocking words kept flooding back to her.

Free pass. *Free pass.* FREE PASS???

"Okay, sweetie, this is getting dire. You have to stop glaring at your party guests." Evie McGraw, Suzanne's newly in love and disgustingly happy cousin, steered her behind a potted ponderosa pine. "What's going on with you? You've been planning this event for so long, and it came out great. You should be dancing a jig right now."

Suzanne could barely look at Evie. The glow of her joy was just too much. "I don't want to rain on your love parade, Evie. Just go be happy and don't worry about me."

Evie's silvery eyes widened. "Let me guess. Is it Logan?"

If she wasn't such a genuinely kind and compassionate person, it would be hard to be related to someone as beautiful as Evie. But Suzanne had very few family members who had actually stuck around in her life. So her relationship with Evie meant the world to her—more than Evie knew.

"You can skip the 'I told you so.'" Suzanne signaled to a passing waiter, who nodded as he headed to refill his tray of sushi rolls. "I'm sure it's just normal engagement jitters."

"I didn't say anything."

"It's written all over your face in big capital letters. I know you don't like Logan. Hang on." With an eagle eye on the area roped off for kids' games, she spoke into her little walkie-talkie to one of the other volunteers. "Someone needs to liven things up in the kids' area. They look like they just got assigned homework."

Evie raised her eyebrows. She was wearing a lilac linen sheath dress and had a camera slung over one shoulder. "So back to those jitters..."

Suzanne whooshed out a breath, wishing she could expel all the hurt in her heart with that one exhale. "I don't want you to be mad at him. That's *my* job."

"I promise to *try* not to, is that good enough?"

Evie waited patiently, but Suzanne wasn't quite ready to spill her news yet. "Where's Sean?"

At the mention of her new boyfriend, Evie lit up. "He'll be here. They just got back from a fire in Utah this morning. They have to debrief, unload their gear, do inventory, all sorts of details like that. But they're planning to come."

"They?" A funny little jump of excitement twisted in her stomach. Sean Marcus, Evie's boyfriend, was the leader of the new wildfire crew that had just moved into Jupiter Point. Through Sean, Suzanne had gotten to know the other members a bit. Actually, one of them in particular had quickly made himself one of the most popular people in town. Josh Marshall's charm did nothing for her, of course. She had no idea why everyone liked him so much. All he did was joke around like a boy who'd never grown up. A six-foot-plus, blond-streaked, more-fun-than-should-be-legal boy.

"He's bringing a few of the guys, I'm not sure who."

Oh great, now she'd be wondering *if* and *when* Josh was going to show up. Ugh—never mind Josh. He wasn't her type of person. He wasn't serious about himself and his future.

Not like Logan, who was studying for the California Bar Exam and was sorting through job offers. And who had just knocked her world upside down.

"Have you ever heard of the concept of a 'free pass'?" Suzanne lowered her voice to pose the question to Evie, who was in the midst of framing up a photo of the strings of twinkle lights shaped like stars.

Evie clicked off a few shots. "In what sense?"

"Well, Logan just dropped this whole idea on me. He says that since we're getting married, and we're about to swear off all other sexual partners for life, we should agree to a free pass now, while we're still just engaged."

Evie lowered the camera, revealing an expression of horror. "You might have to spell this out for me. You're saying he wants to sleep with other women until you get married?"

Suzanne winced. It sounded terrible when Evie phrased it like that. "He's being practical. We're still young. Isn't it better to get it out of our system now than to cheat later on?"

"Why isn't it cheating now? He's your fiancé."

"He says it's only cheating if he's doing it behind my back. He doesn't want to do that, so he came to me first. He said that's the only part of being married he's worried about. So he wants to deal with it now rather than later when it could ruin our relationship."

It had made sense when Logan explained it—sort of.

"Think of it as a preemptive strike," he'd said on the phone, just minutes before the party started. "It's better to face facts head-on. I'm a man. I'm facing a lifetime ban on sex with other women. That could breed resentment and everyone knows resentment is a relationship-killer."

Luckily, the conversation had taken place on the phone so he couldn't see her slamming her cell phone repeatedly into her passenger seat. "I don't know, Logan," she finally managed when she got control of herself. "What's the point of being engaged if you're going to..." She didn't even want to say it out loud for fear she'd lose it and yell at him.

"Not just me. This applies to both of us. Listen, sweetheart. You're the one I want to marry. Our life is going to be exactly what you always wanted. Everything will be how you planned it *after* the wedding. I'm being very honest with you. Isn't that worth something?"

Yes? No? She didn't know what to think. Her mind had been in a whirl ever since that conversation. Logan was everything she wanted in a husband—or so she'd thought. He had the same goals she did. A stable, successful life, a home, eventually a family. Not too soon, they both agreed. Only when the time was right and they could afford to give their children absolutely everything they needed. Her dream was to give her kids the happy childhood that had been ripped away from her. And Logan could make that happen.

But only if she went along with this free pass idea. The alternative—losing Logan—ugh, she didn't want to consider that. She was tired of dating, tired of facing life alone. She'd been alone since the age of fifteen. Everyone thought she was the town social butterfly, but in her mind, she was

5

more like the town chicken with its head cut off. Logan's proposal had made her so happy. So what if their chemistry was off and they didn't laugh at the same things? They *wanted* the same things. Logan was her future. She needed to be practical.

No, she wasn't going to let this little pothole derail their relationship. *Stick to the plan.*

"He's trying to save our relationship from future resentment," she told Evie with all the confidence she could muster. "I think it's very reasonable."

"He's a lawyer." Evie put her camera lens cap back on. "He can make anything sound reasonable."

"Yes, but that doesn't mean it *isn't* reasonable."

"Well, how does it make you feel? That's the most important thing."

Like screaming. Like stomping her feet. Like throwing Logan's diamond ring down a gutter...well, maybe not that. Suzanne appreciated nice things and didn't like waste. "Like I just slipped on a banana peel and fell on my ass," she admitted.

"In that case, you need one of these." Their friend Brianna appeared, with three champagne flutes clutched in her hands. She handed them out one by one.

Normally Suzanne didn't drink during an event that she had planned. But this one was basically done, and dammit, she could use a mood-lift.

She took a sip. "Just so you know, you are enjoying the best of Napa Valley's new sparkling *champenoise*, with a hint of blackberry liqueur, just enough to provide a refreshing tartness but not enough to overwhelm the palate."

Details. It always came down to details.

Brianna took an enthusiastic swallow—more of a gulp, really. "Nice. Great party, Suzanne. I just wish the kids were having more fun. Can't we set up a volleyball game or something for them?"

Suzanne drained the rest of her champagne and squinted in the direction of the play area. Half a dozen kids slouched around two picnic tables. Most were staring at their phones, looking bored. "I know, they look like they're on detention. I arranged for balloon animals and face-painting. But none of them are going for it."

Now that she looked closer at the kids, she saw they were older than she'd anticipated. None of them had a speck of paint on their faces—not counting the emo-Goth boy with all that black eyeliner. The balloon animal *artiste* sat off to the side, looking at his own phone.

"I think they're a little past balloon animals," Brianna said dubiously.

Suzanne tugged her lower lip between her teeth. Okay, so that *one* detail hadn't gone so well. "Oopsies. You know, I wouldn't mind a balloon animal. A sad panda or something." She craned her neck, looking for another waiter with more champagne.

Evie and Brianna both laughed. "You're adorable, do you know that?" Brianna pinched her cheek, which seemed ironic considering that she was about a foot shorter than Suzanne. "Do you want me to get something going for them? Charades is always fun."

Suzanne shrugged and tipped the flute to her mouth. She couldn't drum up any enthusiasm for this party anymore. Logan had promised to be here to lend support. Instead he was in Palo Alto, probably taking full advantage of his free pass.

Details. Details were important. What did the details say about Logan?

No. It didn't matter. She and Logan would work it out. They had to.

She beckoned to Seth, one of the waiters, who hurried over to them with another tray of drinks. She took one and downed about half of it before even realizing it.

"How's the champagne supply holding up?" Suzanne hiccupped. "Asking for a friend."

Evie and Brianna exchanged glances of alarm. So silly. She could handle a little champagne. It took the edge off, that was all.

"We're in good shape, boss." Seth gave her a conspiratorial wink. "Enjoy yourself, you've earned it. The party came out great."

She smiled at him, the fizzy effect of the champagne making it an extra-wide grin. "Dyn-o-mite."

She giggled and swallowed more delicious fizziness. Had she really just said "dyn-o-mite"? God, champagne was the best thing ever invented. Logan didn't know what he was missing. He could be at her side, watching the sun glide toward the Pacific, listening to the happy chatter of party guests, admiring the perfection of her meticulous planning.

"Oh wait!" Brianna said suddenly. "The kids don't need me. They have hotshots."

Suzanne jerked back to attention. Sure enough, three of the new Jupiter Point Hotshots—Sean Marcus, Josh Marshall, and Rollo Wareham—were pushing aside the balloons and striding into the kids' area. In jeans and flannel shirts, they looked like wild men compared to the rest of the guests. Rugged good looks didn't begin to describe it. Their physical fitness level was insane. They all looked like they could have run up the mountain to the observatory without breaking a sweat. For all she knew, they had.

"Oops, I forgot to tell them this was a formal party," Evie whispered. "Sorry, Suzanne." She raised the camera and took a few more shots. "Make that sorry not sorry. Good Lord, they're photogenic. Every last one of them."

Suzanne heaved a sigh, pretending to be annoyed. Better to look annoyed than fascinated, which was her usual response to the sight of Josh Marshall. Had he even combed his hair? Did he *ever* comb his hair? It always tumbled around his face as if he'd spent the day at the ocean. Or just gotten out of bed. Which, given the amount of flirting he

9

did, was pretty likely. And did he always have to have that teasing sparkle in his eyes and that "I love trouble" grin?

Would he ever bother to grow up?

"It's okay. I'll handle it." She took a fortifying sip of champagne, then beelined toward the hotshots, ignoring Evie's and Brianna's attempts to stop her. This was her event, damn it, and Josh Marshall had no business cruising in here as if it was some kind of block party.

She ducked past the balloons at the edge of the play area. One of them swung back and bumped her in the nose. She brushed it aside and blinked her eyes back into focus. Josh—of course it would be Josh—had caught the entire embarrassing moment. A wide grin took over his face. That smile would make the panties melt off any girl, Suzanne most definitely included.

Except she refused to fall for that carefree vibe of his. It was *so* not her thing, at least not anymore. Carefree was for kids.

"What are you guys doing back here?" she asked as she reached them.

"Checking out this rockin' party you have going on." Josh tucked his thumbs in his front pockets and cocked his head at her. "I'm all for outdoor education." And he winked.

Winked.

As if outdoor education was something naughty. And of course now all sorts of images were hightailing it through her brain. Josh at the beach, in nothing but board shorts.

Josh jogging shirtless up a mountain trail. Josh chopping wood, muscles flexing as he wielded the axe—and guess what? No shirt.

She shook her head to clear it of all those unwelcome Josh Marshall images.

"The outdoor education is for the kids," she said stiffly.

"Yeah, I hear this whole event is about the kids." He cast a glance at the group of young people who had finally put away their phones and were listening to the two of them. "Having fun, kids?"

Shrugs. A few "whatever" glances. Suzanne sighed and admitted defeat. "Suggestions are more than welcome. You're more or less still a kid, right, Josh?"

Sean laughed, then hid the sound behind a cough when Josh glared at him. "I'm...uh...going to say hi to Evie." Sean whisked himself away.

Josh dug into his pocket and came up with a small, well-worn leather sack that fit into the palm of his hand. He addressed the moody group of young people.

"You kids like hackeysack?"

Suzanne started to laugh in anticipation of the mockery that suggestion would receive from the kids. But that wasn't what happened. Their faces lit up and they gathered into a loose circle. Josh flashed a grin at Suzanne.

"You can thank me later," he whispered. "Actually, you can thank me now by bringing me a beer."

"This isn't a beer kind of party," she snapped. "I budgeted five hundred dollars for kids' entertainment and you're telling me all I needed was that little sack?" She pointed at the item in his hand.

"Please don't insult the hack," Josh said solemnly. "Right, kids? The hack is a thing of beauty and a gift to all mankind."

The kids, who had all clearly been brainwashed, laughed along with him. How did Josh do it? He had them all eating out of his hand.

Disgruntled, Suzanne watched as he dropped the little pouch onto his foot and flicked it into the air. The emo boy caught it on his knee, then kicked it across the circle to someone else.

"He's like the Pied Piper," Rollo murmured in her ear. "Just go with it."

"I need more alcohol," Suzanne muttered.

"Coming up."

Rollo must have departed, because she didn't hear him say anything else. Her attention was riveted on the sight of Josh playing with the kids. For such a physically tough guy, he moved with an amazing amount of grace. Apparently you weren't allowed to touch the hack with your hands, so the players had to twist their bodies or fling their feet into the circle to snag it. This gave her an excellent opportunity to watch him in action. His reactions were so quick, his movements incredibly nimble. He was like a cat out there. A

lean one, with lots of muscles, and a smile that made everything more fun.

Another flute of champagne appeared in her hand. "Oh, I
shouldn't," she told Rollo. "I'm actually working."

"And you're doing an awesome job." He clicked her flute
with his and drained his glass. "Everyone's raving about the
party." He indicated the sweeping view of the Pacific off in
the distance. The setting sun spread liquid gold across the
horizon. "Nice setting."

"I can't take credit for the sunset," she pointed out. "Or
for the kids having so much fun. They were bored out of
their minds before. I guess I should thank you guys."

"Thank *him*." Rollo gestured toward Josh. "Handy guy to
have at a party."

Fine. She probably should thank Josh. He'd corrected the
one big oversight in her party planning. And you really
couldn't stay annoyed with a guy who was doing a scissor
kick in mid-air while his blond hair flew around his face.
Feeling suddenly charitable, she raised her voice. "Thank
you, Josh."

Her gratitude seemed to trip him up. He got a foot on
the hack but then whipped it in the wrong direction—right
toward her. With perfect aim, it winged through the air and
dinged her champagne flute.

Champagne splattered all over the front of her favorite
cream silk dress. The best thing about the dress was the little mesh cutouts at the waist and neckline. With champagne

drenching her, it was now the worst thing about the dress—the liquid went right through the mesh onto her skin.

She gasped in shock and stared down at the wreck of her dress. Then looked up and met Josh's apologetic gray eyes.

How dare he show up here and ruin everything? Well, everything that hadn't already been ruined by Logan.

Someone deserved to be yelled at. But Logan wasn't here and Josh was.

She shoved her glass at Rollo and marched toward the gray-eyed hotshot.

CHAPTER 2

Josh braced himself for Suzanne's furious approach. She was clearly a little buzzed; it looked like she'd forgotten the party, forgotten the Jupiter Point movers and shakers gathered on the observatory grounds. He had to save her from making the situation even worse.

As soon as she got close enough, he slipped his arm around her waist, nudging her off-balance so she was forced to cling to him. Moving quickly, he steered her away from the kids' picnic tables and gestured to Rollo to take over the hackeysack game.

He walked her in the direction of the observatory's lobby, taking care to smile at everyone they passed, as if an indignant Suzanne wasn't spluttering next him.

"What do you think you're—"

"Keep it cool, Suzie Q. I know you want to whip my ass, but that'll just get people talking."

"I don't care," she said through gritted teeth. "It would be worth it."

"Fine. I'll let you do whatever you want to me. In private." Most women he knew would be all over that offer. But Suzanne always put him off balance, even when she'd had too much champagne.

"I don't want to do anything in private with you." She brushed at the front of her dress. "You're more than enough trouble in public."

"It was an accident. Obviously." He steered her through the door of the empty lobby. A display of photos taken by the observatory's infrared telescope populated the cavernous space. "I never like wasting champagne."

"You think you're so cute and funny," she hissed. "You're at the party for one minute and my dress is completely ruined. You're like...like...Loki. God of Mischief."

"Really? Aw, you're too sweet."

At Suzanne's look of pure fury, he backed down.

"Seriously, Suzanne. I was just trying to give the kids some fun. They looked like they were at a wake."

"You're not helping." The corners of her mouth trembled and turned down. "I worked really hard on this party."

Oh bloody hell. Was she going to cry now? "Here's the bathroom," he said quickly, opening the door for her. "Go on in, I'll be right back."

"Where are you going?" Halfway through the door, she looked up at him with a look of alarm. Her eyes, he noticed suddenly, were really something. At first they looked blue, but up close he saw they had more depth in the color, more of an ultramarine, like the ocean above a sudden drop-off.

"To the bar." When her eyes widened with indignation, he clarified. "Club soda is the best way to get alcohol off fabric. Tried-and-true method from the ranch lands of Texas."

"Fine. Just hurry. If you see Evie—"

"I'll tell her we have it under control and she can go back to making out with Sean. They haven't seen each other in a week."

She nodded and whisked behind the door, closing it firmly behind her. As he headed back out to the bar, he acknowledged the contradiction that Suzanne was both his kind of girl, and a girl he knew to avoid. He had a weakness for long, lanky blondes, especially sassy ones like Suzanne. He enjoyed teasing her to no end, and loved the fireballs she lobbed back at him. Suzanne could definitely hold her own in verbal combat.

As for the avoiding part, that was simple. Suzanne was engaged. Besides, she'd made it crystal clear that she looked on him with utter disdain. She never laughed at his jokes. In fact, she seemed to take offense at the entire concept of joking around. Sometimes he wondered if he'd accidentally insulted her at some point without knowing it. He'd even questioned Evie about it over dinner once.

It shouldn't bother him—there were plenty of other girls to hang out with in Jupiter Point and elsewhere. After a solid week of back-breaking firefighting in the Utah wilderness, during which the crew had kept a summer wildfire from taking out an entire town, he was exhausted. All he wanted to do was sleep for the next twenty-four hours. But when Sean had mentioned this party, and he'd realized Suzanne would be here...well, he'd hopped in the shower and dragged his ass to the observatory.

Face it. He had a bit of a thing for Suzanne. She got his motor running with her sass and that long blond hair she liked to fling over her shoulder. She was like a tall, refreshing glass of extra-tart lemonade on a summer day. Tangling with her was like a dive into whitewater rapids—exhilarating but also humbling.

And *that* was why it was best to avoid Suzanne. Unrequited interest in a girl who was engaged? No, thank you. He preferred to keep things nice and easy, all around. Better for everyone.

At the bar, he grabbed a handful of napkins and a bottle of club soda, then quickly made his way back inside the lobby. He tapped on the door of the restroom. "Room service," he called.

"Ha ha." She swung open the door, more vigorously than she probably meant to. Because there she was, in her underwear. Her tiny, silky, sexy underwear. "Eeek!" She shrieked and pushed it closed again. "I didn't mean to do that," she called through the barrier. "This door is very well-oiled."

Josh stared blankly at the blond wood of the door, which was about two inches from his face. He didn't even see it. All he could see was the mental image of Suzanne in all her lean, golden near-nudity. Her long hair had come down from its uptight knot and flowed freely over her shoulders in lemony streams. She still wore her high strappy sandals, which made her legs look absolutely endless. Suzanne Finnegan was a goddess. A freaking goddess. A prickly, beautiful, *engaged* goddess.

And now she was saying words like "well-oiled." *Avoid, avoid, avoid.*

"I'm...uh...going to leave the club soda right outside the door, okay? There are some napkins here, too, just in case." Did his voice sound as strained to her as it did to him? He adjusted his jeans over the very uncomfortable bulge that had developed.

"You said you were going to help me."

"I *am* helping you. I got you club soda. It's right here, next to the door."

A pause, during which he took a careful step back.

"Josh Marshall, haven't you ever seen a girl in her underwear before? It's no different from a swimsuit."

"Of course I have. Many girls, in and out of underwear." He closed his eyes, hoping the image of mostly naked Suzanne would disappear. It didn't. Apparently it was branded onto his retinas forever.

The door swung open again and Suzanne poked her head out. She looked right, then left, then grabbed his wrist and yanked him inside. The door swung quietly shut behind him.

Damn, that thing really *was* well-oiled.

He glanced around the bathroom—anything to avoid staring at Suzanne. "I was always curious what women's restrooms were like."

"Don't be gross," she said. "Or I won't make out with you."

"Excuse—what?" He squinted at her. Even through narrowed eyes, she looked mouthwatering. He didn't know which part of her statement to address first. "I'm not being gross."

"Good." She reached for the front of his shirt and twisted her hand in it, tugging him closer. "Let's make out."

He leaned backwards and dug in his heels. Normally he'd be very interested in that offer, but there were a few things he wanted to clear up first. "Uh...why?"

"Why not? Don't you want to?" She released him and put her hands on her hips. Her slim hips in those tiny silk boy shorts.

He groaned silently. All she had to do was drop her gaze to his groin and she'd see how much he wanted to...and...too late. He clenched his jaw under her scrutiny.

"Ah. I see that you do." A mischievous smile played across her mouth.

"That doesn't make it a good idea. Aren't you engaged?"

The smile disappeared, as if he'd reminded her of something sad. "He wouldn't mind."

"The hell he wouldn't. Any man would." If he was engaged to Suzanne, he'd rip apart any man who dared to make out with her. Of course, he had no intention of getting engaged to Suzanne or anyone else.

"Logan says that we should have a free pass up until our wedding day. He thinks it's good for our relationship." She leaned toward him, her lips pursed. He caught her by the forearms and held her away from his body. If she got too close, he'd no longer be interested in doing the right thing in this situation.

"First of all, how much champagne have you had?"

"I wouldn't mind a little more. Next question."

"Okay, even with this crazy 'free pass' thing, what makes you think you won't both regret it if you actually go through with it?"

"Hang on now, big guy." She lifted a finger and waved it drunkenly in his face. "I've definitely had too much champagne for a long question like that. Short ones only, please."

"All right. Why me?"

She frowned up at him, those pretty eyes darkening to a deep sea-green. "What?"

"Why use your free pass on me? You don't even like me."

She leaned forward and spoke in a conspiratorial whisper. The girl definitely had a good buzz going. "Guess what? I *do* like you, Josh Marshall. You're very cute. And I bet you look even better without all that." She waved at his torso, apparently indicating his clothes. "Besides that, you're *here*. And Logan isn't. And he was supposed to be here so he could see what a great job I did, but he's always busy and sometimes I don't even know why he proposed to me because most of the time he's at Stanford and he only comes here on weekends and sometimes not even then, and I just...I just...want someone to *be* with. I don't like being alone. I've been all alone forever. Do you know what that feels like?"

Her gaze clung to his. A sheen of tears turned them into jewels. His heart gave a slow heave, like an engine turning over. He didn't want her to cry. He couldn't stand to see her in pain. He'd never seen this side of Suzanne before. Usually she was quick with a comeback, with a breezy confidence about her. He'd assumed that was who she was—the girl who had it all together, who knew exactly what she wanted out of life and how to get it. He'd never imagined that she might be vulnerable like this.

"I do," he said gently. "I know what that feels like." He slid his hands up her arms, along her smooth skin, until he reached her shoulders. "But you're going to get married, and then you won't be alone. So why would you take a chance on messing that up?"

She sniffed and blinked back her tears. As he watched, he saw the truth of what he said sink in. *Way to go, Marsh. A hot girl is practically naked in front of you and you take a pass.*

"You may have a point." She spoke in a small voice as she wiped away a tear that had managed to sneak through. "But he would never know. And he gave me the free pass. I think he wants me to do something so he doesn't feel guilty."

Wow, the red flags with this relationship were really piling up. This free pass concept seemed a little fishy, if you asked Josh. Either commit to a girl or stay single. Don't try to have it both ways. Of course, he had no doubts about which camp he belonged in. Team Single all the way.

But maybe he just didn't understand the mysterious ways of engaged couples. "How about a kiss?" he suggested.

"Just a kiss?"

"Yes. Just a kiss. Not enough to cause any trouble, but enough so you can know that you did something with the free pass."

She ran her tongue across her lower lip, which was pink and plump and practically begging for his touch. "No one needs to know except us."

"*We* don't even have to know. We can pretend it didn't happen if we want. It's just a kiss. We'll probably be laughing about this tomorrow."

Laughing was better than crying. With relief, he saw her expression brighten and her tears evaporate. "You're really smart, Josh! That's a great idea. Just a kiss. No biggie."

"Exactly. No biggie," he agreed.

"No harm, no foul."

"Don't ask, don't tell."

"Easy come, easy go."

"One up, one down."

"What?"

He shrugged, having no idea what he'd meant with that one. "Baseball, maybe?"

"Come here, you." Grabbing his lapel again, she yanked him toward her and this time he didn't resist. He slid his hands down to the soft indentation of her waist and snugged her against his pelvis. She lifted herself onto her toes and craned her neck, straining toward his mouth. He bent his head—she was so tall in her heels that he barely even had to—and for a long moment simply hovered his mouth over hers. Anticipation crackled between them. He felt her nipples harden against his chest. His cock was doing exactly the same thing.

If they were going to have only one kiss, he might as well make it a good one.

He ran his hands up her back, savoring every smooth inch of that long, elegant curve. When he reached her head, he cradled it in both hands, tilting her face to the perfect angle, where he could devour at will. Her eyes drifted half-closed and her lips parted. She looked as if she were dreaming.

He brushed his lips against the soft, tempting mouth open before him. An electric vibration sizzled directly to his brain. He slid his tongue along the sleek flesh of her upper lip, then nipping the lower one until she opened farther, on a soft moan. He tasted champagne and a sweet wildness that had him driving deeper, sweeping his tongue inside the delicious cavern of her mouth.

She wrapped one long leg around his hip. He felt the heel of her shoe against the back of his leg—the visual of that nearly drove him nuts. He clamped a hand on her silk-covered ass and pressed her mound against his groin. His cock pounded with nearly painful arousal. He bent her over so he didn't lose his balance as he ravaged her mouth.

Moaning, she grabbed the back of his shirt and held on tight. Being Suzanne, she gave just as good as she got. Their tongues touched and teased in a wicked twining dance. Every stroke generated more electricity, more sparks, more need. The shock of it made him light-headed, and he had a sudden image of the two of them floating in zero-gravity space, locked together in a kiss as hot as a supernova.

Quick footfalls sounded outside the door and a female voice called, "I'll be out in a sec. Don't you go anywhere. Oh, look, someone left a club soda out here."

They broke apart, staring at each other in a sort of daze, trying to reorient themselves. "Someone's coming," Suzanne finally whispered.

Josh shook himself out of his stupor. Sweeping her off her feet, he whisked her into the stall where she'd left her dress. He pulled the door closed behind them just as the outer door opened. He squeezed his eyes shut, cringing as the woman hurried to the sink, her heels clicking on the tile floor.

"Hi, it's me," the woman said. Suzanne pulled a worried face, but Josh put a finger to her lips before she could say anything. "Yes, it's going fantastic, like a dream. All signs point to getting lucky tonight."

Suzanne clamped both of her hands over her mouth, eyes wide with mirth.

"You were right. I'm definitely going commando from now on. It just puts you in the mood, you know? I think he can sense it. We're connecting on a whole different level. Like, pheromonially. Like, my pheromones are speaking to his pheromones. You know? We're pheromonially compatible."

Suzanne's shoulders were quaking with silent laughter. Josh bent to her ear and whispered, "I hope you're taking notes. That commando thing is worth checking into. Not that I don't love these." He trailed his finger along the waistband of her panties.

In response, she tickled him in the ribs. He made a sound that caught the woman's attention.

"Hello, is someone in here?"

"Yes, just fixing my dress," Suzanne called. "Don't mind me. Good luck with your date."

The woman "hmmphed" and left the restroom. As soon as she left, Josh pushed open the door of the stall. He hurried to the door and snagged the club soda still sitting outside.

When he ducked back in, Suzanne was already dressed and twisting her hair back into a knot. Staring into the mirror, she waved off the soda. "Never mind. It's already nearly dry and right now it's the least of my worries."

"Oh yeah? What's the worst of your worries?" He tucked the club soda into her bag in case she changed her mind. "That she might have caught us eavesdropping? She shouldn't worry. I'm erasing that from the memory banks starting now."

"No, it's not that." She finished with her hair and turned to face him. A troubled expression darkened her deep blue eyes. "Logan has...well, he's never kissed me like that."

Josh shoved his hands into his pockets. "What do you mean, 'like that'?"

"Don't worry, it's a compliment. To you, I mean. And I must have had a lot of champagne or I wouldn't be saying all this. He's never kissed me like...like he couldn't ever get enough. Like he wanted a kiss more than breathing."

Oooooh. Suddenly this seemed like a tricky situation. He didn't want to come between Suzanne and her fiancé. A fiancé was a solid thing to have, and Josh had nothing solid to offer. He and Suzanne were completely different and they were headed in opposite directions. He couldn't allow her to think that anything else was on the agenda.

"I like breathing too. It's almost as good as kissing," he quipped.

"But the *way* you kissed me..."

"I know. It was amazing." He preened like some kind of cocky asshole. "I've been told I'm a champion kisser. Don't let it worry you."

Frowning, she pulled a shimmery blue shawl from her bag and draped it across her front, where the champagne had spilled. "So you kiss everyone like that?"

Her tone of voice was dubious, and he couldn't blame her. That kiss was not a regular everyday kind of smooch. It was more of a once-in-a-lifetime thing. He needed some time to figure out why it felt that way. For now, he had to laugh it off.

"Listen, if Logan needs a few lessons, I can probably work with him," he said, mock-seriously. "But my kind of skill and experience doesn't come cheap."

Ah, there it was. Suzanne's patented "look of scorn." He didn't usually care much for that look, but right now, it was for the best. "I'm sure we'll muddle through without the mighty Josh Marshall's kissing lessons."

"Good. After all, you probably picked up a few tips yourself during the kiss."

Shaking her head in disgust, she pushed past him. "You know what? I think I'm going to block the whole thing from my mind."

He followed her across the tiles toward the door. "I would too, but there's no way I'm forgetting the way you moaned. 'Ooooh, Josh. Oooh, baby. Oooh, that feels so good.'"

She flung open the freakishly well-oiled door, making it bang against the wall. "I didn't say anything like that, you idiot."

"There was moaning."

"There *will* be moaning if you don't stop saying silly stuff." She clicked down the hallway in her little silvery strappy sandals, which made him remember how it felt when she wrapped her leg around him.

Which practically made him moan right there in the hallway. "See you around, Suzie Q," he said in a voice too low for her to hear.

CHAPTER 3

Josh slept badly that night. It had been a brutal fire season so far, and it was only August. The hotshot crew had been working nonstop and everyone was on edge.

And he kept having that dream. The one where he was back in the fire shelter in Big Canyon, with the wildfire roaring over him. Over all of them. Fire and death raining from the sky. In the dream, the wind kept whipping the thin aluminum fabric away from his body, exposing him to the blast of the furnace of flames. Then it changed, and he was hiding under a bed and the howl of the fire turned into voices yelling. Familiar, beloved voices.

He woke up sweating and shuddering, and blinked at the sun filtering through the casement windows. They were set high on the concrete walls of the dorm, which was an old Army barracks that had recently been transformed into a fire and rescue compound. From the angle of the sun, it was still early. In the summer, it was hard to shake the habit of waking up at dawn.

He jumped out of bed and pulled on his workout clothes. His lifelong habit was to run first thing in the morning, no matter what time it was or what he'd done the night before. From personal experience, he could confirm that running was the best hangover cure around. The other guys teased him about his punishing workouts. But he enjoyed beating his body up. It temporarily blocked out the crap that still bounced around in his head.

He jogged lightly down the hallway, feeling every sore muscle he'd acquired during the last week of cutting line. In the mess room, he spotted Kit Evans, who was kicking back on the old couch with a paperback. "What's up, Kit?" he asked the young Texan, who didn't look up.

"I'm not running with you, so forget it." He turned a page. It was a sore point with the crew that Josh always woke up chipper.

"Am I the only morning person in this whole crew?"

"Yes." Kit raised his book higher to hide his face. "Leave me alone."

Josh gave up on Kit and cruised over to the table, where Rollo huddled over a tall thermos of coffee like a mama bear protecting a cub.

"Morning, champ!" Josh greeted him brightly. "What's cooking?"

Rollo clamped his big hands over his ears. "Can you get your sunshiny ass out of here? Go run, or skip to my lou, or whatever."

"Big guy have a wee bit too much champagne last night?" Josh breezed toward the coffeepot, tweaking him in the ribs on his way past. It was a bit like poking a bear. Rollo gave a low rumble of warning. Good thing Josh had his Adidas on. He picked up the pace and jogged out the front door. Who needed coffee anyway?

"Marsh!" Rollo yelled after him. "Answer your damn phone. If it goes off one more time this morning, it's going under my boot."

Warily, Josh turned, still jogging in place, to make sure Rollo wasn't trying to lure him back for revenge. But the big guy didn't really operate that way. Rollo was all heart. Well, heart and a lot of beard. He made the lumberjack look work like nobody's business. But right now his soulful blue eyes were looking a little bloodshot and he was brandishing a cell phone in his big fist.

"Sorry, man." Josh jogged back and took the phone from him. He'd left it plugged in to charge last night and missed five calls. None of them from the lovely and amazingly kiss-able Suzanne, sadly. All of them from his brothers. He handed the phone back to Rollo. "Here. Got your boots on?"

Understanding flashed across Rollo's face. "Family drama?"

"Not talking about it."

"Come on, bro. You gotta at least see if it's an emergency."

"You don't get it. It's always an emergency. And yet, it's never an emergency." But he took the phone back and clicked on the first message, which was from his brother Chad.

"Dude, you gotta call Mom. She let the bull out of the pasture last night. He went and trampled all of Dad's turnips. He's mad as hell."

Josh erased that message, and the next one, which was from his brother Andy. "Dad just drove a tractor over Mom's alfalfa. He's going crazy and he won't listen to either of us. Will you call him? Please, bro. You gotta do something."

Erase.

Next message, from Chad: "You know what, Josh? If you're going to be fifteen hundred miles away, the least you could do is help us out long-distance. Just give a fucking call, would you? They're trying to kill each other."

All of Josh's good-morning cheerfulness evaporated like mist at noon. His parents had fought their way through marriage and were in the midst of the slowest, most agonizing divorce in the world. It had started when he was still at home, in high school. And it was *still going,* eleven years later. They were officially separated now. But neither was willing to let go of the ranch, so they'd divided it in two.

Clearly, that was a better solution in theory than in reality.

Josh punched Chad's number and waited, fuming. As soon as his brother answered, he launched into his usual rant. "Listen, moron. If Mom and Dad want to act like immature little kids, there's nothing you or me or anyone can do about it. Why do you have to drag me into it?"

"Who is this?" Chad asked, joking. But Josh wasn't in the mood.

"I spent three years trying to negotiate some kind of truce. I'm done. I told them I'm done. I told you guys I'm done. Why won't anyone believe me?"

"Dad's talking about selling the ranch," Chad said. "I mean, his share."

"Yeah? Good. Because this ranch-sharing arrangement is not working."

"So where does that leave me and Andy?"

"Buy it from him. He'd probably sell it to you cheap."

"He can't sell it cheap because he wants to move to Austin and houses are expensive there. Besides, he thinks I'm in league with the devil. You know, Mom."

Josh closed his eyes and pinched the bridge of his nose. Even at such a distance, the toxic atmosphere of the Marshall family drama filtered through the phone. "I don't know what to tell you, Chad. You have to get out and find some other kind of life for yourself. Forget the ranch. They're going to drive it into the ground anyway. There won't be anything left when they're done throwing the dishes at each other."

"It's easy for you to say. You wanted to leave. You never wanted to stay in the first place."

The three brothers had been very close. But he was the youngest and the only one still at home when all hell had broken loose. His brothers had both been deployed, while he'd been stuck at the ranch, collateral damage from the worst divorce in Texas.

He'd left as soon as he could, and he hadn't been back since, not even for holidays. He didn't understand why his brothers stuck around. "Why don't you come out to California and get a break from that crap."

"Nah, I got too much work to do here. Cindy's pregnant."

"Really, man? Congratulations."

"Yeah. Thanks." Chad sounded happy, but Josh had to wonder. This poor kid would have grandparents who had once gotten into an armed standoff that required the sheriff's intervention. Was that the right family to bring a child into?

"Listen, I gotta go," Josh told him. "We just got back from a big-ass fire. I have a ton of catch-up to do."

Chad grunted. "Some days, I think a wildfire would be a cakewalk compared to this. Later, man."

Josh hung up. He agreed with that statement one hundred percent. He'd rather risk his life in a wildfire any day than suffer through one more bitter fight between the two people who had given him life.

He stepped inside the mess hall to ditch his phone.

"All good?" Rollo asked as he palmed a muffin from an open box on the table. He was looking slightly more human, now that he'd consumed an entire thermos full of coffee.

"Sure. Peachy."

Rollo tossed him a pager. "Take this with you. Apparently the entire interior of Alaska is up in flames."

Josh groaned and pocketed the pager. "Seriously? Some-one better tell Boise that I need my beauty sleep." Boise was where the National Wildfire Coordination Center was lo-cated. They were the ones who decided where each hotshot crew would be sent.

"You sure do. Can't fight a wildfire looking like that." Rollo stretched out his long legs and propped his stock-inged feet on the mess hall table. Where they ate dinner—rarely, since they were mostly out in the field. Josh decided not to pick a fight about it.

"Where'd you get off to with Suzanne last night?"

"We made out in the ladies' restroom. She took off all her clothes, but she left her spiky heels on. It was freaking hot."

Rollo released one of those rolling-thunder laughs that seemed to come right from his gut. "You're hilarious."

Josh winked, just to make sure Rollo took it as a joke.

But the joke was at least partially on him, because now that damn image was implanted in his brain again. Suzanne rocking those boy shorts that showed off all her long, lean muscles. As he launched himself up Heart Attack Hill, he lingered on that memory. Then another one took its place. In this one, she wore that vulnerable, heartfelt expression while she told him that Logan never kissed her "like that."

To chase that image from his head, he focused on the narrow trail that wound uphill through groves of pine and birch trees. He gratefully drew clean air into his lungs. The air in Jupiter Point was always so fresh and clear—it was one of the reasons the stargazing was exceptional here. Just one of the things he liked about this place.

Another one being the girl who'd been wrapped around him last night.

What kind of man was Suzanne engaged to, anyway? What did she see in him? All he knew about Logan Rossi was that he was going to be a lawyer and that he'd suggested that he and Suzanne get a free pass to make out with other people.

So far, he didn't like the guy at all. Suzanne deserved better. But what the hell could he do about it? He couldn't exactly offer her an alternative. Given the *Twilight Zone* that was the Marshall family, no one would ever expect him to follow that path.

Maybe he could be a kind of "big brother" to Suzanne. Yeah, that was the way he'd play it. He'd keep a close eye on her and this Logan jackass. If he saw any more danger signs, he'd...do something.

If he had to kiss her again, well, anything to help out.

CHAPTER 4

When Suzanne arrived at the office of Stars in Your Eyes Events and Tours on the Monday after the YWCA party, a young Asian couple was already waiting at the door, flyer in hand.

"Good morning. Are you interested in one of our honeymoon packages?"

"How did you know?"

She smiled at them. "It's the happy glow. I can spot it a mile away. Come on in."

She unlocked the front door and gestured to the two honeymooners to take a seat. The sunny office was filled with scenic shots of various romantic locations around town. Jupiter Point wasn't on par with Hawaii or the Caribbean or other top honeymoon destinations, but the town had carved out a niche for itself thanks to its prime stargazing. Night picnics on the beach—complete with linen-covered tables and torchlight—private tours of the observatory with a chance to name a star, a sunset cruise on the sailboat *That's Amore*...there were so many ways to weave stargazing into a honeymoon.

She'd been working at Stars in Your Eyes since high school. When the owner, Marlene, had made her a full partner, she'd expanded the business into big event planning. Since she excelled at planning, she loved her job—when she was in an optimistic mood.

The rest of the time, it could be depressing.

Like when she was comparing the bliss in a newly married couple's faces with her own troubled state of mind.

Plastering on a bright smile, she got to work. "Do you enjoy sailing? There's nothing quite like a private sunset cruise."

The husband shook his head, placing a protective arm over his bride's shoulder. "She gets seasick. We'll take a pass on that. We were looking at the nighttime stargazing picnic package."

"Of course. That's a wonderful one." As she smiled and walked them through the choices, she really wished he hadn't used the word "pass."

As in, "free pass." As in, what the hell, Logan Rossi?

She was dying to ask the newlyweds if they'd had a free pass before their wedding. But luckily, she managed to get through the rest of the booking without completely embarrassing herself.

After the honeymooners left, she decided that this day was going to need a big hazelnut latte. Normally she would go around the corner to Evie's gallery, which had recently added an espresso bar. But she didn't want to hear about Sean and the other hotshots—especially Josh. She wasn't ready to talk about what had happened between them.

So she walked the extra three blocks to the Venus and Mars Café. It had the look of a French outdoor café, with its ironwork chairs and black awning. Its logo was a white cameo silhouette of a couple facing each other, with the merest sliver of space between their noses.

It reminded Suzanne of Josh and the way his face had hovered over hers, those gray eyes so unexpectedly serious. For such a playful guy, he kissed with impressive, knee-weakening intensity. It wasn't just the kiss, either. It was the way he'd looked at her, the way he'd handled the whole situation.

Josh had opened Suzanne's eyes to another side of him.

Of course, then he'd ruined it by acting like a jerk again. Which was the "real" Josh Marshall? Not that it mattered. One kiss meant nothing compared to wedding plans. That was just common sense.

She ordered her latte to go but lingered on her way out the door. She wasn't ready to face more deliriously happy couples. Surely there must be someone here to chat with.

Yes! Merry Warren, a reporter for the town weekly, sat at one of the little round tables in the bay window. With her tortoiseshell glasses halfway down her nose, and her wild frizz of brown hair confined by a red scarf, she was pounding the keys of her laptop. A newspaper sat under a mug and a scone. Merry was always so focused when she worked. She forgot about mundane things like the breakfast waiting right under her nose.

Suzanne hesitated, not wanting to interrupt the creation of her next masterpiece, but finally Merry looked up and beckoned her over.

She sat down with a happy sigh. Sipping a hot beverage—any beverage, really—while chatting with a friend was one of her favorite pastimes.

"How's everything in the honeymoon business?" Merry asked after they got the preliminaries out of the way.

"To be honest—and off the record, of course—I think they're all under the influence."

"All your clients are drunk? Hmm, sounds like they might have somethin' in common with journalists." Merry pulled a comical face.

"Yes, but they're drunk on *love*. That's even more dangerous than whiskey or whatever journalists drink."

"We're not too picky."

"Well, apparently my clients aren't either. They marry just about anyone they fall in love with. What kind of way is that to make a decision?"

Merry's eyebrows drew together, creasing the smooth brown skin of her forehead. "Isn't that the usual way? Or so I hear. Haven't had to make that call yet."

"Just because it's the usual way doesn't mean it's the best way. Just look at the divorce rates in this country. Do you know how many times I've sat with a newlywed couple and thought, eh, fifty-fifty chance you'll make it? There are exceptions, of course. Like Sean and Evie. They're soul mates.

But that doesn't happen very often. Mostly, people choose their mates for the wrong reasons."

Merry broke off a piece of her blueberry scone. "You have this all worked out, don't you? Go on, then, hit me, I'm all about the facts. You have a solution for this problem?"

Suzanne took off the lid of her latte and blew on the foam. "I do. In my humble opinion, no one should leave their future up to emotion. Emotions change. The only reliable way to secure your future is to make a real commitment." When Merry started to protest, she held up a finger. "But there's a catch. The commitment has to be with someone who *doesn't* make choices based on emotion. Both parties have to be equally logical and practical."

Merry looked at her as if she were crazy. "Girl, you are just depressing the hell out of me now. You're saying only two coldhearted people can ever make a marriage work?"

"No. Of course not. You don't have to be coldhearted to be practical. Take me and Logan. We know why we're getting married. We want the same kind of life. And we're willing to commit to each other to achieve that life."

"Are my ears bleeding yet? Because they sure feel like they are."

Suzanne frowned at her friend. "I was sure you'd agree with me. You always talk about research and facts and all that."

"Fact is, I'd rather be alone than have the kind of marriage you describe."

"Hey." Feeling rather wounded, Suzanne took shelter in her latte. "It's the only way to guarantee that it'll work. If you just go by emotions and love, anything could happen."

"No one can guarantee anything. Not when it comes to romance."

Suzanne propped her elbows on the table and rested her chin in her hands. "Well, I can try, can't I? What if all it takes is careful planning and execution of the plan?"

"And what if you're dreaming, Suz?"

Suzanne let out a long sigh. "Darn you and your facts. You ruin everything."

Merry laughed. "Not the first time I've heard that. Okay, changing the subject. Did you see this week's *Gazette*?"

"I saw last week's, has anything much changed?"

"Ooh, burn. Are you out for revenge now?"

"I'm just teasing. What big breaking news do we have in town this week?"

"Well, aside from the killer photo spread of our new hot-shot crew—"

Suzanne snatched the paper toward her. Josh was right there in full color, doing pushups with his muscles bulging out of his workout shirt.

"Oooh, that got you going," Merry teased.

Yeah, well...why wouldn't it? He was insanely attractive. And she remembered exactly how good he felt pressed against her body.

"But that's actually not what I meant to point out. Did you know that we have an honest-to-goodness fairy-tale castle in this town?"

Suzanne's heart nearly stopped.

As far as she knew, there was only one castle-like house in Jupiter Point. She knew every nook and cranny of it.

Was Merry talking about—

She scrabbled through the pages of the newspaper. "Where? Where'd you see it?"

"Take it easy, hon. It's in the real estate section. I just happened to see this grainy little photo, but then I looked it up on Zillow. It looks like an enchanted castle. It even has a name. Casa di Stella. Check it out."

She turned her laptop so Suzanne could see. But Suzanne didn't have to look at it to know what she would see. A Victorian whimsy of a house covered with climbing ivy, with two turrets and a drawbridge out front. It used to have a sort of moat, though now it was more of a swampy home for frogs.

"Why is it in the paper? Is there a story on it?"

"No, no. No story. But it just went on the market. It's being listed at half a million dollars, which isn't too bad if you consider that it's practically a *castle*. Are you okay?"

Suzanne nodded dumbly. *It was for sale.* Old Mrs. Shrew must have finally decided she couldn't maintain it anymore. Not that she ever could, with all those pets of hers. But why the hell hadn't anyone told Suzanne? Jupiter Point Realty knew that if it ever went on the market, Suzanne wanted to be notified.

"Let's go check it out," Merry was saying. "I bet there's a story there. Don't you think?"

"Oh yes. There's definitely a story."

"You know something about this place, don't you?"

"You could say that."

"Well, spill it, girl! You can't torture a reporter like that."

Suzanne couldn't drag her gaze away from the photo in the online real estate listing. "Well, I don't know *all* of the story. But I did live there from the age of eight to fifteen."

"Get the hell out!"

"It's true. My parents bought that house when we moved to Jupiter Point. My mother fell in love with it at first sight."

There was much more to the story, but she didn't feel like dredging all that up now.

Merry turned the computer so they could both see the listing. She read aloud. "'Historic Jupiter Point home is every childhood fantasy come true.'" She clapped her hands in glee. "Is that true? Was it your childhood fantasy come true? Did flocks of little tweety-birds fly through the window to help you clean the kitchen?"

"That's not nice." Suzanne had loved that house with every inch of her child's heart. It had crushed her when they'd lost it.

"Sorry. I'm just...hey, I grew up in Brooklyn. I'm a little out of my league here. Look, it says 'Vintage interior, period details.' Well, you know what that means. Sketchy plumbing. Now we have something in common."

The rusty color of the water that flowed from the kitchen sink had never bothered Suzanne. And she'd learned to use a toilet plunger early on. To her, it had been part of the fantastic adventure of living in a real castle. "Who needs plumbing when you have a drawbridge?"

"True that." Merry continued reading from the ad. "First time on the market in twelve years. Call for showing."

"Okay." Suzanne put the lid on her to-go cup and rose to her feet. This couldn't be a coincidence. It must be destiny—written in the stars. She was engaged and her beloved childhood home was back on the market. Everything was coming together in perfect harmony. That was what happened when you planned carefully. "I'm on it."

"You're going to go see it?"

"I don't need to see it. I'm going to buy it."

Ignoring Merry's stunned expression, Suzanne tossed her latte in the trash bin on her way out the door. The need to act now, to stake her claim before anyone else fell in love with that photo in the paper, drove her forward. She picked up the pace and practically jogged the ten blocks to Jupiter Point Realty.

With Merry on her heels.

"How are you going to buy it, girl? Are you a secret millionaire?"

Merry, who was about eight inches shorter than Suzanne, had to jog to keep up with her. Suzanne slowed her pace, even though the thought of losing the castle to someone else made her want to scream.

"Of course not. But I've been saving up for a down payment since I was sixteen and scooping ice cream at the Milky Way."

They reached the storefront of the real estate office, which had listings posted on the glass for passersby to peruse. Casa di Stella was posted front and center in a featured position. Suzanne resisted the urge to pull out a black sharpie and scribble "sold" on the glass.

"It's still posted, that means it's still available," Merry pointed out. She adjusted her laptop under her arm. It looked as if she'd stuffed it haphazardly into its case when she'd bolted after Suzanne. "Don't panic. Take a moment and tell me why you've been saving up for this eyesore all these years."

Suzanne turned on her. "Take it back. You can't call it an eyesore."

Merry nearly dropped her laptop. "Are you kidding me?"

"No. I'm not. I love every inch of that place." Tears sprang to her eyes, shocking even her. "Every dilapidated inch. We had to sell it when my dad went bankrupt in the big market crash. I swore I'd get it back someday." Merry touched her arm with a remorseful look.

"Sorry, Suz. I didn't know it meant so much to you. I think it's crazy fantastic and if you buy it, I promise I'll come paint walls or drawbridges or whatever you have to do to fix up a castle."

Suzanne threw her arms around her friend. "Really? You'd really do that?"

"Sure. Of course I would." Merry seemed to be soothing her the way she would a volatile two-year-old. "It must have been so sad to leave it."

She had no idea. It wasn't just the house—everything had fallen apart after the crash. Her parents had fled the country when it turned out her father had done some frantic and illicit things to cover his ass. They still couldn't come back without risking prosecution.

Suzanne shook off the memory. "It's okay. I always knew I'd get a chance to buy it back. I've been planning for this ever since." Critically, she surveyed her outfit. Sleeveless royal-blue top, pinstriped pencil skirt, kitten heels. Professional but not uptight. Luckily, she even had her prized Kate Spade clutch with her. "How do I look?"

Merry gave her an "a-okay" sign. "Lookin' good, girl. I'd sell you a castle if I owned one."

"Good isn't quite good enough. I need to look— inevitable." She pulled out a comb and ran it through her hair, then tied it in a low ponytail. Peering at the plate glass, she saw that she looked every inch the young professional about to make an offer for the house of her dreams. She drew in a deep breath and glanced at Merry, who looked highly amused by her storefront toilette.

"Good luck, baby doll. I need to get to work, but if you line up a showing, you better call me. I want to know how much painting's in my future. Come here. Hug for good luck."

They hugged one more time, then Merry hurried down the street toward the *Mercury News-Gazette* building. Suzanne stepped closer to the listing taped on the glass. Details were always important, and maybe there was something in the description that would help the Realtor look more favorably on her. Lord knew her financials weren't her strong point. She could afford the down payment, but barely. But her history with the house, her familiarity with its drawbacks, her emotional attachment to it—maybe that would all count for something.

As she scanned the description, she stumbled across a line that made her freeze in her tracks.

"Seller prefers families with children. Contact only if you meet seller's criteria."

CHAPTER 5

With an exhausted groan, Josh squatted onto a mossy log and cracked open an MRE. The crew ate the flavorless meals in silence. They'd spent the morning cutting a chain—hacking vegetation to "mineral" so the fire would have trouble reaching the fuel. It was back-straining work and Josh could feel it in every inch of his body.

He'd heard it said that hotshots were the most physically fit of all types of firefighters. Generally speaking, it was probably true. But more importantly, backcountry fire-fighting required a certain kind of mental toughness because of the sheer length of time it took to battle a wildfire. You could be doing the same back-grinding work for sixteen hours at a time, then the same thing again the next day. And the next.

It took stamina. Or lunacy. Luckily, Josh had plenty of both.

On the plus side, the scenery was incredible. How often did a guy get to take a break while admiring a waterfall tinkling down a slope of slender white birches?

Sean Marcus, who was sitting next to him on the log, finished his MRE and tucked the empty wrapper into his pack. "Let's mop up those last few hot spots then go help the Scorpions."

"What do you think, boss? Home tomorrow?"

"It's looking good."

"Excellent. I have a hot date with a hot tub." Josh licked out the last bit of mush from the foil package.

"Yeah? Who's the lucky lady this time?"

"No lady. Just a hot tub. They have a good one at the gym in town." Wildfire fighting was dirty, grimy, sweaty work. When Josh got back to the base, he always spent half a day just getting clean. In Colorado, he'd even been known to book himself a spa day at the end of the season. The other guys teased him about it, but he didn't care. He liked being clean. So sue him.

"After you're all nice and clean and tidy, want to come to an engagement party?"

Josh's gut went tight as a drum. "Suzanne and what's-his-name?"

"What? No. It's for someone else. You might know them. Sean and Evie."

The relief that flooded him made no sense. Suzanne was already engaged. What difference would a party make? Then the import of Sean's words sank in. "Wait. You two are *engaged*?"

"Yup. We're not making a big deal out of it though. Evie doesn't want to step on her cousin's big moment."

There went that annoying stomach punch again. Of course Suzanne was still getting married to Mr. Free Pass.

That was what she wanted, and she seemed like the kind of girl who got what she wanted.

"Hey, man, congratulations." He punched Sean on the shoulder, then, since that seemed like an underwhelming level of excitement for his best friend's news, he punched him harder.

"Ow."

"Honest to God, I never thought I'd see this day. The ultimate lone wolf brought down by the town sweetheart."

"Evie's a lot more than that and you know it." Sean narrowed dark green eyes at him. On one topic, the man refused to joke around. Josh could respect that.

"Of course I know it. She's gorgeous, she's kind, she doesn't lob insults at a guy or act like he's a juvenile delinquent just because he likes to joke around." He unfurled himself from the log, stood up and rolled his shoulders.

Sean followed suit. "Talking about anyone in particular?"

Josh picked up his pack and fastened it on his body. It held everything he needed out here. Extra gas for the chainsaw, rain gear, an extra warm layer, some flagging, and of course the all-important emergency fire shelter. That thing had already saved his life once.

Why did he keep thinking about the Big Canyon burnover? And having nightmares about it? He was starting to think that something had happened to him during it—something important. It had changed him. He just hadn't figure out how yet.

"Eh, doesn't matter." Even though he was answering Sean's question, he also addressed that remark to himself and his memories of the burnover. It didn't matter. He was alive. Free to live his life the way he wanted. Nothing had changed.

"Actually, I have a question for you, Romeo. If you're officially engaged you should have no trouble answering."

"Shoot." Sean donned his pack as well and picked up his Pulaski, the favorite tool of the hotshots. He waved to the rest of the crew that lunch was over.

"What would you think of the concept of a free pass?"

"No idea what you mean." Sean unscrewed the top of his canteen and glugged down a long swallow of water. Dehydration was a real hazard for hotshots and something Sean paid close attention to. "Make sure to hydrate!" he called to the crew.

"This isn't Zumba class," Josh grumbled, even though he pulled out his own canteen. "A free pass apparently is when an engaged couple decides they can screw whoever they want until they actually take the vow."

Josh wished he had a camera to commemorate the expression on Sean's rugged face. "What the *fuck*?"

"So you wouldn't be in favor of something like that?'

Sean glared him with something like menace. "Whose dumbass idea is that?"

Tim Peavy, a rookie and Jupiter Point local, was listening curiously from several yards away. "I have an opinion. Anyone want my opinion?"

It occurred to Josh that maybe Suzanne didn't want everyone knowing about the situation. "It's a hypothetical. Forget I asked."

The crew set off for the half-mile hike to the location of the Fighting Scorpions, the crew that both he and Sean had been part of during the burnover. Josh didn't need any more information about the free pass idea. Sean was the best example of an "in love and engaged" man that he knew. If Sean had reacted like that to the concept, his question was answered.

Logan was a dick who had no business being engaged to Suzanne.

Suzanne, who would most likely be in attendance at Sean and Evie's engagement party, since she was Evie's cousin.

"Hey, Magneto," he called to Sean, who was striding a few yards ahead. "Count me in on the party. It's like a bachelor party, right? Cigars and strippers?"

"Don't you dare."

"I can wear my thong. The girls love it."

"Idiot."

*

"Logan, you promised." Suzanne stood just outside the door of the Orbit Lounge and Grill, where she was supposed to be meeting Logan. Who was apparently still in Palo Alto. "This one isn't optional. It's mandatory."

"I'm sorry, babe. My interview is tomorrow morning. I can't get back in time."

Suzanne swallowed down her bitter disappointment. Of course Logan couldn't miss an interview. Their future hinged on him getting hired. "Can you come afterwards? I told the Realtor you'd be at the showing this week. They want the buyer to be family-oriented, so my fiancé should really be with me."

"I can't commit to that. It's a multi-level interview. I have to meet with every department and go out to lunch with one of the junior partners. It's just a house, Suz. Why is it so important?"

Grrr. She'd explained it to him last weekend, when she'd flown to Palo Alto to surprise him and show him the listing.

She smiled and waved at Mrs. Murphy, who owned the used bookstore next to the Sky View Gallery, Evie's place. She was kindhearted but a notorious rumormonger. The last thing Suzanne wanted was word getting out that there might be trouble with her engagement.

Which there wasn't. She and Logan were totally on the same page. Even if that page had some bad words on it. She kept her voice nice and even as she answered his question. "I've wanted that house back ever since my family went broke. It's the most wonderful place on earth, and I know that you would fall in love with it if you would just," *get your ass here when I need you,* "give it a chance. It has lots of extra space so you can entertain your clients there. And it's a steal. Mrs. Shrew is unloading it because she wants to go back to Hong Kong."

"But we're going to be living in Palo Alto."

"Yes, but for weekend getaways, it's perfect."

"Hm." For the first time, Logan lost the condescending tone he'd been using every time Suzanne mentioned Casa di Stella. "That's worth thinking about. But I can't make it, so you'll have to handle this alone. Love you, babe."

He ended the call, leaving Suzanne ready to throttle her phone in sheer frustration.

"Cool it, princess." Josh's laughing voice, warm and as deep as smoked honey, spoke in her ear. "If you need to throw something, I have a hackeysack you can borrow."

Suzanne turned around, her best glare cued up and ready to launch, only to stop short when she caught sight of him. Instead of his usual jeans and flannel, he wore gray trousers and a black button-down shirt. His tumbling blond locks were neatly combed for once, although the stubborn wave in his hair suggested that wouldn't last. He must have just shaved, because his face showed not a speck of stubble and she caught a haunting trace of spicy aftershave.

She caught herself leaning forward to inhale more of it.

His deep gray eyes gleamed in the low-lumen streetlights Jupiter Point used to reduce light pollution. Part of her wanted to sit back and just enjoy the sheer visual treat that he presented.

His expression shifted from playful to concerned when he scanned her face.

"What happened?"

"Nothing." She forced her mouth into a smile. "Everything's great. Are you here for Sean and Evie's party?"

Her fakery didn't throw him off for a second. He kept his gaze on her. "Not buying it. Who was that on the phone?"

"Why is that any of your business?"

"Because." He paused, as if trying to think up a rational reason why he might have a right to question her. "I got stuck in the ladies' room with you."

Laughter burst out of her. "So?"

"You know how they say when you save someone's life, you're responsible for that person? Same principle applies. Your life is now my responsibility."

She tucked her phone into her little black clutch with the sparkly starburst pattern. "Maybe *your* life is *my* responsibility. You could look at it that way too."

"Fine. Then you have a responsibility to fill me in." He flashed that irresistible, panty-melting grin, the one that put that ridiculously kissable groove in his cheek.

"You are so ridiculous."

"I'll take that as a compliment. " He took her by the arm and steered her toward the front entrance. The warmth of his body had a strange effect, both soothing and exciting. She never felt that way with Logan.

Then again, it wasn't a fair comparison. Logan didn't do physical work like Josh did. Of course he didn't have the same level of musculature.

It's not about the muscles, something inside her whispered. That's just part of it. Most of it is Josh, his playfulness, his grin, the thoughtful expression she sometimes caught in his gray eyes.

Inside, they located the group of Evie and Sean's friends who had pushed together several tables in the quietest part of the bar. The glow-in-the-dark stars scattered across the ceiling cast a gentle, eerie glow over the space. Fuchsia and indigo lava lamps illuminated the tables and booths. A techno electronic beat pulsed from the dance floor. Normally, Suzanne loved hanging out at the Orbit; it was so campy. But this was the third time Logan had failed to show up for an event.

Evie flew to greet them, kissing and hugging them both.

"Cuz, I love you but I have to say this is not the way I would have planned your engagement party," Suzanne murmured in Evie's ear, eyeing the beer bottles and bowls of pretzels on the tables.

"I know. But with Sean's schedule we didn't want to plan something then have to cancel it if the crew got allocated somewhere."

"Allocated," Josh said with a lift of his eyebrow. "Look at you, using fire-service jargon. Welcome to the family."

Evie laughed and gave a fond glance at her fiancé, who was listening closely to Evie's father, known universally as the Dean. "Sean gave me a study guide. He said if I'm going to have any clue what he's talking about over the next fifty years, I'd better get the vocabulary down."

"What's a Pulaski?" Josh fired the question at her.

When Evie couldn't quite come up with the right answer. Suzanne gave it a stab. "A move in women's gymnastics?"

"Wrong. What does BLM stand for?"

"Bureau of Lame Munchkins," Suzanne shot back.

"Wrong. What role does an Incident Commander play?"

"In bed or out of bed?" Suzanne asked in her most innocent voice. Evie burst out laughing, while Josh threw up his hands in defeat.

"Never marry a hotshot," he told her. "You'd be the end of him."

Suzanne made a little face at him. "I think I've earned a drink, don't you?" she asked Evie.

Sean chose that moment to appear with two bottles of beer. "Can someone take these so I can do something more interesting with my hands?"

Suzanne and Josh exchanged a glance. "Should we help them out?" Josh asked in a dubious voice.

"You know what they'll do as soon as his hands are free," she answered in a conspiratorial whisper. "And they aren't even married yet. It's shocking."

"It's an outrage to decent people everywhere." Josh put a hand over his heart, as if he could barely handle the shock.

"I might faint if I see any more googly-eyes over there."

"Yup. I need a beer just to recover."

They both laughed and Suzanne held out her hand to accept a beer bottle, only to find Evie and Sean looking at them strangely.

"Uh...what's going on with you guys?" Sean asked as he handed over the bottles. He slid his arm around Evie's waist and nuzzled her hair.

"Nothing." Suzanne bristled. "What are you talking about?"

"You were...kind of bantering. Like a comedy team or something." Evie tilted her face so Sean could land a kiss just below her ear. "It was cute."

Suzanne shot Josh an uneasy glance. It was true; they'd had a sort of groove going for a minute there. She supposed it was safe to say they connected on a certain level. But just the most superficial level.

And the physical.

But that was superficial, too, wasn't it?

Josh stepped into the awkward moment. "Actually, Suzanne was about to fill me in on her conversation with Logan. Her fiancé," he added pointedly, as if reminding everyone.

"Right, where is Logan? I thought he was coming tonight." Evie frowned, as much as she could while continuing to beam happily in Sean's embrace.

"He has an interview. I completely understand. He probably won't make it here for a few weeks. The thing is…" She trailed off, biting her lip. Evie already wasn't Logan's biggest fan. Once she heard about Logan missing the house showing, that would be one more strike against him.

But as usual, Evie was perceptive enough to understand the situation without Suzanne explaining. "That means he'll miss the showing. Aw, sweetie, I'm sorry." She reached out a comforting hand to squeeze Suzanne's shoulder. "I'm sure you can reschedule it. Especially when you explain that your future lawyer husband is interviewing for his future well-paying job."

Was it her imagination, or did Josh stiffen at that glowing description of Logan? "This will be the third time I have to cancel. They weren't happy the last two times." She worked at the label of the beer bottle with her thumb. She had no intention of drinking—not with Josh so close and so appealing. She didn't trust herself, not after the champagne incident at the observatory.

He wasn't drinking either, she noticed, and wondered if it was for the same reason.

"Are other people looking at the house?"

"I'm sure they are. I'm not Mrs. Chu's first choice anyway. She wants to sell to a family and my ring's still on the wrong finger." She waved the hand where her diamond sparkled.

Sean scratched his head and squinted at Suzanne. "What am I missing here?"

"Remember Casa di Stella, the house Suzanne's parents used to own? She wants to buy it back, but the seller wants a family to get it. But Logan keeps—" Evie broke off suddenly and looked from Suzanne to Josh. "Hang on. Does anyone know what Logan looks like?"

"Not me," said Sean promptly. "I've never laid eyes on the guy."

"As far as I'm concerned, he might as well be imaginary," Josh agreed. "Never seen him."

Evie rolled her eyes at them. "I don't mean you guys." She turned to Suzanne. "Has Mrs. Chu or the Realtor ever seen Logan? Would they know if someone else came with you instead?"

Suzanne had to think about it. "I doubt it. When he comes to Jupiter Point, we mostly stay in. We sometimes go out to dinner but Mrs. Chu is practically a hermit, so we've never seen her. Lisa, the Realtor...well, it's possible. But she just had a baby and this is her first month back at work. She probably has other things on her mind."

She trailed off as the implications of Evie's question sank in. "Do you mean someone else could pretend to be Logan?"

"Did you ever tell them the name of your fiancé?"

"No. I don't think so."

Evie shrugged. "You just need someone to accompany you in a fiancé-like capacity. Normally I wouldn't suggest something like this, but I'm slightly outraged by the fact that Mrs. Chu is making such crazy demands. Is it even legal?"

"I have no idea, but Mrs. Chu never liked me. I didn't behave very well after she bought Casa di Stella," Suzanne said gloomily. "I'm probably the last person she wants to sell it to."

"Then Josh will be even more helpful. Everyone likes Josh."

Next to her, Josh broke out in a coughing fit. "Wait...what? Did I just hear my name in connection with the term 'fiancé'?"

"Fiance-*like*," Evie emphasized. "Suzanne needs someone who will convince Mrs. Chu that she's a suitable candidate for home ownership, with a husband and children right around the corner."

Just then the group of guests chatting with the Dean waved to her, and she said a quick "excuse me" to Suzanne and Josh. "I'll let you two work out the details," she whispered as she pulled Sean back to the party. "But it's a genius idea."

Suzanne reluctantly dragged her gaze to meet Josh's. He looked torn between bewilderment and amusement. He looked around at the dark interior of the Orbit Lounge. "Is this place literally a black hole? I walked in here a happy single guy, and now Evie has me pretending to be engaged so I can buy a house."

"*I* am going to buy the house," she corrected. "And I can reschedule the showing again. It's not a problem." She put her bottle on a table and looked around at the party. It had lost its appeal. She'd left the house with her spirits sky high, dressed in her favorite fuchsia halter-top dress with the ruffled skirt. She was supposed to be here with her fiancé at her side, for once. Logan had promised—he'd *promised*. And now she might lose Casa di Stella forever. A family with kids would move in, and those kids would love it and leave it to *their* kids and—

"What's so special about this particular house?" Josh was asking. He snagged a bowl of pretzels from the closest table and offered it to her.

"It's not important." She didn't have the heart to explain it one more time. She chose a pretzel from the bowl and touched her tongue to it, letting the flavor of the salt soak in.

He made a funny sound, like a subterranean groan. "You just licked your pretzel."

"Yes. I always do that. What's the matter?" She did it again. "You should try it. The salt kind of dissolves against your tongue and your saliva moistens the pretzel and— what?"

He cleared his throat. The poor man really did look uncomfortable. She frowned, wondering if she'd done something terribly inappropriate. Then she saw him shift his stance just a bit and realized...oh.

He was getting turned on by watching her eat a pretzel.

"Seriously?" she asked him. She licked it again, more slowly this time, dragging her tongue across the hard crystals studded along the pretzel's surface. "Mmmm. That's sooooo gooood," she crooned.

"Okay," he said quickly. "I'll do it. I'll do the house thing. Whatever you need. Just don't eat any more pretzels. I can't take it."

She gave a little burble of laughter, then another, feeling as if tiny bubbles of delight were flooding her entire being. As a notorious social butterfly, she was used to flirting. She never got shy around men. She liked the male gender, and enjoyed spending time with most men. They usually liked her, too.

But she wasn't used to someone as hellaciously hot as Josh Marshall looking at her with quite that combination of raw desire and carnal knowledge. That look promised all sorts of naughtiness.

If his kiss was any indication of the things he knew...hoo boy.

Scratch that thought. She was engaged.

Engaged to someone who was about to sabotage her chances of getting her dream home, if she let him. "So you're saying you'll pretend to be Logan?"

He grimaced. "I'll pretend to be your fiancé. But I won't pretend to be *him*. We'll just have to work around it."

She thought it over. It could possibly work. She would introduce him as Josh and act all lovey-dovey, as if they were a couple. Mrs. Shrew and the Realtor would be expecting her to arrive with her fiancé, and would automatically jump to that conclusion. If she never specifically *called* him her fiancé, she couldn't be accused of lying. It would be tricky, but it could be done. She nodded and offered her hand to shake on it. "Okay. Thank you, Josh. This really means a lot to me."

They touched palms. The contact sent ripples up her arm and down to her lower belly. She snatched her hand away as if she'd been electrocuted.

Josh cleared his throat again. She wondered if he'd felt the same unsettling sensation she had. "So...when and where do you need me?"

CHAPTER 6

The heat wave that had gripped the West for the past month finally broke, and the nation's firefighting crews got a brief respite. No one expected it to last, but Josh and the other Jupiter Point Hotshots took full advantage. When they weren't catching up on their sleep and doing their daily PT training, they held big barbecue feasts at the base and helped out with local fire mitigation efforts like brush-clearing.

Jupiter Point was definitely growing on Josh. In his firefighting career, he'd been based in Colorado, Arizona, and now California, and he had friends in all those places. He always enjoyed getting to know the towns where he spent his summers, but he was never tempted to settle down in them. A good, friendly relationship was as far as he wanted to go.

That principle applied to many areas of his life, actually.

He didn't really understand Suzanne's obsession with one house out of the many charming homes Jupiter Point had to offer. But he was willing to help her out, the way a big brother type of person would.

Suzanne picked him up in her red Miata at the base about a week after Sean and Evie's engagement party. She looked fresh and pretty in a crisp, mint-green cropped blazer and white linen pants. Her hair was pinned into a low knot at the base of her neck and she wore little diamond studs in her ears. He wondered if Logan had given them to her to match the diamond ring on her finger.

Screw Logan.

What was wrong with the man? Was he so confident that he didn't think he had to pay attention to his fiancée anymore?

"I've been thinking about how to handle this," Suzanne told him as she aimed the Miata toward the foothills. "I'm going to introduce you as Josh, except kind of like this." She coughed, burying the word "Josh" in the middle of the sound. "Don't worry, I've been practicing it."

He looked at her with an incredulous laugh. "Please tell me you're joking."

She grinned at him. "Yes, but Mrs. Chu is hard of hearing so we don't have to worry about it. I already told Lisa what's going on, so don't worry about her. Your job will be to charm Mrs. Chu with your smile and dimples and all of that."

"So now I'm supposed to be a fiancé who's flirting with another woman?"

"Why, is that so out of character?" She gave him a wicked sidelong glance.

"Watch the insults, babe. I could do or say anything in there. You don't want to piss me off."

Her expression instantly transformed to something more sober. "No insult, I promise. I just meant that we should make use of your overwhelming masculine charm."

"You know I can hear the mockery in your voice, right?"

She turned into a section of Jupiter Point he'd never seen before, where the homes were grander and set farther apart, hidden behind groves of cypress and eucalyptus. Her posture tightened, her shoulders hunched forward. He realized she was nervous.

"Hey, don't worry so much. It'll be okay." He touched her neck, sliding his fingers under the silky bundle of hair. He massaged gently until her shoulders relaxed. "Uncle Josh is here for you."

The corner of her mouth turned up. He couldn't help remembering how her lips tasted, like fresh rose petals dipped in champagne.

"Oh, one more thing," she added. "The owner's name is Mrs. Chu, not Shrew. I occasionally call her that because she hates me, but please wipe that from your mind. Mostly, I'll do all the talking. You just have to shake hands, flash your dimples, and act like you want to spend the rest of your life with me."

"Shrew, not Chu. Rest of my life. Got it," he repeated.

"No! It's Chu. Choo choo choo. Like a train. You know what? I'm going to say you have laryngitis. That way you don't have to say a word."

He threw his head back and let the laughter roll out of him. "I was joking, you little crazy pants. We've got this in the bag. You can just relax and start writing your down payment check."

She turned onto a driveway so long and curving, he couldn't see the house yet. "Okay, we're almost here. No more joking."

He put up a hand, Scout's honor style. "No more joking. I don't know why you want to tie yourself down to a mortgage payment, but whatever. I'm here for you." He gazed at the parade of tall cypresses lining the drive. What was this place, some kind of mansion?

And then they came around a curve and a vision appeared before him.

He blinked to make sure it was still there.

Yup. There was no denying it. The house—or castle—looked like something from a children's fairy story, with kind of a *Secret Garden/Red Riding Hood* vibe. Or maybe *Rapunzel,* based on the two shingled turrets that couldn't possibly have any practical purpose. Thick ivy climbed up the walls; he could just imagine the rats shimmying up and down the vines. The deep green leaves looked as if they were wilting in the August heat. He spotted gaps where shingles should be and shutters that used to have paint—possibly apricot-colored, based on the shreds that remained.

"Turn the car around," he told Suzanne.

"What?"

"I'm not going to help you buy this house. It's a money pit. It'll ruin your life."

She kept driving forward, her jaw set. "You said you'd help me. If you go back on your word now, you'll be a promise-breaking, untrustworthy jerk."

"I can't in good conscience let you throw your hard-earned money away on this—"

She slammed on the brakes and the Miata jerked to a stop. She turned on him. "The only time I've ever been truly happy in my life was when I lived *in that house.*" She jabbed her finger in the direction of the monstrosity. "The only reason I can afford it is that I've been saving up since I was sixteen and because my parents forgot to liquidate my savings bonds when they left the country."

He stared at her in shock. "Left the country? When did that happen?"

"When I was fifteen."

"*Fifteen?* And they left you behind?"

She rubbed the heel of her hand across her forehead. "It was fine. I didn't want to go. I lived with Evie and the McGraws. But right after they left, I stayed here by myself for almost two months. I had no problem taking care of myself. I would have stayed forever if Mrs. Chu hadn't bought it out of foreclosure. I love the place."

It was all starting to come together now. This wasn't just any other house to Suzanne. It had much deeper significance. To be honest, based on her breezy spirit and sassy attitude, he never would have guessed she had so many troubles in her past.

He heaved a sigh. "You know that entire house is a fire hazard, right? I ought to put my yellows and greens on just to go inside."

"What's that?"

"Nomex. Fire-resistant. But we'd be better off in bunker gear."

She laughed. "That's actually not a bad idea. Remember how I mentioned Mrs. Chu doesn't like me? Well, she has good reason. When she first moved in, I refused to leave."

Oh, this just got better and better. "Do I want to know the details?"

"I...well, I might have done some Beetlejuice-type things. Me and my friends. We wanted her to think it was haunted so she'd go away."

"How did that work out?"

She took her foot of the brakes and cruised slowly toward the eyesore looming ahead. "Not very well. Mrs. Chu is one tough cookie. On the bright side, my community service was awesome. I got to know the girls at the YWCA and I still volunteer there. I planned that fundraiser for free, you know." She smiled at him impishly.

He was still laughing when she parked the car in a cobblestone courtyard that served as driveway and parking area. Suzanne was full of surprises, most of them darker and edgier than he ever would have imagined. She had an unexpected rebellious streak that really appealed to him. He could just picture her as a mischievous fifteen-year-old dropping water balloons from the turrets and moaning through the heating vents.

As they walked across the decrepit drawbridge, which seemed to be rotting into the swamp below, he draped his arm over her shoulder and pulled her close. At first she stiffened in surprise, but he bent to her ear and murmured, "Well, hello, Mrs. Chu. I can't wait to spend the rest of my life here with Suzanne, replacing shingles on this monstrosity. Do I have that right?"

Her lips curled up at the corners in that adorable way he'd really grown to appreciate. Suzanne's smiles always started like that, as little divots on each side of her mouth, growing into a full-fledged, wide grin that took over her entire face.

He loved seeing her smile.

He looked up to see a tiny elderly Asian woman in a tailored black business suit planted at the front door, arms crossed over her chest. The nervous-looking Realtor hovered behind her.

"You," spat Mrs. Chu, looking at Suzanne. "You have a nerve. You think I will sell you this house? Pfft."

"It's been almost ten years, Mrs. Sh—I mean, Mrs.—you." Suzanne was obviously rattled by Mrs. Chu's laser-guided glare. He was amazed she hadn't melted into a puddle already. Instead she was babbling and about one second from calling the owner a shrew.

"Hi there." He dropped his arm from around Suzanne's shoulders and strode forward with his friendliest grin and his hand held out. Experience taught him that most people weren't so outright rude as to refuse a handshake, and once you touched someone's hand, it was harder to hold on to your antagonism. "You must be the queen of this here castle." He added a hint of Texas twang to his voice, as the down-home cowboy thing also seemed to disarm people. "I've never seen anything like it in all my life. When Suzanne described it, I almost didn't believe her. It's like a fairy tale come to life. You must be a visionary woman, Mrs. Chu."

"Visionary, absolutely," said the Realtor, seizing on his compliment with an expression of massive relief. She aimed a vague wink at Josh. "That's so very true."

Mrs. Chu didn't look as impressed, but she did shake his hand and allow Josh and Suzanne to step inside the house. She jabbed her finger toward their shoes and pointed to a basketful of little slip-on disposable booties. "Either take off your shoes or put those on."

Josh looked askance at the worn floorboards, which had maybe been varnished once upon a time, or maybe not. Hard to tell. What was she trying to protect?

He glanced at Suzanne, who was slipping off her flats. Damn, did he have to take off his cowboy boots? He didn't want to leave them lying around for the mice. Gritting his teeth, he grabbed a couple of booties and sat down on a little bench situated next to the door.

As he pulled the booties over his boots, he scanned Casa di Stella's interior, which was just as quirky as the exterior. The high-ceilinged entryway was lit by a chandelier dripping with cut glass. An actual cuckoo clock stood guard next to a spiral staircase that disappeared into the dusty shadows of the next floor. A balcony overlooked the foyer. Old-fashioned wallpaper covered the walls in a pattern of roses and water stains.

He startled when Suzanne took his hand. "Honey, it's even better than you described." He brought their clasped hands to his lips. A fiancé would do that, right?

Mrs. Chu was watching them narrowly. "This house must have new life." She spoke like someone used to being obeyed. "I purchased for my grandchildren, to encourage them to visit. But now, all they want is Pokemon Go. This," she waved at the entryway, "big waste. No one here to enjoy. It needs young people, children who like this sort of thing."

Josh wondered if by "this sort of thing," she meant rotting floor beams and stained wallpaper. "I can't imagine too many kids who wouldn't love it, Mrs. Chu. Even I would have, when I was young."

Now, not so much.

Suzanne started to say something, but he squeezed her hand. His take on the situation was that Mrs. Chu was never going to warm up to Suzanne. Best to keep the focus on him.

"Who was the original owner?" he asked.

Translation: Who would be insane enough to create this fantasyland?

Lisa stepped in to answer that one. "One of the early Disney animators retired here to Jupiter Point. He had twenty grandchildren and, just like Mrs. Chu here, wanted to give them something fun to look forward to in their visits. It was built in the nineteen-sixties and most of the original structure is still intact..."

They followed her through the downstairs rooms as she pointed out the various unique features of the castle. You had to pass through a tunnel to reach the kitchen—that feature, he definitely would have loved as a kid. She pointed out little reading nooks nestled into window seats and a miniature table perfect for a tea party. She talked about the turrets, and the sheltered stargazing platform that stretched between them. The whole house had secret passageways and vents that carried sound from one section to another.

Josh noticed that Suzanne kept gazing around at each new room as if greeting an old friend. She didn't say much during the tour. When Mrs. Chu and the Realtor ducked their heads to enter the kitchen tunnel, he pulled her aside. "Everything okay?"

"Of course. I haven't been in here since I was fifteen, that's all. It's just...it's strange. It looks the same, but it doesn't smell like my family anymore. Know what I mean?" She pointed at the tea table, which held a complete set of little china teacups and saucers. "My mother loved that. She always wanted me to have tea parties with her, but I thought it was stupid. I was more of a tomboy."

Josh eyed the squat little teapot. "Any chance there's alcohol in that?"

Suzanne giggled. "Might have been, knowing my mother. She lives in her own little world. She's never worked for a living, never lived on her own. My father is twenty-five years older than she is and treats her like some kind of doll.
"

"Where is she now?"

"They live in Costa Rica. It's very affordable."

Lisa yodeled to them from the other end of the tunnel. "Come see this absolutely adorable kitchen! The tea kettle actually sings! Like literally sings!"

"You know," Josh whispered to Suzanne, "I can feel my balls shriveling up a little more with each step. This is literally the most emasculating house on the planet. By the time we're done, I'll be skipping around in pigtails."

She giggled as he ranted. Ducking into the tunnel, she took his hand. "Oh come on. It's not that bad."

"You should have warned me. I would have pumped some iron and eaten a few steaks to juice up my testosterone levels. They're just about depleted."

"I'm sure they're just fine. Don't firefighters come with an extra dose anyway?"

"That's right, baby. We do. I'm worried about Logan though. Do you think he has what it takes to withstand the girliness?"

Suzanne made a face at him over her shoulder as they picked their way through the short tunnel. "He's going to be a badass divorce lawyer, so I think he'll be fine."

"This just gets better and better," he muttered.

"Divorced people need lawyers too."

"Believe me, I know." His parents had each hired and fired several, but he didn't want to talk about that. He shouldn't rag on Logan's profession. It wasn't even the worse thing about him. The free pass proposal still took first place in that respect.

Then again...he watched Suzanne's cute little rear sway back and forth, just as sassy and saucy as the rest of her. Maybe the free pass wasn't such a bad idea after all. Maybe it meant that Suzanne had free rein to compare and contrast. Maybe it was the perfect exit ramp. Maybe it was his duty to show her the kind of man she really deserved.

The *kind* of man.

Not to say that he was the *actual* man she deserved. Because if this castle represented the kind of life Suzanne wanted, they existed in two different worlds, him and Suzanne. He'd prefer an emergency fire shelter during a burnover to this ridiculous structure.

But that wasn't the point. The point was that Suzanne was so much more than a beautiful, tart-tongued, blond knockout. He could read between the lines of her history and see her vulnerable heart. She deserved someone who understood that about her. Someone who looked past her sexy surface.

CHAPTER 7

Suzanne had to admit that without Josh, the showing would have been a disaster. It wasn't a typical showing anyway. She wanted to buy the place no matter what condition it was in. If any "showing" had to be done, it was on Suzanne's part. She had to show off her fiancé and convince everyone that even though she was technically still single, a husband and family were right around the corner.

And Josh did it. His relaxed manner, his easy smile, his cowboy-drawl charm all wove a magic spell over both Lisa and Mrs. Chu. The owner actually smiled at him when they left. Sure, that smile dropped as soon as her gaze touched Suzanne. But hey, they'd all seen it. She'd also mentioned that she was going back to Hong Kong for a few weeks and Lisa would be in charge.

Thank God.

All in all, it was a fantastically successful day, and Suzanne could have hugged Josh for helping her out.

In fact, she did hug him. Mrs. Chu had already gone back inside, so the embrace wasn't designed to impress her. It wasn't designed at all; it was a completely spontaneous outburst of affection for the man who had taken time from his day for her sake.

"Thank you thank you thank you," she told him as she flung her arms around him.

"Mmm, I can already feel my masculinity coming back," Josh murmured after a few moments had ticked by. "You must have magic powers."

"No, *you* do. That woman is like every mean principal I ever had, and she was eating out of your hand."

"She's not so bad. She bought a castle for her grandkids to play in, how bad could she be?" He ran his hands up and down her spine, just barely grazing her ass. She melted against him, going liquid inside. She remembered exactly how his calloused hands felt against her skin.

"That's true." Suzanne dropped her arms and took a little step backwards. The temptation to just surrender to their attraction was incredibly strong. But she couldn't. She didn't want to. Well, she *wanted* to—but she didn't want to think about what it could mean, or where it could lead. "Maybe I was jealous because I was on my own."

She laughed it off, as if it meant nothing anymore. But Josh didn't seem fooled by that. "If I ever meet your parents, I might have a few things to say to them."

She unlocked the doors of her Miata and skipped around to the driver's side. "Yeah, well. That won't happen. My mother could come, but she never leaves my father. She's afraid to travel alone. It's too bad, because I know she misses my aunt Molly."

"Molly McGraw is a darling." Josh swung into the passenger seat.

"How do you know her?" Since Molly had an advanced case of Parkinson's, she rarely left the house.

"I helped Evie with that new ramp they put in. Apparently power tools are not the McGraw family's forte. I asked where their tools were, and she showed me a drawer full of compasses and protractors. There might have been an X-Acto knife, too."

As they drove back to the street, sunny afternoon light sliced through the cypresses along the drive. "First Evie, now me. Do you just go around helping people out?"

Josh shrugged. "I was trying to earn points with my crew boss's girl."

Suzanne doubted it, but let it go. "I want to do something nice for you now, since you helped me out. How about a hot fudge sundae at the Milky Way?"

"It might take more than that to make us even, Suzie Q. There was a *singing teakettle*."

She laughed. "Pizza first? With extra pepperoni?"

"You're getting there. But do I have to remind you about the booties?"

"Fine." She threw up her hands in surrender. "You pick. I had no idea you were so hard to please."

"I *am* hard to please, and yet you do it so well."

She snorted and focused her attention on the road ahead. She didn't want to see how much he'd surprised and touched her with that comment.

*

Uh-oh...had he offended her? Had he let his attraction to her run away with him? But it was true—Suzanne did please him. Looking at her pleased him, so did touching her, and inhaling the fresh fragrance that drifted from her hair. So many things about Suzanne pleased him.

She interrupted the short, awkward silence as if nothing had happened. "I could show you some of the fun stuff I arrange for honeymooners."

"In the bedroom or out?"

She laughed. "Do you make a joke out of every single thing?"

"No," he said, in his most serious voice.

Even though she got the joke and laughed, he kept a straight face. "There are a lot of things I don't joke about. I never joke about fire, especially wildfires. I never joke about racial stuff. I've heard that kind of joke on the fire lines, but I don't like it. It doesn't add anything, you know? I never joke about gays. It just makes you look homophobic. And that makes you look gay."

She slanted a narrow-eyed glance at him. "Is that supposed to be a joke?"

"Okay, so I do joke about *joking* about gays."

"You're crazy." She shook her head as they approached the quaint downtown area with its old-fashioned lampposts and cedar-shingled buildings.

"Do you have something against jokes?"

"Not per se, no. But there ought to be some serious mixed in with the jokes, don't you think?" She stopped the car outside the Milky Way Ice Cream Parlor. "How about we start with an ice cream cone and go from there?"

They ordered two double-scoop cones—heavy on the chocolate for her, while he chose an all-green combination of pistachio and mint chocolate chip. He tried to avoid the sight of her little pink tongue lapping at the ice cream as they strolled down Constellation Way.

"I think I'm finally starting to get used to the ubiquitous stargazing theme," Josh mused as they passed the Rings of Saturn Jewelers.

"Are you ready for the Jupiter Point history lesson I give my honeymoon clients? They always ask me when all the stargazing stuff started."

"Sure. Shoot." He savored the cool sweetness on his tongue, happy to listen to her pretty voice.

"After they built the observatory, the Milky Way was the first business to cater to the tourists who started coming. Then the Goodnight Moon B&B opened and it was completely booked from like, day one. The owner noticed that the bulk of the guests were couples. One night, he went around the breakfast room and counted three couples celebrating their anniversaries and five on their honeymoons. He told his sister about the strange coincidence. It was a total lightbulb moment. Jupiter Point used to be more or less a fishing village, but that industry was having a tough time. Her husband was a fisherman and every year his catch was going down. So they decided to sell their boat and open Stars in Your Eyes. She advertised in the wedding announcement sections of newspapers in San Francisco and Los Angeles, other places all up and down the West Coast. It all just took off from there."

Josh was so mesmerized by the sound of her voice that he'd forgotten his ice cream until it dripped onto his hand. "That's where you work, right?"

"Yes. I started working there in high school. I just love all the history here. It's so unique, you know? Did you know we have a town motto?"

"Wait, let me guess. 'Jupiter Point: We're All from Planet Mars.'"

She laughed, tossing her head back. He admired the line of her throat, which was just as long and vibrant as the rest of her. "No, goofy. It's 'Remember to Look Up at the Stars.' I like it. I actually use that phrase to remind myself that my problems aren't really that big, if you look at the whole scheme of things."

"Yup. A wildfire will do the same thing."

"Mmm." Having consumed all the ice cream mounded above her cone, she stuck out her tongue to lick the cone itself. He dragged his gaze away from the tempting sight. "You were in that burnover, weren't you? The one they're making a movie about?"

"Yes, I was there. I asked if Matthew McConaughey could play me. They said they'd try."

She gave him a sidelong, up-and-down scorcher of a look. "I'm sorry, but you're much cuter than he is. And a lot younger. They could do better."

He was surprised into momentary silence. Since when had Suzanne decided to start complimenting him? He should wear booties over his cowboy boots more often.

"So where do you live when it isn't fire season?" she asked him as she nibbled on her cone. The evening light gave her eyes a deep cobalt sheen.

"Nowhere."

"What do you mean, nowhere? Where's your stuff?"

"I have a storage unit in Boulder. I leave stuff at a few friends' houses every winter. But a house would just be a waste of money for me. I travel in the winter."

Suzanne had stopped in the middle of the sidewalk. Passersby swirled around her as she stared at him, her ice cream cone forgotten. "Are you telling me you're homeless?"

"I guess you could say that." He shrugged. "I don't need a home. I spent last winter surfing in Baja. I lived in a little palapa not far from the beach. The rent was about a dollar a night. I make enough money during the summer that I can do whatever I want in the off-season. I was thinking I might go to New Zealand this winter."

"But don't you...I mean, what happens when you...you have to have a *home*. At least a home base."

"Not really." He didn't understand what she was so upset about. "I use the hotshot base as my address. You can do everything online now anyway. It works out great. No bills, no debt, no renting out my place or worrying about something happening to it when I'm gone all summer."

The appalled look on her face made him laugh out loud.

"But...I mean...what about later on?" They reached the Goodnight Moon B&B, with its night jasmine vines cascading over a wrought iron fence. The fragrant blossoms were just starting to open, glowing like little stars in the deep green tangle.

"What do you mean?"

"Well, you're, what...late twenties? My age, or maybe a little older?"

"I'm twenty-seven."

"You can't live like a hobo forever. Don't you want to settle somewhere, have a family?"

"Nope." He stuffed his mouth with a huge chunk of ice cream in the hopes that she'd drop the subject. But this was Suzanne and she had a level of determination he'd already learned to respect.

"You want to just travel around forever? Don't you want to have kids?"

"Nope."

"But you're so good with kids!" Again with the compliments. This was starting to make him nervous. "I watched you at the party at the observatory. They loved you. Even the emo ones."

"Kids are a lot of fun. I like how they think. And they like me because I take them as they are. I don't look at them and think they should be different, the way most adults do." He raised a pointed eyebrow at her.

She made a little face at him. "Point taken. But you're not a kid. You're a man." She swept a quick glance down his body. He liked how that felt. He liked that she was aware of him in that way, even though he wasn't crazy about the critical tone in her voice.

"I'm glad you noticed."

"Yeah, well, you know I did." Even in the near darkness, he saw the flush rise in her cheeks. "But being a man involves more than just the equipment."

"Right. You have to know how to use it too. I've been working hard on that part."

She quickly turned back to her ice cream. "I'm sure you have. But of course that's not what I mean. I mean you have to be responsible. You have to set goals for the future. That's the part I'm wondering about."

The hell if he was going to defend his choices to her. If fighting fires and saving lives and property wasn't enough for her, then whatever. She didn't know anything about him and his life. He decided to turn the question back on her.

"I suppose you and Logan will be expanding your perfect family before too long."

"Of course. We're planning to wait until Logan's law practice is more established, but when it's the responsible thing to do, we will."

"Hmm." The less he said about Logan, the better. Every time the dude's name came up he felt his hackles rise.

"What does that mean, *hmm*?" The edge in her voice increased with every word she spoke. She cocked her hip and planted one hand on it. Her long hair flowed over her shoulders, the moon glow giving it a soft, lemon-blossom sheen.

"No meaning. Christ, Suzanne. Relax."

"See, that's the problem with you. You're too relaxed. If you want to get anywhere in life, you have to be organized and work hard. You can't just roam around the world whenever you feel like it." She gestured with her ice cream cone, nearly hitting a woman who was passing behind them. The woman gave them a wide berth.

"Who says I can't? I've been making my decisions since I turned eighteen. I can do what I want." He finished his ice cream cone and brushed his hand on his pants.

"That's fine for an eighteen-year-old, but you're supposed to be a grown-up by now." She took a step forward, but he snagged her arm before she could escape.

"Okay, that's it. You don't know enough about me for that lecture. Maybe I have good reason not to get married." He did—damn good reason. But he wasn't going to explain it to someone so determined to think the worst of him.

"Well, I suppose it's best if you don't get married. You'd have to stick with it, stay in one place and all that. And I don't mean Neverland."

And there she was—the Suzanne who always needled him and seemed to look down on him from some great self-righteous height. So much for the compliments. "Think what you want about me. At least I don't need a ridiculous rundown castle to be happy."

Ice cream dripped into her fingers from the mostly-finished cone. "And that's exactly why we're completely different and should have nothing to do with each other."

"Do you hear me arguing?"

For a moment they simply glared at each other. The sweet, wistful fragrance of the jasmine wound between them, like a cat purring against their ankles.

The porch light of the Goodnight Moon B&B winked on. An older man in a sweater vest called to them in a low voice, "Pssst. You two, arguing on the sidewalk. You're a real mood-killer for my guests. Would you like your honeymoon ruined by strangers having a lovers' quarrel?"

Suzanne rounded on the man. "Sorry, Benito, but you're way off. This isn't a lovers' quarrel."

"Nope. No honeymoon for us," Josh added. "*That* would be a disaster."

"Just keep it down, would you? Or better yet, move along." The man shook his head and went back inside.

"Great," muttered Suzanne. "Now everyone in town is going to think you and I are fighting."

After a long stare, he let out a hoot of laughter. "We *were* fighting."

"I know we were fighting. But it wasn't *that* kind of fighting." She finished her cone, licking the last drops of ice cream off her fingers. He tried not to think of pretzels and her tongue.

And despite everything she'd said to him, he wanted her. He wanted to sweep her off her feet and make her eyes go wide with desire. He wanted to kiss that luscious, tart-tongued mouth. He wanted to show her he wasn't what she thought.

The air between them practically vibrated with tension— the best kind of tension. She felt it too; he saw her eyes widen. His hands twitched. The desire to reach out to her was so intense, he had to curl his hands into fists to stop himself.

No. Just...no. The reasons tumbled through his head. She was engaged. She wanted marriage and an absurd house and all sorts of things he didn't. She looked at him as some kind of overgrown kid. She jumped to assumptions and thought his freewheeling lifestyle was all wrong.

No doubt about it—he and Suzanne should have nothing more to do with each other.

At least they could agree on that.

CHAPTER 8

After her parents had left the country in a mad midnight scramble, Suzanne had Casa di Stella to herself for two months, until the McGraws insisted she stay with them. During that time, she used to explore the empty house, poking into the rooms that used to be off-limits. One of those was her father's study, which contained shelves and shelves full of books on business and investing. To feel close to her missing parents, she'd curl up in her dad's study and read those books as if they were bedtime stories.

That was when a huge revelation had changed her attitude about everything. Her father, she learned from those books, had taken foolish risks with his business. If only he'd been more careful, more logical and goal-oriented, maybe she'd still have a family and a real home.

The lesson? *Be practical. Make a plan. Stick to the plan.*

From then on, she clung to those principles like a lifeboat in a storm-tossed ocean. Her more freewheeling, fun-loving side was no longer in charge. Nope. Those childhood days were over.

The first rule she'd learned was to focus on the things she could control, not the things she couldn't. She couldn't control her parents. She couldn't control the financial disaster happening around the country. But she could focus on her own life. She could make a plan for herself.

Make a goal and work toward it. That made sense to her. Even when nothing else did.

So she'd created a Dream File filled with everything she wanted in her life. Dream Files were good—they kept you looking ahead, aspiring for greater things. She consulted it often and added to it whenever she wanted. The most recent addition was Logan and their wedding plans. But long before that, getting Casa di Stella back had been goal number one.

Over the next few days, Suzanne poured her energy into that goal. She chased down every piece of information Mrs. Chu asked for—which was a lot. She got her partner, Marlene, to write a letter of recommendation; she unearthed her college transcripts, her high school transcripts.

The one thing she couldn't control was her thoughts and the way they strayed to Josh Marshall. The morning after their fight on the sidewalk outside the B&B, she woke up groaning at her own rudeness. Why had she spoken to him that way? He'd gone out of his way to help her out—he'd put booties over his boots!—and how had she thanked him? By insulting his entire lifestyle! So what if he wanted to travel in the winter? What was wrong with that?

After a solid hour of scolding herself, she called him to apologize. But the crew had been sent to a fire in Northern California and she couldn't get through.

Fighting a fire. Risking his life. While she was planning a moonlight cruise for a couple who wanted to watch the Perseid meteor shower from a sailboat.

Josh probably hated her by now, and she couldn't blame him. She'd been completely out of line.

That weekend, Logan came to visit her for the first time in a month. She picked him up at the little airport that served the entire county, about an hour away from Jupiter Point. Normally she loved watching him descend the escalator from the arrivals level. He'd usually be checking his phone for everything he'd missed on the short flight. He always carried a messenger bag packed with his laptop and whatever books he was using at the moment. Even though he wasn't as physically fit as, oh, say, a wildfire fighter, he knew how to present himself, how to carry himself with confidence. Maybe even arrogance, a bit. But that didn't matter. He was a brilliant lawyer; he had a right to be arrogant.

When he reached the ground level, he finally looked up from his phone. He stashed it in his pocket as he shot her a quick smile. "Hey, cutie," he said, bending to brush a kiss on her lips.

At the last second, she turned her head away and his mouth touched her cheek instead.

"Cold sore," she improvised when he looked at her questioningly.

"Bummer. Better stay away from me, then. I can't get sick. Too much studying."

"Do you have to study all weekend?" She pouted a bit as she threaded her arm through his. "I was thinking we could start making plans."

"That's your thing. I just want to fucking sleep. It's been brutal, all these study sessions."

Was it really just the studying that had been taking all his time? Or was it the free pass? She shoved the thought aside.

"Sure, of course I can make the plans. It's what I do." She pretended to preen. "I'm the planner extraordinaire of the entire Jupiter Point area. Speaking of which...how would you like to drive by Casa di Stella on the way home?"

One downside of having Josh play stand-in was that she couldn't exactly arrange another showing with a different man. But she could at least show him the outside. Hopefully he'd get inspired by her vision of it. Unlike Josh, who just saw it as a ridiculous eyesore.

"Maybe another time." Logan gave a massive yawn. "I've had less than three hours of sleep over the past two days. I'm toast, babe. I want sleep and a cocktail. Maybe some sex. That's all I can handle."

"Sure, I understand." Suzanne decided not to mention that Evie had invited them over for dinner. Or that there was an outdoor festival at Stargazer Beach. Or any of the other fun things she'd lined up.

Logan was going to be a lawyer, an extremely successful one. She'd have to get used to him being busy and exhausted. It was the price they had to pay for the kind of life they wanted.

Just as he'd warned her, he spent much of the weekend asleep. When he wasn't sleeping, he ranted about the professor who'd refused to give him a recommendation, a member of his study group who wasn't holding up her end, and how hard it was to get a job at the top law firms these days, the famous ones in the big cities.

"But Logan, I thought we agreed you were going to stay in the central or Northern California area?"

"I'm hoping. But I have to see who makes the best offer. You gotta go where the money is."

Go where the money is. A chill settled through her. Did she want to go where the money was? Where was that? Would she even have a say in where they went? "What if the money's in Hong Kong or something?"

"I guess we learn Chinese. Don't worry about it. Whatever we have to do, right? Eyes on the prize."

"Eyes on the prize."

But what was the prize? More and more, she wasn't sure she knew. Ask her two weeks ago and she would have said "security" and "a nice life" based on a solid financial foundation.

The night before Logan left, she woke up to feel him spooning her, his erection prodding between her legs. She stiffened, but he didn't seem to notice. He parted her thighs.

She pulled away as revulsion swept over her. "Sorry, I'm way too tired," she muttered, putting an extra six inches between them.

"But I'm leaving tomorrow. And we haven't had sex once."

Anger shimmered through her, anger she hadn't really known was there. "Look, Logan. You can have your free pass, but you can't also have sex with me. Sorry, it doesn't work that way."

He fell back to his side of the bed, his silence confirming every suspicion she had. "You're making too big a deal out of that," he finally muttered. "But whatever."

A few seconds later she heard him snoring. She rolled onto her back and covered her face with her hands.

She'd just turned down sex with her fiancé, and it wasn't even hard to do.

The truth was, sex with Logan wasn't all that exciting. And she *liked* sex. She'd never been shy about it. But she saw sex as something both people should enjoy if they were going to bother with it. She'd never understood why someone would fake an orgasm—until she'd gone to bed with Logan.

But with Logan, she was willing to ignore so many things. She tried to be understanding of his schedule and his exhaustion level and all the pressure he was under. He was going to be a bigshot lawyer and that was part of the deal. She had to support his brilliant career.

A snore rose from his side of her bed. She scooted a little farther away, relieved to put even more distance between them. She didn't even want to lie next to him right now. She wanted to flee to the couch in the living room of her little condo. Usually she enjoyed the feeling of his warm body snuggled next to hers. She loved not feeling alone.

What was different now?

Two words: *free pass*.

She gave a long sigh. The free pass had opened a wide crack between them, and now she wondered if it had always been there. She couldn't help comparing Logan to Josh. She and Logan definitely didn't have the kind of chemistry she had with Josh. But chemistry was just a physical fluke—it didn't mean anything. Being with Josh was also more fun than being with Logan. Josh actually paid attention to her and listened to her.

But there was no point in comparing. Josh was a free spirit with no interest in a family. And she'd insulted him, too. She should just put Josh out of her mind.

Easier said than done. She fell asleep thinking of the hungry way Josh had touched her. She wanted him to do it again. She didn't trust herself with a free pass around Josh Marshall.

As she was driving Logan back to the airport for his 6 a.m. flight the next morning, she took the bull by the horns. "We need to talk about this free pass idea."

"Non-negotiable."

"Excuse me?"

"I'm not willing to negotiate on that point."

"Are you using lawyer language on me? That's not cool, Logan. Just say it in normal people language."

He dropped his sunglasses over his eyes, even though it was barely dawn. "Fine. I need the free pass."

"But what if it's—"

"I don't want to feel trapped until I actually *am* trapped. And that's all I'm going to say."

Trapped? *Trapped?* "You don't want to feel trapped?" she repeated, stunned.

"I thought you understood that. It didn't bother you before. What's going on, are you on your period?"

Oh. No. He. Didn't.

She took both hands off the steering wheel and ripped off her ring. The car veered toward the shoulder. He reached for the wheel, but she slapped his hand away and grabbed it herself. With the other hand, she dashed her ring to the floorboards on the passenger side. "There you go. You're officially un-trapped."

"*Suzanne.* That ring cost five thousand dollars. Get a grip." He bent down to retrieve the diamond solitaire. She got a minor twinge of satisfaction over the fact that he had to push aside a crumpled Doritos bag first.

"I just can't believe you said that. You used the word *trapped.*" Her nostrils flared the way they always did when she was angry. "You're the one who proposed to *me.*"

"I know. I know I did. And I still want to get married, I think."

"You *think?*" If she weren't so angry, she'd be crying right now. Or would she? At the moment, all she felt was hot outrage.

He stared at the ring cradled in the palm of his hand. His look of raw confusion made her think she was seeing the real Logan for the first time all weekend.

"Maybe it's just the stress, Suzanne. Everything's happening at once. Exams, interviews, wedding stuff. As soon as my exams are over, we'll take a little vacation, how's that? We can go to the wine country or something."

"Can I drink *all* the wine? I think I'll need it." She pulled up outside the terminal. "You're here. Better get out while you can. I might *trap* you here until your plane leaves." She was so furious she wanted to push him out the door.

"Suzanne, relax. Come on. Give me a break here."

She flung her arms to the sides. "But how can I relax when I have this poor helpless man in my trap?"

"Can you just *let it go?*"

"Can you just be real with me for a minute?" she shot back. "What's going on, Logan? First you want a free pass, now you think I'm a trap. I just want the truth. The one thing I can't handle is a bunch of lies." So true. All the lies leading up to her father's financial collapse had made everything a hundred times worse.

Logan adjusted his messenger bag over his button-down shirt. His metrosexual look used to appeal to her, but now it struck her as too slick.

"Let's keep the dialogue open," he told her as he slid out the passenger door. He put the ring on the seat. "This is yours, whether you wear it or not."

She blew out a long breath and turned her little Miata back to the highway toward Jupiter Point. *Keep the dialogue open?*

What did that even mean? Was that a legal phrase or an "I have no idea what else to say" phrase?

She needed a hazelnut latte. And one of the Venus and Mars Café's legendary sticky buns, the ones drenched in caramel sauce and studded with pecans.

CHAPTER 9

Josh lay flat on the ground, face-down inside a flimsy sheet of a tent. Only a thin layer of aluminum shielded him from the inferno consuming the entire world. A blast furnace raged outside. He was going to die. If he so much as lifted one elbow, the shelter would flip up and leave him completely exposed. The fire would melt his flesh from his bones and suck the air from his lungs.

Don't do it. Do it. Don't do it. Do it.

He fought the reckless compulsion to try it out—just see what happened—how bad could it be?

Do it.

Then the tent was being ripped away and he was completely exposed to the elements, so he curled up in a ball and rolled under the bed. Voices peppered the air with accusations and jabs, louder and meaner and...Stop. *Stop it.*

Josh woke up gasping, drenched in sweat. He swung his legs over the side of his cot and buried his head in his hands.

Fuck. He hated these dreams, and they were coming every few nights now.

"You okay, man?" Tim Peavy stood in the doorway. He wore workout clothes and held a free weight in one hand. "Heard you shouting."

"What was I shouting?"

"Something about 'stop, stop.'" Tim flexed his biceps for a forearm lift.

Josh released a long breath. "Weird dream. I get them a lot ever since the burnover."

"I get it. I had a few nightmares after Afghanistan."

Josh nodded, swiping a hand through his hair. He looked closer at Tim and noticed shadows under his eyes. Tim was married to his high school sweetheart, and they had a baby due in a couple of months. Maybe the stress was getting to him. "Did you have one last night? What are you doing here so early?"

"Came out to get a workout in before Rosario wakes up. You up for it?"

"You're on." He got out of bed and pulled on a t-shirt. The two of them went outside into the gray light of dawn. A hint of pink glowed over the hills behind the base. Once again, Josh was struck by the sheer beauty of this territory. One last star still shimmered in the achingly clear sky.

"That's Venus." Tim dropped into pushup position in the wet grass.

"How do you know that?"

"My dad's a fisherman. We used to watch the stars out on the boat."

Josh rolled his shoulders to stretch out. "Nice place to grow up, huh?"

"I used to think it was boring as hell. I couldn't wait to get out. But it's not bad being back. Home is home, you know?"

"Right." He took a spot next to Tim and planted himself on his knuckles. Maybe that was true for someone like Tim, who grew up watching the stars on a boat with his dad. For Josh, home was not home. Home was wherever he woke up that morning. "Ready?"

"Born ready."

"And...go."

They both launched into a rapid-fire sequence of pushups. Hotshots were required to be able to do twenty-four pushups in under a minute, but since they were all competitive alpha types, the crew liked to push the limits.

Josh felt his lungs start to expand, his blood pump faster. "Fifty," he shouted as they reached that number. "Tired yet?"

"Not even breathing hard," Tim gasped.

They kept going in synchronized rhythm. Oxygen flooded Josh's brain. He sucked in the fresh morning air, feeling alive and energized.

Something soft and wet stroked the back of his calf. Grass, maybe? He shook out his leg and the thing disappeared. "Sixty!"

"Keep going."

Up and down, up and down. The sensation of soft and wet came back again, this time on his other calf. "What the fuck?" He glanced over his shoulder and caught a furry face looking back at him.

A dog? It was a floppy beast of a dog, with raggedy ears pointed straight up and a pattern of brown splotches on his white coat. Not so white at the moment, it was more of a dirty gray.

The dog nuzzled his lower back and nipped at him. "Hey! Stop that."

But the dog seemed to think Josh was playing. He gave a little jump of excitement and rolled onto his back. He arched his back and squirmed in ecstasy against the wet grass. Then he flopped himself onto his belly and crawled *under* Josh, blocking his pushup motion.

"I call interference." Josh came up on his knees and glared at the dog, who somehow managed to look both mischievous and guilty.

Tim collapsed on the ground, practically crying with laughter. "You should see your face right now."

Josh addressed the pup. "Are you working for my opponent? How much did he pay you? I'll double it if you go bite him on the ass."

The dog inched closer to him, ears perking up.

"You got a new fan." Tim shook out his arms and wrists. "And don't blame him; you would have lost for sure."

Josh scratched the dog between his ears. Its eyes closed in bliss. "Whose dog is this? I've never seen it before. He doesn't have a collar. Or maybe it's a she?"

"It is a she." Tim pointed to the area that made it obvious. "Figures. You get all the girls."

"Well, I don't want this one. What should we do?"

"Hey, not my problem." Tim grinned at him. "She's in love with you, not me. But there's a good vet in town. I'll take you if you buy the coffee."

Josh tickled the pooch under the chin. She cocked her head to the side, her bright eyes fixed on him. "Where'd you come from, pup? Do you have an owner somewhere?" He turned to Tim. "Is there a shelter in town? We can see if someone's been looking for her."

"Yeah, there's a shelter. But it looks to me like she's been wandering for a while. She looks hungry."

Josh examined her sides, where ribs showed through her dirty coat. "Yeah, she does. I think I have some beef jerky in my pack."

When he tried to go inside, the dog followed close at his heels. "Pooch," he told her. "I'll be right back. Stay." At that command, the dog sat reluctantly. At least she had some training. That meant she probably had an owner somewhere. Maybe he reminded her of her owner. He jogged into the dorms and found a package of beef jerky. He also pulled on some jeans and grabbed his wallet. When he got back out, Tim was snapping his fingers at the dog, trying to get her to follow him.

She wouldn't budge until Josh stepped onto the grass, when she actually leaped into the air in a dolphin-like spiral. Tim shook his head. "You are so screwed, Marsh. You got yourself a dog."

"No, I don't. No dog."

"You can't say no to that face, can you?"

Josh looked at the dog's jaunty mixture of white and brown patches, the white areas dirty from whatever mysterious wanderings she'd been on. His heart gave a twinge. Saying no would definitely be a challenge. But it had to be done. How the hell could he keep a dog? *Where* would he keep a dog? Most of the time the base was empty. Most of the year he wouldn't even be in California.

"Tell you what," he told the dog. "If you can change yourself into something small, like a snail, I can keep you. Or maybe something useful, like a flashlight."

"That's just wrong, Marsh. I'd take her home with me but my wife's allergic. There's a chance the baby is too, so I can't even risk it."

"Ain't that convenient?" Josh drawled. "The old 'wife and baby' excuse. Didn't know it would come in so handy, did you?"

Tim cackled and pointed him toward a black Jeep Cherokee. Since Tim lived in Jupiter Point, he got to sleep at home and use his own vehicle to get back and forth. He opened the door for the dog, who hopped in and took one of the backseats as if she'd done it a million times.

From Josh's comprehensive investigations, he knew the Venus and Mars Café made the best coffee in town. The base was a few miles outside of Jupiter Point, and by the time they made it downtown, the café was just opening up.

Since it was still too early for the shelter or the vet's office, they decided to pop in for coffee first. Tim used a ratchet strap to fashion a dog leash for the pup.

"Sorry about this," Josh explained to her. "You'll have to wait patiently on the outdoor patio and pretend you aren't grungy and stinky."

"She's the perfect hotshot dog, if you think about it," Tim said as he looped the leash around one of the fence posts. "No one's grungier or stinkier than a wildland firefighter coming off the lines."

"You got that right. Maybe we should have washed her first." He looked dubiously at the dog. She would probably be cute once she was clean.

"No one's going to be here this early. We'll be in and out."

"Stay...um, doggie." Josh used the voice of command he used to use with livestock at the ranch, but the word doggie definitely detracted from the effect. "She needs a name too."

"That's easy. Stinky?"

"Filthy?"

"Hairy?"

Josh was still laughing, looking over at his shoulder at the plaintively whimpering dog, when he collided with a woman coming out of the Venus and Mars.

She squeaked and lifted her to-go cup high away from her body, but it was too late for the massive chunk of cinnamon roll that was now smeared across her shirt. Her blond hair draped in long strands across her shoulders as she stared down at her chest.

"Oh shi— Suzanne?" He grabbed her by the elbow to steady her. "Damn, I'm sorry about that. I wasn't looking. I—"

Suzanne looked up at him, but instead of the irritation he'd expected, her eyes were dark with tears.

"Are you okay?"

"No." The tears brimmed over, spilling down her cheeks. "I'm not okay. I needed that sticky bun. You have no idea how much."

"I'll get you a new one. Come on." With his hand still on her elbow, he steered her back to the counter. But instead she veered for the little hallway where the ladies' room was located.

"I'll just be here, ordering you a new pastry," he called after her.

"Okay," she said faintly as she disappeared around the corner.

The dreadlocked barista handed him a paper plate with what looked like a small mountain of caramel and nuts. "You better do something, man. She's been crying ever since she walked in here."

"But I'm not...she's not...I don't know what's—"

114

Tim gave him a shove. "I'll take care of Snowball. You watch out for Suzanne."

"Snowball? What makes her a Snowball?"

"She's got no balls." Tim snickered, as if he was making the most brilliant point in the world.

"Okay, then." On that note, Josh went after Suzanne.

She hadn't gotten far. The back screen door of the café was half open. Suzanne leaned against the wall, wiping wet paper towels across her blue boho-embroidered top. Tears were trickling down her face.

"Uh...I got you a new one." He held out the sticky bun, but she waved him off.

"Give me a second. Honestly, when I'm anywhere near you, I should just take off my top. Pre-emptively."

"Not going to argue with that plan. And really, why stop with the shirt?"

She wrinkled her nose at him. "You think you're cute, don't you?"

"No. Nope. Not at all. I think I'm studly as fuck."

Finally she laughed. "Nope. I think 'cute' is more like it. What are you doing here? I thought you were up north."

For some reason it pleased him that she was keeping tabs on his location. Or maybe it was because of Sean. "We got back yesterday. But thanks for noticing."

"Well, I called you. I wanted to...um...apologize for my rudeness the other night. I had no reason to speak to you like that."

Right now, he was a lot more worried about the tracks of tears down her cheeks than her attitude toward him. "Don't worry about it. You aren't the first woman to have a problem with my footloose ways. Of course, I was sleeping with the others, so it made more sense, but—"

She burst into tears. He tried to touch her, but she swatted his hand away. "Damn it, I'm angry, not sad," she said fiercely. "I don't want to be crying over him. I'm *not* crying. I'm *not*."

Him. Logan, no doubt. He hated that guy.

"Of course you're not crying over him. It's perfectly obvious that you're crying over that sticky bun on your blouse. Which is my fault, so I guess that means you're crying over me. And I'm standing right here so you might as well just hit me."

Just like that, her sobs shifted into laughter. Her shoulders shook with it as she wiped tears away with the heel of her hand. "How do you do that? One minute I want to strangle someone—you, most often—the next I'm laughing."

"Well, it is a gift, it's true. But I bet I can make you want to strangle me again." He lifted her sticky bun to his mouth and bit into it, closing his eyes in mimed ecstasy. "Mmm, cinnamon roll."

"You are such an idiot." Finally, smiling, she took the thing away from him. "I suppose you deserve a bite, just for not being an asshole like the rest of your gender."

Uh-oh. "Seriously? You're going to blame an entire gender for something Logan did? If someone's going to represent us, I want a vote on who it is. And it wouldn't be him."

"You don't even know him."

"Fine. Introduce us." He reached for the sticky bun and plucked off a pecan. She tore off a piece of the pastry and handed it to him.

"You want to meet Logan?"

"Not really. But since your life is my responsibility now, I suppose I should. It's my big-brother side coming out. This is twice now that I've caught you crying over him. Three strikes and he's out."

She crinkled her forehead at him as she nibbled on the bun. "You're not my big brother."

His gaze lowered to her upper lip, which had accumulated crystals of caramel syrup. As he watched, she swiped her tongue across it. No, definitely not her big brother. But nothing else either, he reminded himself. "When's he coming back?"

She gave a gloomy shake of her head. "We're keeping the dialogue open on that one."

He snorted. Whatever that meant, it didn't sound like any fun. "Well, Suzie Q, I can't say that I know much about marriage or long relationships or really anything beyond...mmm...a month. But to me, it seems like there should be a good misery-to-orgasm ratio. Like a hundred orgasms to one tear."

He traced a finger down her cheek, feeling just a hint of the wetness that had been there. "Not asking for details here, just something to think about."

But she surprised him. "When you have sex, does the woman always have an orgasm? And don't pull any of your macho crap on me. It's a genuine question. The kind of thing I might ask a big brother, if I had one."

He nearly choked on the pecan he'd just popped in his mouth. "That's not the sort of thing a girl asks her big brother."

She pounded his back to help him get the pecan out, but kept looking at him expectantly. "Okay, then answer as a friend. I really want to know."

He finished chewing the pecan as he readied his answer. It wasn't the kind of thing he was used to discussing with women he wasn't sleeping with. But he and Suzanne were obviously forming a unique kind of relationship.

"All right, then. The answer is no, the woman doesn't always have an orgasm. I always *want* her to. I always do whatever I can to make it happen, and it usually does. But sometimes it just doesn't, for whatever reason. I feel bad about that, and aim to make it better the next time. But if I said that every woman I've slept with had an orgasm every single time, that would not be true."

Something shifted behind her expression. He wondered if he should have lied instead of giving her an honest answer. Would she now think less of him? Maybe see him as a selfish prick in bed? Not that it mattered. They weren't headed to bed anyway. She was engaged—tears or no tears.

"What about faking it? Has a woman ever faked it with you?"

"There have been times that I wondered." He shrugged. "I like to think not. I try to be everything a woman wants, but maybe sometimes I fall short. And maybe she doesn't want to tell me, or she doesn't know *how* to tell me what she needs. Sex isn't always cut and dried for a woman. So if a woman feels that she needs to fake it, I guess I can't judge her for that. Or myself, for that matter. I'm all in, every time. Whatever she needs. If that doesn't work, well, maybe we're just not compatible."

She was listening to him with an expression of absolute fascination. And maybe even...respect? If so, that was something new. "Thanks for being honest," she told him. "That means more than you know."

"Well, sure, anytime. Nothing to hide here, because this happens to be an area I'm extremely confident about." He grinned at her. This conversation was getting entirely too serious. Time to bring back the jokester. "Of course, showing is even more educational than telling. Just something to think about."

"Oh, I absolutely agree. You should definitely show me how to fake an orgasm. I beg you, please."

"What?" He gave a scoffing laugh. "There is no way I'm showing you that. That is beyond the scope of the big-brother responsibilities."

"Please?" She batted her eyelashes. "Pretty please with sugar on top? Literally?" She pulled out an especially cara-mel-soaked piece of sweet roll and held it a few inches from his lips. "I will hand-feed you the rest of this sticky bun if you mimic one good fake orgasm. It doesn't even have to be the entire orgasm. Just a moan or two."

Her eyes held such a wicked challenge that he couldn't resist. Hell, at least she wasn't crying anymore. He ran a hand across his torso and moaned, exaggerating the sound. "Oh, baby. That feels amazing. Touch me there. Right there. Oooh, yeah. Oh, baby." He flopped his head back and forth, going now for comedy instead of accuracy.

Suzanne burst out laughing. She put her hand over her mouth to block the spurts of giggles.

"More. Oh yes. Don't stop." He was really getting into it now, rubbing one hand back and forth across his chest. "Make me come. Oh yes. I'm coming. I'm coming." He moaned louder this time, and then the sound amplified, as if someone else was howling along with him.

Suddenly the dog came hurtling through the air and launched herself at the sticky bun in Suzanne's hand. The sticky bun flew through the air and landed splat on the ground. The dog pounced on it, sheltering it between her paws and sniffing at it joyfully.

"*Snowball!*" Josh scolded. "Bad dog." He turned to Suzanne. "I'll get you another one right away."

But Suzanne was laughing so hard, tears studded her eyes. "Never mind. I guess it just isn't my day for a sticky bun."

"I'm sorry. She was supposed to be tied up out front."

"She's your dog?"

Josh looked down at Snowball, whose snout was buried in sticky pastry. "No. Absolutely not."

"Are you sure?" Suzanne kneeled down to ruffle the fur on her back. "You should really give her a bath."

"Not my dog. I don't have a dog. I am not a dog-owning person. I am completely dog-free. She wandered onto the base this morning. I'm taking her to the vet or the shelter, whichever I see first."

"Stop that, you're hurting her feelings. I know what we should do!" Suzanne straightened up, face lit up with eagerness. "Let's take her to the beach. I usually stop there before work anyway. Look, her coat is all sticky now. She can play in the ocean, and there's an outdoor spigot where she can rinse off."

"No. No bath. Not my dog—" He broke off as Suzanne took him by the hand. "I'm a busy man, I have things to do, places to go."

"Oh yeah? Like where?" She dragged him back into the Venus and Mars, with the dog trotting behind them, still licking her chops.

"Like the shelter."

"Oh come on. What's the harm in giving her a little fun first? You can't fool me. You like her. Dogs can sense that kind of thing."

"You know something? I really need to stay away from you. First I'm pretending to be a fiancé trying to buy a house, now I'm getting a dog. Every time I see you it's something else."

They'd just reached the sidewalk, where she stopped in her tracks. He stopped too, and the dog piled up behind him. "Speaking of which—" She drew her bottom lip between her teeth. "Any chance you would mind a repeat performance?"

"Why? What's going on?"

She rolled her eyes. "Mrs. Chu has a few more questions. I swear, I've given her every piece of personal information I have, down to my grade school reports and the name of my dentist. Now she wants to talk to *you*. Please?"

With those big blue eyes fixed on him, it was hard to say no. "I don't understand how this is going to work. If she asks me a bunch of questions, she'll figure out I'm not Logan Rossi, future lawyer."

"I have an idea about that."

Just then, Tim called from his Jeep. "Dude, my wife called, I need to get home. Want me to take you back to the base?"

Suzanne tightened her grip on his hand, holding it with both of hers. "I'll drive him back, Tim. We're going to wash the dog."

"No we're not," Josh insisted.

"It's a public health issue. Look at her."

"The vet can handle it."

"There might be bikinis involved," she whispered.

Instantly Josh turned to the Jeep idling at the curb. "See you later, Tim."

Suzanne laughed, her face as bright as a sunflower.

CHAPTER 10

In her little red Miata, with the top down, they zipped toward the ocean. Between the morning sunshine and the gorgeous blonde at the wheel, Josh wasn't complaining about life right now. He hadn't been to a beach since he'd left Baja, and he missed the good old Pacific Ocean.

Stargazer Beach was a pebbled stretch of shoreline at the base of the cliffs. He knew it was a popular hangout among the Jupiter Point teenagers, but at this hour, he and Suzanne had it to themselves. Since the parking lot was empty, Suzanne snagged the best spot, right next to the path that wound through the scrubby beach grass to the sand.

Josh got out and stretched, with Snowball right on his heels.

"I'll meet you at the water," Suzanne said as she grabbed a striped beach bag from her trunk. "I have to do something first."

"Changing?"

"No, I just have to check something."

He watched curiously as she headed toward a grove of eucalyptus trees set back from the beach. "What are you doing?"

"Don't worry about it. It won't take me a second."

But he didn't want her wandering off by herself, so he caught up with her and strolled at her side. She shot him an impatient look. "You don't have to play bodyguard. I come down here every morning."

"For what?"

"Just to check and see if anyone's here." They reached the shadowed grove of trees. Their long branches were so sweeping and thickly leaved, they created a sort of cave. A dark, creepy one, if you asked him. But it didn't seem to bother Suzanne. She pushed back a branch and peeked inside.

"Hello?"

No one answered.

Josh, peering over her head, saw definite signs of recent habitation—a crumpled Coke can, a dirty balled-up t-shirt, a stray scrunchie. "Someone used to be here."

"Yeah, I saw a girl here yesterday. Runaways know about this place and they spread the word." She reached into her beach bag and pulled out a business card and a plastic jar of peanut butter. She placed both items on the ground and backed away.

"All right. I'm done. Race you back to the car?"

She dashed off, her bright hair flying behind her. He gazed after her, too surprised to move at first.

Suzanne came down here just about every morning to leave stuff for runaways? What else did he not know about this woman?

*

If anything could make a tall, tousle-haired, ripped fireman even more attractive, it was a dog. Even though Josh kept claiming he had no interest in keeping the mutt, Suzanne could tell he was completely full of it.

Suzanne loved Stargazer Beach and always kept beach gear in her car. While Josh was racing Snowball across the sand toward the ocean, she changed into a bikini top and cutoff shorts. She dug around in her gym bag for a small bottle of shampoo and ran after them.

But the fun, easy task she'd envisioned went completely off the rails the second Snowball caught sight of the water. The dog was hilariously afraid of the incoming waves. She barked at the line of foam skimming toward her across the sand, then chased it as it receded into the ocean.

"You know, I always thought the job of dog-shampooer was ridiculous, but now I'm kind of seeing the point," she told Josh as she squirted shampoo at Snowball. "Maybe we *should* take her to a professional."

"No way. Now that we're here, we got this."

It took fifteen minutes of romping around with her, but Josh finally got the dog into the water. While she wriggled and squirmed and chased the spray, Suzanne rubbed shampoo into her coat. By the end, they were all covered in foamy suds and Suzanne was laughing so hard her stomach hurt.

"I'll go rinse her off," Josh said, heading for the spigot at a half-jog, so Snowball would follow him. He stripped off his t-shirt as he ran. Suzanne gazed in awe at all that firm browned skin stretched over the most defined back muscles she'd ever seen. His sun-streaked hair swung nearly to his shoulders as he whistled to Snowball.

She turned back to the ocean before he noticed the way she was gawking. He was so sexy, it just wasn't fair. How was she supposed to pretend she wasn't wildly attracted to him? As she waded into the water, the waves lapped against her knees, the strong surge of the incoming tide swirling around her. The fresh sunlight spangled the surface with crystals. The salt-and-sea-creature smell brought her right back to childhood, when she used to come here with her parents and look for seashells.

How could they have just left her behind?

She startled. Where had that thought come from? It was silly. She'd chosen to stay. They'd *had* to leave.

Or had they? They could have stayed and gone through the legal process. Maybe her father would have gone to jail, but maybe not. Maybe a good lawyer would have gotten him a good deal. And she would still have a family. She skimmed her fingers across the cool surface of the water.

Jesus, why was she even thinking about this? Hadn't she gotten over all that by now? She was fine. More than fine. She was on track to achieving the life she wanted. There was no point in mourning the past.

Snowball barked from the beach, while the sound of splashing came closer. Shivers danced up and down her skin as Josh waded to her side. All her sad thoughts vanished into thin air.

"You know something?" Josh's deep voice murmured in her ear. "Considering you've had two sticky buns down your top today, I think I know what you need."

"Really? What do I need?" She was already smiling. There was something about Josh's voice that triggered an almost automatic thrill in her lower belly.

"A bath."

"What?" She shrieked as he picked her up in his arms and tossed her into the ocean. She went under in a big splash. Cool water closed over her head. Spluttering, she surfaced and launched herself at him. Laughing, he didn't even fight her, just let her topple him into the waves.

"Woohoo!" he hollered, shaking the water out of his shaggy hair. "Now that's what I'm talking about."

"You are so dead."

"No, I'm not. You need me. Who else is going to play 'Logan' in your little soap opera?" He grinned at her unrepentantly.

She splashed a big rooster tail of water at him. He dove underwater. When he surfaced and rose to his feet, water streamed down the muscular ridges of his torso, to the waistband of his cargo shorts and beyond. The wet fabric clung to his thighs and other parts. He looked like a sun-bronzed sea god. She realized she was staring and yanked her gaze away. She spotted Snowball, who paced up and down the sand, yipping anxiously.

"Your dog is getting a little nervous over there."

"Too bad. I'm busy doing something more fun right now." Josh waded toward her and took her by the waist. He swung her around in an arc. "So...something happened with Logan."

"Yes."

"Still engaged?" His playful gray-eyed gaze anchored her as the rest of the world tilted dizzyingly. She grabbed his arms for more stability, but that just made her even more aware of the lean definition of his arms and chest, and his intoxicating sun-salt scent. Her mouth watered and her lower belly clenched with desire.

Question...he'd asked her a question. Right, it was about her engagement.

"Well. I guess so." Even though she'd tossed Logan's ring on the floor of the car, he'd given it back to her. She'd been upset in the moment, but that didn't mean she was ready to call it "over." Maybe this was a normal part of the process of getting engaged. Doubts and second-thoughts were normal, right? "We had a huge fight, but we'll probably work it out."

He nodded and set her back down in the water with a splash. "Did you ever think that maybe it's not supposed to be so much work?"

And just like that, Josh went right back on her blacklist. She stomped through the waves toward the shore. "Says the man who doesn't even have a home! I've never been afraid of work. I've been working since I was sixteen. And I'd never just walk away because it's hard. I made a commitment to Logan. That means something to me. Maybe that sounds crazy to someone like you."

"Hey."

At his sharp protest, she turned to look back at him.

"I committed to *pretending* to be your fiancé, didn't I? You don't see me backing out, do you?"

No, she didn't see him backing out. She saw him standing in the sunlit water, so gorgeous her panties wanted to drag themselves off her body. She saw him actually talking to her, listening to her, playing with her. He hadn't taken his phone out a single time since they'd run into each other at the Venus and Mars.

She put a hand to her forehead. "I'm sorry. I didn't mean that the way it sounded. I just meant, someone who doesn't intend to get married."

"Well, you're right about one thing. I'm a lot better at committing to being a pretend fiancé than the real thing." His smile made her knees a bit wobbly as they made their way back up the beach.

"And I really appreciate it. Believe me. If not for you, I'd have no chance at Casa di Stella."

She flopped onto her favorite beach blanket and half-closed her eyes, letting the sun soak into her. Josh grabbed a towel and whistled to Snowball. She watched them jog down the beach a ways so Josh could dry her off. It was amazing how attached to Josh the dog had become in such a short time.

Or maybe it wasn't amazing. Maybe it was completely understandable.

Her phone buzzed from her gym bag. Lazily, she reached for it. Probably just Logan letting her know he'd landed safely and was back home studying again.

The actual words of the text were nothing like that. *You were right. Let's put things on hold for now. I can't deal with drama on top of exams. Sorry. L.*

She felt Josh's weight settle next to her on the blanket. The hairs on her arm stood up as if his nearness electrified them. She tossed the phone back in her bag and whooshed out a long breath. She lay back and closed her eyes, letting the weight of Logan's words sink in. Strangely, she didn't feel angry or hurt or sad.

Mostly, she felt relieved.

"Everything good?" Josh asked her.

She opened her eyes a crack. Josh sat with his knees bent up, feet apart. The sunlight haloed his shaggy blond-streaked hair and gilded his long limbs. One hand shaded his eyes as he looked out at the ocean. The other casually dug through the thick scruff of fur around Snowball's neck. The dog lay across his feet in apparent bliss.

"Sure."

"What happened?"

"Nothing. Listen...we can skip the house thing. You've done enough already."

Josh frowned down at her. "Okay, what's going on? Half an hour ago you were begging me to help you."

"I know, but..." What was the point? Casa di Stella was supposed to be a home for a family. A happy couple with children. "It's over with Logan," she said in a low voice. "He just sent me a text."

"He broke off your engagement in a text?" Josh sounded appalled, but Logan actually did a lot of his communicating by text. Suzanne didn't find it that strange.

"Well, for now. Until his exams are over." A sort of depression settled over her. Reality sinking in. No longer was she engaged. She was alone again. "Anyway, I can't have you pretending to be my fiancé if I don't actually have a fiancé. And I have no business buying that house anyway."

"Why not? You have enough for the down payment, right?"

"Well, yes, but—"

"And you've wanted it since you moved out, right?"

"Yes."

"So what difference does it make if Logan's being an ass? This is about you, not him."

She stared up at him, shading her eyes against the bright sunshine halo-ing his head. Suddenly a visceral memory took hold of her.

She was lying on her back on the platform behind the turrets of Casa di Stella. She thought of it as her own private stargazing platform because she was the only one who went up there. It was the night before Mrs. Chu was due to move in, and she was supposed to be at the McGraws' already. But she didn't want to go...wasn't ready to go...and that was when she spotted the first shooting star.

Of course she wished on it.

Then another streaked across the night sky, and another. And she'd wished with all her heart for—

She sat up. "Oh my God."

"What?"

"You're wrong. It *isn't* about me."

Josh looked utterly confused. "What are you talking about?"

"When I wished on the shooting stars at Casa di Stella, I wasn't thinking about me. I was thinking...okay, I know I'm not making sense here. I told you I had a rough time after my parents left. I lived alone at Casa di Stella, and I was really angry and upset. It was summer, and I used to ride my bike down here to the beach. One morning, I got here really early and met these two runaway girls, Fiona and Leeza, who were camping out. That's how I first found out that runaways stay in that grove. Anyway, I invited them to stay with me in the house."

"What?"

"It was fun, don't freak out. We had tea parties in the library and played in the tunnel. It was like a big make-believe playground. Then the Realtor started showing the house and Fiona and Leeza got scared off and left. About a week after that, I saw a news story on TV about a runaway teenage girl who was attacked and nearly murdered. It was Fiona. And that's when I realized how incredibly lucky I was. I was scared and lonely, but at any time I could have gone to the McGraws'. So many girls don't have that luxury. Fiona was from here, and her stepfather was abusing her. Bad shit happens everywhere, even in cute little tourist towns."

"Yeah, of course that's true." Josh played with a handful of pebbles, letting them flow from one hand to the other. "But what does all this have to do with the house?"

"Well..." She took a deep breath. "Did you know it has a stargazing platform on the roof between the two turrets? Just before I left, there was a meteor shower. I lay on the platform and watched the stars fall."

Josh leaned over and nudged her with his shoulder. "Not to correct a resident of the stargazing capital of the West, but you know those aren't stars, right? They're chunks of rock hitting the atmosphere and burning up."

She stuck her tongue out at him. "Who's telling this story, anyway? They're shooting stars, hotshot. And I wished on every single one. All of my wishes were for Fiona and Leeza. I wished they'd be safe. I was really scared for them. I wished they'd find a good place to stay. So that's what I'm going to do with Casa di Stella."

"You lost me."

She rose up on her knees to emphasize the seriousness of her announcement. "I'm going to buy it and turn it into a home for runaway girls."

He turned his startled gray gaze on her. "Wow."

"It's perfect. It's practically designed for girls. It's the girliest house on the planet, you said it yourself."

"Yup. Can't argue with that."

Energy surged through her. Details, plans, all cascading into place. The third floor could be transformed into dorms. The living room would become a common room. This was so much better than her original idea about a weekend getaway where she and Logan would entertain his clients. Runaways would appreciate Casa di Stella so much more than any grown-up could.

But first—she had to buy it. And for that, she still needed someone who resembled a fiancé. "Will you get fake-engaged to me again, Josh?"

CHAPTER 11

Suzanne took Josh and Snowball to her condo so she could shower and change. Josh had warned her that he might get called to a fire at any moment, so if she wanted his help it had to be soon. She called the Realtor, scheduled the meeting and took a personal day off from work.

Now she was getting dressed while he sat on her couch, which was upholstered in a bright scarlet color that somehow seemed perfect for Suzanne. She was so full of surprises. At first she'd seemed like a fun girl, someone to joke around with and needle—the kind who gave as good as she got. Someone with just enough edge to keep him interested.

But now he saw her in a whole new way. Her plan impressed him. He had no idea how practical it was, but admired the fact that she wanted to help runaways. And the idea of a fifteen-year-old Suzanne inviting two strange runaways into her house—that was definitely Suzanne Finnegan in a nutshell. She was a secret rebel with a generous heart and an unpredictable streak.

He listened to the sound of her rummaging in her bedroom and tried not to picture her getting undressed. Impossible not to, since the image of her tall form in boy shorts and bra was never too far from his mind.

Back to business. They still had the problem of convincing Mrs. Chu to sell the house to Suzanne.

"The showing was just the preliminary, this is the main event," she'd told him. "Now she wants to actually talk to us in person. Grill us, really. She might ask for other stuff, like your bank statements or whatever."

He didn't like any of that, but he'd told her he'd help and he would. The stakes were higher now; there were runaways involved. How could he say no to that?

"I see only one way to make this work," he called to her.

"Please, I'm all ears. I can't think of anything that doesn't involve hacking into Logan's bank accounts."

"Nah, no need for that. Let's keep Logan out of it. The solution is simple. You need to get engaged to *me*. Josh Marshall, member of the Jupiter Point hotshots."

She appeared in the doorway wearing a cream wrap blouse that tied at the waist. His fingers itched to untie it. Her long lemon-gold hair was smoothed over one shoulder while she messed with the back of her shirt. She looked as delicious as a lemon meringue pie. Her color scheme made her eyes look an even deeper shade of ocean than he was used to.

"You're saying you're willing to pretend that you, the actual Josh Marshall, are engaged to me, Suzanne Finnegan? In a public sort of way?"

"As crazy as it sounds, yes, I am. For the runaways."

"You're willing to sit there and get interrogated by a crabby, judgmental lady from Hong Kong who hates my guts?"

"She likes me." Josh stretched out his legs and interlaced his hands behind his head. "She is a woman, after all."

She narrowed her eyes at him. "If you're going to be my fiancé, we have to do it right. You have to swear off all flirting. You can't make me look bad. You can't go out with anyone else, either. What if Mrs. Chu sees you with another woman?"

"Well, what if she sees you with Logan? Come to think of it, what if Logan hears that you're engaged to some firefighter? If we're going to do this, it works both ways."

Her face fell. She slumped against the wall, looking completely defeated. Josh fought the urge to rush to her side and wrap his arms around her.

"You're right. This is never going to work. I don't care what Logan hears, but the fact is, everyone knows I'm engaged to a lawyer from out of town named Logan. The only way it would make any sense is if I tell everyone about—" Suddenly she brightened. "Wait. Let's review. You and I were spotted at the YWCA party coming out of the bathroom. We also came to Sean and Evie's engagement party together."

"We walked in at the same time," Josh corrected.

"Close enough. Then we were seen at the Venus and Mars Café. And possibly at the beach. With our newly adopted dog. It's perfectly clear what's been happening."

Maybe it was clear to her, but definitely not to him. "You're going to have to explain it to the simple-minded fireman over here."

"We've been falling in love."

"*What?*" He sat up so suddenly he banged his shin against the coffee table. "No one's talking about love here. This is a fake engagement, remember?"

"Relax, big guy. You're just a rebound, anyway."

"WHAT?" That sounded even more unappealing. "Back up. Way up."

"It's simple. We just have to give people a believable explanation. Hang on." Holding up one finger, she dialed a number. "Yes, Mrs. Murphy? I need to cancel that book I ordered for Logan. Yes, I'm fine. It was a mutual decision... Definitely for the best... Yes, I totally agree. Well, I wouldn't say that, but Josh is definitely a very nice guy and he's been so supportive...okay, thank you. I'll stop in very soon and thank you in person."

When she hung up, she must have caught the stunned expression on Josh's face. "What?"

"What the hell was that?"

"That was me spreading the word that Logan is out of the picture. And that you might be stepping up."

"With one phone call?"

"One very well-placed phone call." She whipped her still-damp hair into a ponytail, slid a hair tie off her wrist to anchor it, shouldered her tote bag, and held out her hand to him. "Ready?"

"One condition."

"What's that?"

"Hand me the car keys. I need to be in control of something around here."

*

In her Miata, after a stop to buy more appropriate interview clothes, Josh came up with a few more questions. "So we're supposedly in love and maybe even engaged."

"We can fudge that one a little. Mrs. Chu already thinks we're engaged, that's all that matters. And Lisa knows you're you. I mean, that you're not him."

"Are you going to tell your friends what's really going on? Because I don't want to lie to the crew. They wouldn't believe me anyway, not with my track record."

She rolled down the window and let the wind play with her ponytail. "Can you tell them you're doing it as a favor to me? Because of some legal issue or something? They might believe that."

He thought about it. "Sure. I'm a good guy. I do favors all the time. They're usually sexual, but—"

"Ha ha."

"Speaking of which, next question. Are we having sex?"

"Look at you." She turned in her seat to give him a scorcher of an up-and-down look. "Of course we're having sex."

Now that was promising. This wasn't the first time he'd caught a hot look from her, but he wasn't sure how serious they were. Maybe there would be a silver lining to this pretend engagement. "Tonight?" he asked hopefully.

"Not *actually* having sex. Good Lord, I barely know you."

"I can fill in a few blanks if you want. No criminal record, no debts, no enemies that I know of. Well, maybe Logan. And maybe Mrs. Chu once she figures out I'm a big fraud."

"Don't worry about them. Think about the bigger picture. Think about the runaways."

"It's a good cause, that's for sure. Good enough to go without sex, though?"

"Well." She whooshed out a breath. "You're forgetting something."

"What?"

"I'll probably know you a lot better after we're done with this meeting."

*

She was so right. Mrs. Chu welcomed them to Casa di Stella with a smile like a shark, with Josh playing the role of chum. She had tea and a spread of Chinese pastries waiting for them. They all sat around the glass-topped table in the backyard, under a gazebo dripping with wisteria. Josh couldn't help thinking what a wonderful place it would be for traumatized teenagers. It had an otherworldly, timeworn atmosphere. Tall brick walls around the entire perimeter made it feel safe from the entire world.

Suzanne's vision held a lot of appeal.

But first, they had to get past the shark patrolling the entrance. And the shark definitely had a nose for blood. "Who are your parents? Where do they live? Are they married?"

Josh nearly sloshed hot tea onto his lap, and returned the cup to its saucer. This interrogation would not be helped by hot liquid. "My parents are divorced, but they both still live on our ranch in Texas."

"You visit often?"

"I visit never."

"What is wrong?"

"I'm busy, and you know..." He cast around desperately for a distraction. "I've been spending all my time here in Jupiter Point getting engaged." Suzanne scooted her chair closer to his and leaned her head against his shoulder and smiled up at him adoringly. But it didn't throw Mrs. Chu off for a second.

"Divorced parents, no good. Not good for children."

"No, it isn't." He could definitely agree with that. "It's very bad for the children, which is why I intend to never get divorced."

Of course, his solution was to never get married in the first place, but he left that part out.

"That's good. No divorce. Once you marry, that's it." She looked from one to the other. "How many kids?"

"Two." He looked at Suzanne in surprise. They'd both said "two" at the exact same moment.

"Ah. You discuss already."

Josh smiled, letting Suzanne answer that one. "It's just one of the many things we've discussed. We talk a lot. That's one of the great things about our relationship."

"How you meet each other?" she demanded, turning to Josh.

"Through friends. My best friend is engaged to Suzanne's cousin, so you see? One big happy family." Josh stroked Suzanne's hand, but when he saw Mrs. Chu frown at the gesture, he stopped.

"When is your wedding?"

When Suzanne tried to answer, she stopped her with one commanding motion of her hand. "I want to see what he says. You, I already talk to."

Oh, crap. If Suzanne had already answered this one, he was screwed. He had no idea when she would have scheduled her hypothetical wedding. Time to scramble. He lifted Suzanne's hand to his lips.

"For me, it can't happen soon enough. Every morning, I wake up wishing we were already married, that I didn't have to wait a single minute before I see her beautiful face again."

Her hand jerked in his, but he held it tight. The moment seemed to slow until it felt like thick honey from a bottle. Where had those words come from? They were supposed to be facetious...but they weren't. They seemed to rise from somewhere deep inside, some part he wasn't used to looking at. Would Suzanne think he'd lost his mind? Or that he had amazing acting skills?

Instead of looking at Suzanne, he sat back and met Mrs. Chu's gaze. His words had touched her, clearly. She sniffed and dabbed at her eyes with a linen napkin. As soon as she composed herself, she went right back into interrogation mode. "You say your family has a ranch?"

"It's more of a farm than a ranch. Alfalfa and horses, and a few sheep."

"And you? Why you here? Why not home on ranch? Family is important."

In Josh's opinion, sometimes it was more important to avoid your family. "I'm better off as a firefighter. It's a tough job, risky and dangerous. Saving communities like Jupiter Point, Big Canyon, it's very satisfying. I'm good at it, and I think I do more good for the world by keeping it from burning down."

"Big Canyon? When the firemen were trapped? That was you? The movie?"

"That was me. So you've heard about the movie." He grinned at Mrs. Chu. "It was touch and go for a while, we didn't know if we'd get out of there alive."

He glanced at Suzanne, who was perched on the edge of her chair ready to pounce if the conversation took a wrong turn.

"What did you think about?"

"Excuse me?"

"When you think you about to die." Mrs. Chu's accent got stronger the more comfortable she got. "When you face death, you see things different. What did you see?"

"I saw…" Images flashed in triple-speed through his mind. The jokes he'd made to make everything feel normal. The flaming debris hitting his leg. The sound of a tree exploding a few yards away. The firefighters calling to each other over the inferno's roar. Holding tight to the sound of each other's voices. Each in his own little shelter, but not alone, not while they could hear each other. The emptiness of knowing that once he stepped out of that shelter, he would be alone. He would always be alone. Because that was the only way to be free. "I saw nothing. Thought nothing."

"Nothing?"

"Nothing. Except for wishing that I had a selfie stick. World's first burnover selfie. I could have been rich and famous."

Mrs. Chu sniffed and turned to Suzanne. "He always make jokes?"

"Always," Suzanne said solemnly. "Something tells me that he was joking even then. Right, Josh?"

"Of course. Why wouldn't I be?"

She rolled her eyes, then apparently remembered that they were supposed to be starry-eyed over each other. She plastered a radiant smile on her face and blew him a kiss. "And that's exactly what I love about you. Laughing in the face of danger."

The word "love" had a weird effect on him, like a guitar string twanging an off-key note. This was roaming into dangerous territory now.

Thank God Almighty, his pager beeped just then. "Excuse me, ladies." He checked the device, which had a message from Sean. *Get you're a** back to base. We're heading to NoCal at 1500 hours.*

Adrenaline shot through him. They'd been following the massive wildfire eating through the forests of Northern California. The only reason they hadn't been deployed there already was that they'd been fighting the Arizona fire when it first broke out. They'd all figured it was just a matter of time before they got the call.

Now time was up.

"I have to get back to the base," he told Suzanne. "T-minus two hours for takeoff."

All the teasing playfulness drained from her face. "Where are you going?"

"That fire up north. It's been in the papers. Fifty homes already destroyed." He turned to Mrs. Chu. "Ma'am, thanks for the tea. If you decide to sell your lovely home to my beautiful fiancée, believe me, you couldn't make a better choice. She'll take excellent care of it."

"She?" Mrs. Chu frowned suspiciously. "Why not you?"

"Of course, me too. Sorry, I'm not used to having a fiancée. It's all so strange and new...and great, of course. Really, incredibly great."

Suzanne, who had also risen to her feet, snickered just a bit. "Don't strain yourself," she whispered in his ear. "You might pull a muscle trying to convince yourself how great it is."

He took her hand and tickled the palm with his thumbnail, an annoying trick from fourth grade that he'd never forgotten. She elbowed him in the side. He put his arm around her, managing to pull her hair in the process. She gave a muffled squeak that she masked with a cough.

But Mrs. Chu saw none of that. Josh made sure that all she saw was a smiling, madly in-love couple walking hand in hand out of Casa di Stella.

CHAPTER 12

Suzanne held Josh's hand until they reached her car, well out of sight of Mrs. Chu. Then she pulled it out of his grasp.

"Have you ever moved past elementary school? I can't believe you actually pulled my hair."

"It's the pre-fire nerves. I have to work them off somehow. And since sex is off the table..."

"You are impossible." She unlocked the car, but didn't get in. Josh let Snowball out to relieve herself. As soon as she was done and capering back to his side, he bent down to ruffle her fur. Oh geez, every time she watched him play with his dog, she melted like chocolate on a cookie sheet.

He looked up at her with a frown. "I just realized that I never got Snowball to the shelter or the vet's office. I don't have time now. Sean will have my ass if I don't get back right away. Could you...as my fiancée..."

"Pretend fiancée."

"As my *pretend* fiancée, take care of the dog who keeps pretending she belongs to me?" His coaxing smile would make a nun give in. It was a good thing he wasn't inviting her to bed because she would have no chance of saying no.

She bit her lip and looked at Snowball. Now that she was clean, she was much more appealing. Fluffy, one ear perked up, the other down. Bright, eager eyes. Floppy tail. And Josh had done so much for her already. And she was supposedly "engaged" to him. How could she possibly justify denying him this one favor?

Oh fine.

"Sure, I'll take care of her. But you have to promise to vacuum up every single dog hair from my couch. It's red and she's white. Not a good combination."

He rose to his feet and ushered Snowball into the backseat. "Are you always this uptight about cleanliness? We're going to have a real problem once we move in together."

"We're not moving in—oh, good grief. Would you just get in the car so I can take you to the base?"

He spent the drive making a lengthy list of all the things she had to do for Snowball. Bedtime stories, home-cooked chicken dinners, at least three walks a day.

"Do they have doggie Pilates? Because I noticed she's a little flabby around the middle."

By the time she dropped him off, her face ached from laughing. With a last wave, he jogged toward Rollo and the others, who were loading packs and other gear into two crew buggies that would be their home away from home while they fought the fire up north.

Then he veered back around and loped to the driver's side. He poked his head through the window and claimed her mouth in a fiery kiss.

A flood of sensation coursed through her. Her heart pulsed with excitement. Her palms tingled, so did the soles of her feet. She lost track of where she was. The only thing that mattered was the feel of his lips against hers, the strong sweep of his tongue through her mouth, the electrifying effect he had on her nervous system. By the time he drew away, she was literally trembling.

She swept her tongue across her lower lip, still tasting him. His eyes darkened to a stormy gray as he tracked the motion. Then, in one of his quick shifts of mood, he winked at her.

"Looking out for my reputation. No way would Josh Marshall head off to a wildfire without kissing his fiancée."

"So it's official now?" She was still having a little trouble catching her breath.

"Yup, you're now my official fake fiancée. Mazel tov."

"Seriously. Do you *ever* stop joking?"

"If I do, call a doctor." He winked, reached through the window to rub the top of Snowball's head, and then he was gone.

It wasn't until she was driving back to her condo, heart rate still wildly elevated, that she realized something. All of Josh's joking around had calmed her nerves about the wildfire. Was there a purpose to his lighthearted approach? A method to his madness? Or was he just...Josh?

"What do you think, Snowball? What are we going to do with that man?"

Snowball gave a soft whimper. Glancing at the rearview mirror, Suzanne saw that the dog had settled onto the backseat with her nose resting sadly on her paws.

Suzanne completely agreed with the dog. Josh had taken all the fun and laughter with him.

About an hour later, when she was getting Snowball set up with a water dish, Lisa the Realtor called. "Congratulations, Suz! Mrs. Chu accepted your offer for Casa di Stella. You got it! Can you believe it? I seriously thought you had about a twenty-percent chance of getting it. But you really pulled it out."

"Thanks to Josh."

"Well, sure. But hey—what does that matter? You got the house! Celebrate! Take Josh out and feed him some champagne. He deserves it. Check your email, I'm sending you some docs."

After she hung up, Suzanne did a half-hearted little dance around her living room. Snowball followed along, watching her as if this was some mysterious but fun new game. "We should tell Josh."

Was it her imagination, or did Snowball's ears perk up higher at the sound of Josh's name?

She dialed his number, but got his voicemail. She remembered that he rarely checked his phone when he was on a fire, preferring to stay focused. He'd told her that he often turned it off, tossed it into his pack, and forgot about it.

"This is Josh Marshall. Leave me some love."

She rolled her eyes. Typical Josh. "This is Suzanne. I was hoping to catch you before you left the base. I got the house! *We* got it, I should say, because it was mostly thanks to you. So, thanks. Good luck at the fire. Snowball really misses you. I'll just have to drink your glass of champagne myself, I guess. See you when you get back. Stay safe."

Stay safe.

That was new, worrying about someone's safety. Now she knew how Evie felt every time Sean left.

She called her cousin. "Hey, Evie. Great news. I got the house. I'm buying Casa di Stella!"

"You did? That's fantastic." But Evie sounded just as subdued as Suzanne felt. There was no point in pretending otherwise.

"Sean will be fine," she told her, trying to convince herself as much as Evie. "The crew is really well-trained, and they know what they're doing. They'll be back soon, just as arrogant and filled with testosterone as ever. Probably even more so."

After a short silence, Evie laughed. "Let me guess. You and Josh?"

"No! I mean, yes, kind of. But not really. Ugh, it's complicated." She pictured Josh's laughing gray eyes as he came in for that kiss, and emotion washed over her. Josh's joking, the news about the house, the fact that Snowball was shedding all over her red couch...none of it mattered. She just wanted Josh to be safe. "They'll be okay, right?"

"There's a margarita at the Orbit that says 'of course they will.'"

"Be right there. I just have to feed the dog."

"The *what*? Since when do you have a dog?"

"It's complicated."

CHAPTER 13

The Yellowstone Fire was four thousand acres of flame marching across territory that hadn't burned in about a decade. It had plenty of fuel to keep it going. Along with high winds and dry conditions, that meant that nothing stood in the way of the entire Northwest going up in flames—aside from the legions of firefighters who had flown in from across the country to help out. Four hundred firefighters were on the scene. A major air effort was also underway, with C-130 air tankers deployed to drop slurry along the fire lines.

Josh and the rest of the Jupiter Point Hotshots slept at the Incident Command Center at night—they pitched tents on the grounds of a nearby high school—and drove to the fire lines every morning. There, they attacked the dry vegetation with Pulaskis and chainsaws, taking it down to the ground. The wooded terrain was full of slopes and valleys, so by the end of the day, everyone's legs ached from all the up-and-down climbing.

At night, they'd drive back to the IC in zombie-like exhaustion. They'd stand in line at the catering truck for their evening meal. It was a running joke in wildland firefighting how much the caterers relied on pork and other pig products. The Jupiter Point crew was almost too tired for the usual jokes about it—except for Josh.

According to Suzanne, that's what he was. A joker. So he might as well play it to the hilt.

One night in line for dinner, he ran into Patrick Callahan, also known as Psycho. He and Psycho went way back. They'd shut down every bar in Montana a few years ago. So Josh was shocked to find out that he was married now.

"She's a doctor," Psycho told him proudly as they ate their pork chops and applesauce. "She opened her own clinic in the town where we grew up. It's doing great. Honestly, it's hard to leave in the summer. This might be my last season."

"Wait one mother-loving second here. You're living in the town where you grew up? You're right back where you started?"

"Yup. Lara and I both. Last thing I ever thought would happen." Psycho's intensely blue eyes held a dreaminess that Josh had never seen before. "She was doing triage at a fire back in Nevada. We ran into each other and, wham."

"Just like that? Wham?"

Psycho laughed. "Might have taken a little longer than that. She wasn't my biggest fan at first. She thought I was one step removed from a hoodlum."

"I know the feeling," Josh muttered.

"Truth is, she might be right," Psycho admitted. "Why do you think we do this job? We're crazy. If we weren't doing this, we'd be off causing mayhem somewhere."

"Speak for yourself. I'm an easygoing kind of guy. Give me a beach and a surfboard, and I'll have no need for mayhem." Josh scooped up the last bite of applesauce and crumpled up his paper plate.

"Don't sell yourself short, Marsh. I've known you for a few years now. I've seen you in action. You might joke around, but when shit gets real, you're as solid as it gets." They strolled toward the garbage bins, tossing their trash as they passed. "How about we put this thing away so we can go home?"

Josh gave a thumbs-up, and they bumped shoulders. He ambled back to his tent, past the med tent, where local massage therapists were offering up free back rubs to the sore firefighters. He rolled his shoulders, considering standing in line for a rub. Nah, he'd go for a good night's sleep instead.

The other Jupiter Point guys were nowhere to be seen, so he crawled into his tent, stripped down to his underwear, and stretched his long limbs on top of his sleeping bag.

So Patrick "Psycho" Callahan was married.

Psycho was pretty much the last guy he'd ever imagine going all puppy dog for a girl. It just wasn't his style. He was the ultimate daredevil alpha type, the guy who always seemed to be running, his demons at his heels. But looking into his friend's eyes, he hadn't seen any demons. He'd seen...happiness.

It made him wonder; it really did.

Was he looking at this all wrong? What would it be like to know that someone was waiting for him back home?

What home? He didn't have a home and he didn't want one. If he had a home, he knew exactly what would happen. It would become a battleground, just like everything else did in his family. They would always know where to find him. There would be no escape. It would drive him so nuts that he might walk into a fire and never walk out again.

Nope, he'd made the right choice. Single all the way. This way, he was free to go anywhere, do anything, and have fun with anyone he wanted.

Except for one particular sassy blonde who had apparently moved into his brain and had no intention of leaving.

No matter how much Suzanne kept showing up in his dreams, she was off-limits. He had a feeling the break with Logan was temporary. They'd get back together, they'd move into that crazy house and have two—exactly two—kids. She deserved the life she wanted. Someday she and Logan would look back on this time and laugh. *Remember when you pretended to be engaged to that fireman so you could get the house? What was his name again?*

Yup, that was it. He'd be a goofy anecdote from Suzanne's past. That was definitely all he could handle.

*

The next morning, Josh rolled out of his tent when it was still dark. Sean and Rollo were yawning and stretching in the dim pre-dawn light. The other guys were all still sleeping, though in about ten minutes the whole makeshift tent city would be buzzing like a beehive. "Coffee?" Sean asked.

Josh nodded and fell into step next to them as they all headed for the catering trucks. The generators were already up and running, lights from the long trailer-trucks penetrating through the smoky air. "What's the word?" Josh asked Sean. "Any big changes overnight?"

"The East flank's almost knocked down. Wind shifted south a bit, but it's died down so they're back to dumping slurry today."

Josh nodded at that. Slurry was a fire retardant that was generally dyed either red or pink, for visibility, but no matter the color, it was disgusting stuff. The tankers dropped it on the unburned areas to prevent them from catching fire. Even though the mixture of water and potassium sulfate was nontoxic, no firefighter wanted to be in the vicinity of a slurry dump. Tight coordination between the pilots and the ground crews was vital.

"Hey, I got a text from Evie." They stood blowing on their cups of coffee, the steam rising into the air, tickling their nostrils. Rollo was still pumping the coffee urn to fill up his thermos, which held about five normal cups of coffee. "She said Suzanne got the house she's been after."

"Good for her."

"I hope she knows what she's getting into. It needed work fifteen years ago. I can only imagine what it's like now."

"This is Suzanne we're talking about. She'll make it work."

Sean looked at him strangely. "Anyway, Evie said Suzanne's been trying to reach you. She wants to thank you. The Realtor said it was your charm and good looks that sealed the deal."

"That's okay. She can skip the thanks. It wasn't a big deal."

Sean sipped his coffee. His dark green eyes were bloodshot from days in the smoke. "Everything okay?"

"This coffee tastes like ass, but other than that, sure."

"Then why don't you answer Suzanne's calls?"

Josh swallowed half his coffee before he answered. "Because I never answer calls when I'm on a fire. I helped her get her dream house. She can thank me properly when I get back."

"I saw that kiss. We *all* saw that kiss."

"It's not what you think, believe me."

"Don't mess around with her, Marsh. She's a good person. When my parents died, she made me a card and a mug."

"A coffee mug?"

"Yeah. She was into pottery, I guess. Anyway, yeah, she made this lopsided mug with all these hearts all over it. No one else did anything like that. And then she got in trouble at her school because someone talked trash about me and she set them straight. She was a real scrapper."

"Yeah, a scrapper with a crush." Josh laughed. "Didn't she say she had a crush on you when she was twelve?"

"I don't know about that, but when she stood up for me, it meant a lot. Back then, I thought the whole world was against me. And here's this fierce little blond girl in pigtails getting into a hair-pulling fight because someone called me a loser. I've never forgotten that."

Josh could picture the scene. "She wore pigtails?"

"Yeah. Whenever she could. Her mother, Desiree, was a model or something. She was always curling her hair and trying to make her look like a little doll, but Suzanne would come over to Evie's and stick her head under the faucet. She was more the tomboy type."

It was strange, but Josh thought he could listen to stories about Suzanne's childhood indefinitely. "What makes you think I'm messing around with her? I did her a favor."

"I just know how you roll, that's all. Everyone does."

"Yes, but..." Josh trailed off. He couldn't deny that Sean had a point. His love-'em-and-leave-'em reputation was entirely deserved. He stated it upfront and never veered from it. But everything with Suzanne was upside down and backwards. He didn't know what was what anymore. "It's different with Suzanne. We're friends. I helped her get the house, she's watching my dog. That's it."

"Your *what*?"

"Long story."

Which he didn't have to recount, because just then Rollo joined them. "Are you going to talk about girls all day or are you going to get your candy asses out on the line and cut some chain? Come on!" He roared like a pirate, causing a nearby flock of sparrows to swoop into the air.

"We're just waiting on you, Money," said Josh. They rarely used that nickname for Rollo because it always got under his skin. Rollo came from an old-money, Mayflower family that highly disapproved of his chosen career. They were constantly dangling big bribes under his nose to get him to quit and come manage the family hedge fund or whatever the hell it was.

Rollo snarled at him. Until he'd consumed his first sip of coffee, he wasn't fit for human company. Josh helped him by tipping the thermos up to his lips. After a healthy dose of caffeine, he relaxed and looked around the collection of white canvas tents that made up the IC. "I smell the blood of a wildfire. Let me at it!"

Josh slung his arm over Rollo's shoulder, even though he had to rise on his feet to do so. "Are you going to scare it into submission?"

"It'll be scared once it gets a whiff of you, tell you that." Rollo twitched his nose behind his big beard. All of them smelled pretty bad, since they'd been working nonstop without showering. They had access to the high school's locker rooms, but the thought of the sheer number of filthy firefighters using those showers kept Josh away. His usual routine was to book himself into a hotel room with a shower as soon as they were released from a fire.

They continued to rag on each other as they joined up with the rest of the crew. They geared up, putting on their Nomex outer layers and grabbing their packs. Then they piled into the crew buggy and drove out to the location where they'd be working.

As a captain, Josh's role was to lead the way, chopping down the bigger stuff with the chainsaw. From experience, he knew that the first ten minutes of work could be painful—his body had to get moving again after the strain of the previous day's labors. His approach was to drink about a quart of water so he'd be properly hydrated, then hunker down and work that saw until it felt like it was one with his body. Once you had a groove down, the time passed more quickly.

The sounds of firefighting rose around him. The whine of his chainsaw, the overarching roar of the fire, the yells between crew members. Sean, as the crew boss, was the one in communication with air support. When the C-130 did its first flyover, they all stopped what they were doing and watched the giant air tanker swoop over the treetops about a mile from them, a rooster tail of red liquid in its wake.

"That was a little close, don't you think?" Tim stared up at the C-130 as it headed across the forest canopy. Josh peered at him and noticed that he was plucking nervously at his Nomex coat. Even though Tim was new to wildfire fighting, he'd been deployed in Afghanistan. He should be used to big military-type aircraft.

But this was the first wildfire this summer in which the crew had been working so close to the C-130s. And Tim was a rookie.

"It's all right, they have the best pilots around flying those things," Josh told him, hoping to put him at ease. "They do their thing, we do ours. Just keep on the Pulaski, bro."

It didn't work. Tim got more and more jumpy. He kept looking up toward the sky in the direction where the C-130 had disappeared. He kept stopping and starting, even dropping his Pulaski several times. Josh had never seen anyone get so jittery on the line.

He tried to get Sean's attention, but the crew leader was speaking rapidly into the comm. No matter—he'd keep an eye on the kid himself.

Keep him engaged. Keep him talking.

Josh fell back next to Tim and beckoned Baker to take his spot. Baker gave him a questioning look but didn't argue. They'd all worked together so long they could communicate without speech much of the time.

"Tim, my brother," Josh said in a friendly tone once they were all back at work "How's Rosario doing?"

Tim didn't answer. Maybe that was too serious a subject.

"Have you heard about the movie they're making about us?"

He'd found this topic could light up anyone connected with the wildland firefighting community. It was a hot topic. People were torn between thinking it was about time wildfires got the movie treatment, and fear that it might trigger more lunatic firebugs.

"Yeah, of course." Tim relaxed enough to smile; above his face mask, Josh saw the skin over his cheekbones crease. "I heard they can't get anyone to play you, Marsh."

"You heard right." He paused for a high-five. He always appreciated a nice verbal jab, even if he was the target. "It's hard to find the right combination of looks and fitness, not to mention personality. I think I might volunteer to play myself. Just to help them out, you know."

Tim's gaze drifted away from him, back up to the sky. The C-130 was coming back, trailing a massive spray of red slurry. The closer it got, the more freaked out Tim seemed to get.

He dropped his Pulaski and slammed his hands over his ears.

"Noooo," he moaned, the sound almost unearthly, like a cat yowling in the night.

"Tim. It's okay. Take it easy." Josh stopped his chainsaw and stepped toward him.

But something was seriously wrong with the rookie. His eyes rolled from side to side, as if he was witnessing something even worse than a wildfire. He shoved Josh away, grabbed his Pulaski and backed toward the forest. Toward the fire. And toward the path of the slurry.

Josh strode after him, yelling. "Tim! Listen to me. You're going the wrong direction."

Tim brandished the Pulaski at him as if it were a machine gun. "Stop right there!"

"I'm your friend, Tim. You're going to get hurt if you go that way. You hear me? *Tim!*"

But Tim was too lost in his freak-out to hear anything. He turned and stumbled through the trees.

Josh ran after him. He didn't bother yelling anymore. His voice couldn't penetrate the fog of whatever flashback had gripped the young veteran. Tim was running hard now, tripping over roots, alternately moaning and shouting. The air got hotter as he ran—was Tim intending to run straight into the damn wildfire?

Josh ran as fast as he could through the trees. If he didn't catch Tim in the next minute or so it would be too late. The crew would lose a brother. Rosario would lose a husband, her baby would lose a father. The world would lose a good human being.

Nope, there was no way Josh was letting Tim Peavy run into a fire.

The drone of the C-130 overhead got louder and louder. It was dumping the slurry practically on top of them. It could be incredibly dangerous to be hit with flying slurry. The stuff hit the ground like concrete.

When red slurry slashed through the trees not fifty feet from them, Josh knew it was time to make his move. He launched himself through the air in Tim's direction. He grabbed for his Nomex coat but missed and went crashing to the ground.

A spray of slurry whipped through the air and caught Tim on the back.

He screamed, then dropped to the ground, his limbs splayed out.

Oh fuck. On his elbows and knees, Josh crawled toward him and felt his pulse. Still alive, but unconscious. He had to get Tim out before the fire got to them. They both had their emergency shelters, but with Tim unstable like this, he couldn't count on him not to wake up and rip the thing off him.

He scooped Tim over his shoulder and staggered to his feet. The dude probably weighed a hundred and eighty, minimum. Thank God for all those fucking lifts he'd done down in Mexico. He pulled his bandanna over his mouth and sipped at the air behind the fabric. *Stay calm. Don't panic.*

One step forward, then another. That was all it took. One, then another. One, then another. The world narrowed down to that simple task. Take a step. Breathe. Take a step. Breathe.

Then a tremendous cracking sound split the world around him. Something hit his left leg and he lost his balance. He crumpled to the ground, Tim rolling off his back. He saw nothing but flames, ground, red slurry...then darkness.

Darkness.

But he couldn't stay there. He knew that. He struggled up through the darkness, through the hellish heat.

A series of flashes came after that. In one flash, Rollo was kneeling over him, his kind eyes wild with panic behind his mask. Then Rollo disappeared from view and a huge weight came off Josh's lower half. *Rollo is so freaking strong,* he thought as he went back under in a flood of pain. In the next flash, he saw tall evergreens bending and swaying overhead, as if they were talking to each other. He was still flat on his back, but moving, every bounce and jostle sending pain through his body. He focused on the treetops and the dense black smoke swirling around them. How far was the fire? Who was carrying him? What about Tim?

"Tim," he groaned.

"Right here," came the kid's voice from somewhere behind his head. "I don't know what happened, Marsh. I freaked out. I'm sorry."

He didn't want to hear any of that shit. This was life and death here. No "sorries." He went back under.

In another flash, he was on a gurney sliding into a medevac chopper. This was getting real now. They only called in the medevac for the serious shit. He wanted to ask what was wrong, but there was an oxygen mask over his mouth and his throat was too raw anyway. Just flexing his vocal cords hurt. He spotted Sean, who was rattling off information to a medic. His best friend's face was smeared with black soot and his hair stood on end. He looked almost comical. Josh wanted to laugh, but not as much as he wanted to be unconscious again.

Rollo's voice spoke in his ear. "You're gonna be fine, Marsh. You'll be flirting with the nurses in no time."

He tried to shake his head, but something was holding his neck in place. *No flirting,* he wanted to say. *I promised Suzanne.*

The next thing he knew, he was airborne, with Sean and two medics crammed into the hull of the chopper with him. It was good to know that Sean had his back. All his firefighter brothers did. Knowing that someone had your back—that was the best thing in the world.

Darkness swallowed him up again.

CHAPTER 14

Snowball really detested her new leash. She kept whining and scratching at it, no matter how often Suzanne adjusted it.

"You're so spoiled," Suzanne scolded her as they walked down Constellation Way. "I buy you the most adorable sequin-studded leash guaranteed to drive Josh up a wall, and you do nothing but complain."

Snowball scratched at it for the tenth time that morning, then decided to take a leak on a patch of grass outside the Rings of Saturn Jewelers. Suzanne didn't mind, since that gave her the opportunity to examine the new rings displayed in the case nestled into the bay window storefront. It made her think of Logan, because the last time she was here, they'd spent a good hour perusing wedding ring options.

From inside, Jack Drummond caught her eye, then came to the doorway to chat. He was a burly man with an obsessively neat Van Dyke beard. She'd heard rumors that he spent an hour every day getting it just right. "I'm still holding those rings for you, Suzanne. But I can't hold them forever."

"I know," she said regretfully. "I've run into a slight hitch."

"You dumped the lawyer for the fireman, I heard. That's quite a hitch."

Well, that hadn't taken long. Mrs. Murphy had risen beautifully to the challenge and happily spread the news about Suzanne's love life. The town seemed to accept the fact that she'd switched Logan for Josh just fine. No one seemed to miss Logan, but that might be because Josh was so well-liked.

What would people say when their charade was over?

It didn't matter. This was *her* life. No one else had a say in it.

"It's not quite like that," she told the jeweler. "I promise you'll be the first to know about any new developments." Snowball tugged on the leash, and she gratefully followed.

Sometimes a dog came in handy.

She hurried past the Venus and Mars Café, even though the dog did her best to slow down the pace and scavenge up any breakfast crumbs. When she caught sight of the pretty Dutch-blue awning of the Sky View, she whistled to Snowball. "Behave yourself, rowdy girl. We're going to an art gallery. Dogs aren't usually allowed in, but it's my cousin's so we have special privileges."

She dashed across the street, with Snowball trotting at her heels. Mrs. Murphy was setting up a display in the front window of Fifth Book from the Sun. The theme appeared to be puppets, or maybe it was crash test dummies. Hard to tell. She gave a quick wave at the older woman.

Mrs. Murphy was making wild gestures behind the glass, pointing at her ear, then at the wall. Clearly trying to tell Suzanne something. She wanted to stop, but Snowball gave a sudden yank on the leash and she had to run after her.

Outside the Sky View, she finally got the dog to slow down. "Come on, wild thing. We're going inside, unless you want me to tie you up out here? No? I thought not. Okay, then, behave." She pushed open the door, with its pretty wooden "Open" sign depicting a radiant sun.

"Hello," she called, scanning the display floor with the stunning space photographs taken by the observatory telescope. No sign of Evie. The espresso bar was empty as well. "Evie?"

Something crashed to the ground in the office out back.

"Evie, is everything okay?"

She gripped Snowball's leash tighter, not wanting the dog to go after a mouse or a cat on the loose. But the sound came from neither of those. Evie came hurrying out of the office, her face pale with distress.

"Evie! What happened?"

Her cousin came forward and took her by the shoulders. "I've been trying to call your cell phone. Do you have it turned off?"

"Yes, because I can't carry on a conversation while I'm walking Snowball. What's the matter? Is it Aunt Molly?" Everyone in the family worried about Evie's mother, who had an advanced case of Parkinson's and was rapidly declining.

"No, no. Mom's fine. It's..." She swallowed hard. "It's Josh. He got hurt in the fire up north. They had to fly him out on a helicopter. Sean's with him at the County Hospital right now. He's in surgery but they should know more soon."

Suzanne went completely numb. Just like that, she couldn't feel anything. She stared at Evie, at her beautiful, compassionate face, and felt as if she were floating overhead, as if nothing was real.

Josh—golden-skinned, sun-streaked, muscled, vital, glorious, playful Josh—the most exciting man she knew, the kindest, too—Josh, her fiancé, was—no—NO—it couldn't be—

She backed away from Evie. "No."

"Sweetie, don't freak out. They got him out of the forest before the fire—"

"No!" She took another step backwards, horrified by the thought of a fire nearly touching her Josh.

Her Josh?

"Come on, Suzanne." Evie came forward cautiously. "He's okay. He's alive. And Sean says his vitals were good."

Suzanne stopped backing up and allowed herself to listen to Evie.

"It may just be a broken leg. They're not sure yet. He was rescuing Tim, remember him? Rosario Lopez's husband? He had some kind of nervous breakdown out there, probably PTSD related. Josh went after him and saved his life. But when he was carrying him out, a tree crashed on his leg. He got knocked out. Rollo went in and found him."

She stopped abruptly, biting her lip. She shuddered, and buried her face in her hands. "My God, Suzanne. The fire was so close to them. They all could have been killed."

Evie's tears finally shook Suzanne out of her shock. She stepped forward and pulled her cousin into a hug. Suzanne's mind started working again, plans clicking into place. "Where is Josh now?"

"County Hospital, I told you. But they're going to send him to Jupiter Point in a few days. So we can see him then."

"Screw that."

Evie startled and pulled away from Suzanne. "Excuse me?"

"I'm going there. Now." She was already calculating distances and timing. The County Hospital wasn't too far from the airport. She could get there by mid-afternoon. Maybe he'd be out of surgery by then.

"Suzanne, that's not necessary. He'll be here in a couple of days."

"I'm *going*. I just have to make a couple of calls first." She pulled out her phone and dialed Stars in Your Eyes. "Hi, Marlene, I have a family emergency. Can you handle my appointments for the next couple of days, or get them rescheduled? Thanks, you're the best. Yes, I'll keep you post-ed."

She hung up and dialed another number. The phone at the Realtor's office rang once, twice.

"But Suz, there's no point in going. There's nothing you can do for him yet. I already offered."

"But you're not engaged to him." Another ring. Where was Lisa? She usually had her calls forwarded to her cell.

"Neither are you," Evie pointed out. She was one of the few people who knew the real story of her and Josh.

"I'm fake-engaged to him, and that's close enough! If he was my real fiancé, I'd be there in a flash. Of course I'm go-ing! You would too, if—" Finally, the Realtor answered. "Hi, Lisa. I have to cancel on the signing. Can we reschedule? Of course I still want the house, I just can't make it today! I'll call you when I can reschedule it."

She ended the call. Evie was looking at her strangely. "You're cancelling the Casa di Stella signing for Josh?"

"Of course I am." Maybe it was crazy, but her need to be close to Josh right now overwhelmed everything else. She didn't question it. Didn't question tossing all her plans out the window.

"Come on, Snowball." She snapped her fingers at the dog, then realized that an emergency room was probably on the list of places she really couldn't take a dog. "Do you think you could..."

Evie rolled her eyes and took Snowball's leash. "Somehow I knew I'd end up babysitting this dog."

"Thank you, cuz." Suzanne gave her a fierce hug. "I'll call you from the hospital."

"Tell Josh I'm praying for him. And give Sean a hug. Tell him to call whenever he wants."

Suzanne was already out the door.

*

After throwing some extra underwear and her toothbrush in a bag, she hit the road. She turned on the radio and unfortunately the first news item was about the wildfire.

"Four hundred firefighters are still on the scene of the enormous Yellowstone wildfire in the northern part of the state. Several firefighters have been injured battling the wind-whipped flames. Today, one of the Jupiter Point Hotshots nearly died when a tree struck him as he was carrying a fellow firefighter to safety. Josh Marshall is reported to be in stable condition following surgery on his left leg. The extent of his injuries isn't known, but it is an important reminder of just how dangerous wildfire fighting can be. Marshall is one of the most experienced members of the crew and a survivor of the Big Canyon burnover. He's also a universally well-liked member of the firefighting community, known for his joking manner. His crewmates, several of whom were also part of that burnover, were quite dis-traught."

Another voice followed. She recognized Jim Baker, Sean's other assistant. "He's one of the best guys I've ever worked with. During the burnover, we were all scared out of our minds. Then Josh starts joking around about what we're going to do after it's over, and that helped get us through it. Honestly, I think he saved some lives that day. If people panic, that's when the bad stuff happens."

The reporter took over. "By all reports, some 'bad stuff' would have happened this morning if not for Josh Mar-shall's bravery. Firefighters say they should have this blaze at least fifty-percent contained by tomorrow, thanks to the increased moisture in the air. But many are working with slightly heavier hearts today thanks to the crisis faced by Josh Marshall."

Suzanne switched off the radio, remembering how she'd given Josh a hard time about joking around in the shelter during the burnover. As if it was a bad thing. Turned out, it wasn't a bad thing. It was a Josh thing—and it helped. It saved lives.

Her phone rang. She answered without checking to see who it was, then groaned when Logan answered. "Hey, babe. Just had my last exam."

"Congratulations."

Silence.

"Don't you want to hear how it went?"

"I assume you aced it. Do I need to know any more? We're through, remember? Remember the text you sent me?" When was that, last week? It seemed like a million years ago. None of it mattered anymore, not compared to Josh being hurt.

"I was under so much pressure then. I needed a break. Everything feels different now that I'm done."

"Well, good for you, but Logan—" And suddenly it hit her, with the force of a thousand suns. No matter what happened with Josh, she could never go back to Logan. "It really is through. We shouldn't get married. It was a bad idea to begin with."

"A bad *idea*? What the hell are you talking about? We want the same things. We're perfect together."

"But our entire relationship was based on *selfishness*. Would you give up anything for me? Anything?"

"I was going to give up my freedom."

"You were *going* to. After you got the free pass."

"So it's back to that again."

"No! It's not back to that. It's not about the free pass. I was selfish too. It was all about me and my plans and my perfect dream life. But now—"

Now she was willing to let Casa di Stella go because Josh might need her. And it wasn't even a hard choice. This thing with Josh was so different from her relationship with Logan. He entranced her, entertained her, supported her, made her absolutely nuts, and she wanted to be with him more than she wanted anything else in life right now.

"I think there's someone else."

"*What*? You *think* there's someone else? Is there or isn't there?"

There is someone else. I don't know how he feels about me, but he's all I can think about and now that I've met him, I can't possibly be with anyone else. Not now.

"It's a little complicated. Look, Logan. You're going to have an amazing, successful career and life."

"But I lo—"

"No, you don't. You *wanted* me. But you never really loved me. Let's be real. You wanted a tall blonde who would look good at your law firm Christmas party. You wanted a certain type of wife. There are a million more just like me."

Even though it hurt her pride to put it that way, she believed it. Logan had never seen *her*. He'd never looked past her surface, and she'd never asked him to.

"I don't know, Suzanne," he mumbled. "I'm pretty sure you're one of a kind and I fucked up."

"Goodbye, Logan."

As she hung up, she passed the exit for the airport, which happened to be the place where she'd last seen him. *Goodbye, Logan*, she repeated silently as she flew past the off-ramp.

She kept going, on to the hospital.

CHAPTER 15

Josh's emergency shelter was gone and he was all alone, exposed to the wild heat and wind of the firestorm. Tree branches were dropping from the sky and slamming into his body. A fire tornado picked him up and whipped him through the air. The voices, the shouting, two people yelling terrible things at each other...the heat...

Was he dead? Was this hell?

No, he was back in the Big Canyon burnover. Back in his shelter. Facedown in the dirt listening to the world burn down around him. There was something he needed to remember. Needed to do. Where were the others? *Sean! Rollo!* He tried to call out to them, but his throat was so raw he stopped right away.

Tim. The kid from Jupiter Point running right into the forest. Slurry slashing through the trees. Dead weight on his shoulders. Something striking him from behind.

He woke up with a start. He wasn't in the forest with Tim, or back in the burnover, or hiding under his bed. He was in a quiet hospital room. A monitor beeped. Some kind of mechanical hum pulsed in the background. A soft snore sounded from inside the room. He lifted his head and saw Sean sprawled in a chair backed up against the wall. His head rested against the window sill, his mouth half-open. A quarter inch of dark stubble covered his jaw.

Sean was a good friend. The best kind of friend, the type that saved your life. He wanted to thank him, but first he had some more sleeping to do. Josh let his head fall back on the pillow.

No more burnover flashbacks, he told himself. How about something more fun. Maybe some Suzanne flashbacks. That would be a one hundred percent improvement.

His instructions to his subconscious must have worked. He dreamed about Stargazer Beach this time. Suzanne was playing in the water with Snowball. Her long hair flew in the air like a bright kite. She wore the lacy bra and boy shorts that he loved so much. Water sparkled on her long limbs; she seemed to be covered in diamonds. She ran toward him, a huge smile illuminating her face and everything around her. She tackled him and he crashed back into the ocean. It should hurt—it did hurt, in a distant way. But he didn't care because she was in his arms, whispering to him.

"Hi, Josh. It's Suzanne. I'm right here."

His eyes tried to open but they were so heavy. Was this real or not? He couldn't tell.

Another voice spoke, a deeper one. "I'm sorry, Miss. Who are you? Evening visiting hours are for family only."

"I'm Suzanne Finnegan, his fiancée," Suzanne answered. "We're engaged to be married."

Josh coughed. Fiancée. Wait... What? The coughing fit wouldn't stop, the spasms kept shaking his body, but at least it woke him up. He opened his eyes, wide, to keep them from falling shut again.

Then he blinked, because it turned out she *was* real. Suzanne sat right where Sean had been sitting, lighting up the drab hospital room like a sunny bouquet of daffodils.

"Josh!" She jumped to her feet and hurried to his side. "Doctor, he's awake."

"I'll need to ask him some questions. I think you should go now." The doctor, a small, white-haired man with square tortoiseshell glasses, pulled his stethoscope from around his neck.

But Josh grabbed for Suzanne's hand. He didn't want her to go. He wanted her right where she was.

"She's...my fiancée," he told the doctor. His throat didn't hurt anymore. That was good. How long had he been here? "She should stay."

Suzanne pulled a triumphant face, as if she was one step away from sticking her tongue out at the doctor. That made him laugh. She always made him laugh. He kept hold of her hand and turned his attention to the doctor. "What...happened?"

"You have a crushed femur with a secondary sprain of your anterior cruciate ligament. Possible concussion, bruised ribs, and a few other minor injuries. Overall, you were extremely lucky. It took ten hours of surgery to reconstruct your leg."

"It has six pins in it," Suzanne told him. "You'll never be able to walk through an airport metal detector again."

"I love it when the TSA gets frisky."

Suzanne gave him a delighted smile, but the doctor frowned. "These are very serious injuries. We're recommending that you stay here at least two more nights so we can monitor your concussion and make sure there's no more internal bleeding. Then you can go home and commence physical therapy."

"Home?" Did the doctor mean the hotshot base? He wasn't looking forward to recovering on a cot.

But he had it all wrong. The doctor checked his clipboard. "Texas, correct? We notified your parents. They should be here shortly."

"*What?*"

All of a sudden the monitor went crazy—which made sense since his heart had turned into a racehorse. He sat bolt upright and started to rip off the wires, sensors, whatever attached him to that hospital bed.

"Mr. Marshall!" The doctor strode to the bed and tried to push him back down. "You must stay in the bed. I can't allow you to leave."

Several nurses crowded into the room, one of them carrying a loaded syringe. "Suzanne," he gasped. "Please."

Even though she looked just as confused as the nurses, she didn't hesitate. She stepped in front of the male nurse holding the syringe. "That's not necessary."

The nurse, a burly black man, looked at the doctor for guidance.

"I can't permit him to hurt himself," the doctor said.

"If I have to see my parents, I *will* hurt myself," growled Josh.

Suzanne gave him a shushing, "I'll handle this" gesture. "I'm his fiancée and I'll make sure he doesn't get out of this bed. You have my word."

Josh reinforced that statement with a death glare. Not that he wanted to stay in bed, but he definitely didn't want to be tranquilized when his parents showed up. On the other hand...

"Can you leave that syringe in case I need help getting through this?"

The doctor appeared to have no sense of humor at all. "We don't allow our patients to self-medicate," he said stiffly. He beckoned the nurses toward the door. "Someone will be back to check on you every half hour," he warned.

Josh fell back on the pillows again as soon as all the medical staff had cleared out of the room. "Can someone take me back to the fire lines?" he groaned. "I'd rather be *there* when those crazies show up."

Suzanne pulled the chair next to the bed and sat down. "I can't tell how serious you are. I mean, these are your parents. You haven't really mentioned them much. But it's nice that they're coming, right? I'm sure they're worried about you."

"You don't understand." He lifted his eyes to the ceiling, which, being made of acoustic tile, offered no help at all. "They care about one thing. Both of them. The same thing."

"Well, that doesn't sound so bad."

"All they care about is beating the other one at whatever's going on. It could be...harvesting the first tomato. Or seeing their grandbaby first. Everything is a battleground to them. I bet I know exactly what happened."

"What?" She still looked as if she didn't know whether to laugh or call the nurses back.

"One of them got the call first. Probably Mom. She snuck off the ranch so she could get here first. Then Pop found out about it because they both have spies who tell them what's going on, see. So Pop decided there was no way he wanted to be left out. So now they're both coming, and they'll be at each other's throats the entire time and seriously...where's Sean or Rollo? They can get me out of here."

"Shhh." Suzanne settled herself closer and stroked his hair back from his forehead. Despite his state of panic, he had to admit it felt good. "That sounds completely nuts. I thought *my* parents were odd, but this is...kind of...off the charts."

"You don't believe me?" The way she stroked his hair felt so good it ought to come with a prescription. He relaxed by small, incremental degrees, until finally he was able to fill his lungs with a complete breath.

"When it comes to crazy parents, I believe just about anything. But you can't leave the hospital. So what are we going to do?"

That "we"...he liked that. He really did. It made the panic subside just a little more. "Talk to someone official and convince them not to let anyone with the last name Marshall through the door. If they won't do that, then find Sean and Rollo. Or Tim, he owes me big time. It's his fault I'm in here like a sitting duck. Tell them to barricade the door. Whatever it takes."

Suzanne bit her lip, laughter filling her eyes. "I don't think any of those things are possible. You know something, Josh? I've never seen you like this. If your parents can turn confident Josh Marshall into a babbling idiot, they must really be something."

He shook his head at her, even though it hurt to move any muscle of his body. "Traitor."

"I promise I'll be by your side the entire time. Does that help?"

"Why, so you can take notes on how to drive me crazy?"

"No." She stroked her fingers down his cheek. "I already know how to do that."

Her soft stroking made him relax even more. "That you do," he murmured.

"I'll be here to step in whenever you need. I know—pick a panic button word. Something you can say when you want a rescue."

He wanted a rescue now. Before they arrived. But maybe Suzanne was right and their visit would be easier to endure with her standing by to step in. "Okay. I choose the word..." He cast around for something perfect. "The."

She burst out laughing. "You are amazing, Josh. You really are. With everything you've been through, you still have your sense of humor."

"I wasn't joking." But he couldn't hold on to his straight face and relaxed into a smile. "Okay, I was joking. How about Snowball? That isn't a word that comes up a lot in conversation. If I start talking about Snowball, you'll know I'm in trouble. Also, if my face turns red and steam comes out of my ears."

"Come on. Is it really that bad?"

"I guess you'll see for yourself." He gave an evil chuckle, then let his eyes drift shut. "Now unless you're ready to give me a naughty sponge bath, I should sleep."

"Dream on, buddy."

"You can also give yourself a naughty sponge bath. I wouldn't mind that either."

CHAPTER 16

Even as Josh's supposed fiancée, Suzanne wasn't allowed to sleep at the hospital. She found a hotel room close by, but came back to the hospital before visiting hours started again. She stopped in the cafeteria for a coffee and bagel, and there she ran into Sean and Rollo. Neither of the two firefighters looked as though they'd slept—or shaved— much over the past few days.

"How's he doing?" she asked them.

"We keep getting texts from him about the apocalypse coming." Rollo blew on his coffee. "So I think he's doing well, considering."

"Are his parents here yet?"

"On their way. It's a good thing you're here, because we have to get back to Jupiter Point. We got called off the Yellowstone fire. They want us to gear up for a trip to Alaska."

"But what about Josh?"

"He'll be here for a couple more days, then we'll see. It might depend on how much rehab he needs. The best thing might be for him to go back to Texas."

Suzanne couldn't imagine that being the best thing, based on Josh's reaction to his parents' arrival at the hospital. "Isn't there somewhere he can go in Jupiter Point? I know he'd rather be near you guys."

Sean and Rollo exchanged a glance. "It's possible," Sean finally said. "We're working on a few ideas. The base might work out, if we can make it a little more comfortable. Hey," he gave her a quick, hard hug, "thanks for coming here. I know it means a lot to him."

"But we're not actually—"

"No need to explain." Sean squeezed her shoulder. "I'm just glad you're here."

Rollo gave her a little salute as they headed for the front door. "See you back in Jupiter Point."

She waved goodbye with the sinking feeling of being abandoned. It was all on her now. Josh's "parent-apocalypse" was coming, and she was his only lifeline.

Hey, if Josh could handle Mrs. Chu, maybe she could return the favor with his loving but difficult parents.

*

Ten minutes later, perched on a chair next to Josh's bed, watching the parental Ping-Pong match, she revised her assessment of his parents. "Loving but bonkers" was more like it. Josh's father had the smiling, friendly air of a car salesman, while his mother could have been a spokesmodel at the same car lot. She was slim and polished as a painted figurine. They both liked to talk—a lot. Suzanne had barely said hello to Josh when the two of them burst through the door in a whirlwind of words. As if they were racing to see who would get the first word in.

"Josh, sweetheart." His mother won the race by ducking down to kiss him on the cheek. "Haven't I told you a million times you should quit that silly job? It's just too dangerous."

"Ignore her, for your own sanity." His father strode to the other side of the bed, next to Suzanne. "No man needs his mother telling him what to do."

"He has no sympathy for a mother's feelings." Tears welled in her eyes. "Never has had. Not from day one."

"Mom." Josh groaned and cut Suzanne a desperate look. "Don't cry. I beg you. I haven't had enough painkillers for that. I want both of you to meet Suzanne Finnegan. Suzanne, meet my mother and father. You can call them Anne and Rock. Or Devil and Deep Blue Sea. Either way."

Rock glanced down at Suzanne. "Well, aren't you a treat. Candy striper?"

"No, I'm here from Jupiter Point. I'm a..." Where should she start? "Friend."

"Well, it's nice of you to be here, but now I'm here and happy to take over."

Josh mouthed "don't go," to Suzanne as Anne opened her tote bag and pulled out a big, fluffy stuffed lion.

"I know what my boy needs. See, honey? I brought Mohimbe for you. He always makes everything all better, doesn't he?" She tucked the lion next to Josh's face and smiled triumphantly at Rock. "It's a good thing someone's thinking about someone other than himself."

The side-eye Josh gave the stuffed lion nearly made Suzanne laugh out loud. "That's...a really sweet gesture, Anne," she told the older woman.

Not to be outdone, Rock pulled a money clip from his pocket. "Why is it that women think a ratty old hunk of cloth is the answer to anything? I brought the green, son. Just point me to the person in charge and I'll make sure they treat you right."

"Dad, this isn't prison. You don't have to grease any palms so I get a better cell block." He lowered his voice to a mutter. "On the other hand, maybe it is."

"Don't be stupid. Everything always comes down to the bottom line. If you don't believe me, try getting divorced."

He shot a bitter glance across the hospital bed at his ex-wife, who folded her arms across her chest. "Why'd you even come here, Rock? A child needs his *mother* at a time like this. Not some big lecturing jerk throwing his ill-gotten gains around."

"Ill-gotten? What do you care where it's gotten from when all you do is spend it?"

"I deserve every measly penny after what you put me through."

"Hey, did you hear I got a dog?" Josh broke in with a tone of flat-out desperation.

"Oh honey. You don't have to talk. Just lie back and relax, your mama's got this." She pulled something else out of her bag of tricks—a small atomizer, which she used to spritz the air around Josh's bed. A light sent of rose petal filled the room. "Very healing," she told them all.

Rock coughed deep in his chest. "Is that rose water? You know I'm allergic to roses," he yelled at Anne. "What the devil is wrong with you?"

"Oh dear, really?" She batted her eyes at him. "That's such awful news. Maybe you should step out of the room."

"The hell I will." Rock plucked his handkerchief from the chest pocket of his pin-striped suit. He tied it over his nose and mouth and glared fiercely at his ex-wife.

"Pop, you look like you could fight a fire," Josh piped up from the bed. "Just add some Nomex and steel-toed boots, and you'd be good to go."

His little joke—Suzanne admitted it wasn't one of his best—brought him only a brief glance from his parents, who were still locked into their glaredown. But it created enough of a pause that he was able to jump in and try to change the subject. "How are Chad and Andy? My brothers," he explained to Suzanne. "Neither of them has yet been able to leave the Marshall Vortex—aka Ranch."

"I'm so glad you asked," Anne said brightly. "They're both very excited that you're coming back."

"Coming—*what?*" His monitor began beeping ominously. Anne frantically sprayed some more rose petal fragrance above him. "I'm not coming back."

"Of course you are. You're injured, sweetheart. You need someone to take care of you while you heal. Who better than your own family?"

Rock spoke through his handkerchief, which kept adhering to his mouth. "On this *one* thing, we agree, son. I made space in my shop for you. You can recover in peace there, without any hovering females." He waved the wafting room fragrance away from his face.

"No, I have a much better plan." Anne patted Josh's shoulder. "You can have the entire side porch all to yourself. Remember how you used to like to sleep out there? It'll be just like the old days. But even better, because..." She cast a meaningful look at the fuming Rock. "Well, you know. It will be a lot more peaceful than it used to be."

"There's been some kind of enormous misunderstanding here." Josh's voice was laced with something close to flat-out terror. "I'm not going back to the ranch. It's too far. Look at me. I have a broken fibia. Tibula. One of those leg bones."

"I got a private plane all set to go," boomed Rock. "Only the best for my boy."

"Your father is good for some things," Anne said with a sniff. "As long as he understands that once you land, you're coming right up to the main house, not to his dirty old shop."

"I'm chartering the plane, I get to decide where it lands." Rock yanked the handkerchief away from his mouth and right away started coughing. "Damn you, woman."

"Listen to you, swearing in a hospital. With your son on his deathbed."

"Snowball," blurted Josh.

"Excuse me?"

"Snowball. You know, those disgusting pink snacks? I could really go for one of those. Right, Suzanne?"

Suzanne shook herself out of the paralysis caused by the nonstop interplay between Josh's parents. It was hard to believe it was real, but the evidence was right in front of her. She stood up, using her height to force their attention her direction. "Actually, I don't know why Josh hasn't mentioned this to you yet, but he's going to be staying with me in Jupiter Point while he recovers from his surgery."

She didn't dare to glance at Josh while she made her announcement. What if he didn't want to stay at her place? The idea had just occurred to her, and there was no chance to discuss it with him. But he'd said Snowball—in the most desperate tone she'd ever heard come out of his mouth. The next move was his.

Anne gasped and put her hand over her heart. "What can you possibly be talking about? You would take him away from his family?"

"Not an option," rumbled Rock. "Absolutely not an option. His brothers are counting on him. He can help out around the ranch once he's feeling more like himself. I've gone out of my way to—"

"It's always about you, isn't it?" Anne interrupted. "You think only of your—"

Josh cut them both off. "Suzanne's right. It'll be better for me if I can stay in Jupiter Point. That way I can help out at the base when I get mobile again. Sorry, I would have told you earlier, but you haven't let me speak two words since you showed up."

"See that? I told you he didn't need his mother hovering over him." Rock pointed an accusing finger at Anne.

She spritzed rose oil directly in front of his face.

"You know," Suzanne reached across the bed and snatched the atomizer from her hand, "I'm pretty sure this is against hospital policy. It wouldn't be a hospital without that classic antiseptic smell, you know?"

"Why, you—" Anne looked outraged by Suzanne's intervention.

"Don't say it," Josh warned, struggling to sit up. "Say anything you want to me, but don't go after my friends."

"I'm betting she's more than a friend. Young love, eh?" Rock wriggled his eyebrows toward Anne. Now that she was no longer armed with room fragrance, he stood taller. "I remember those days. Best time of life. What kind of work do you do, Suzanne?"

"I work at an agency in Jupiter Point called Stars in Your Eyes. I...uh...help newlyweds plan their honeymoons."

In the biting atmosphere created by the Marshalls, her job sounded absolutely absurd, like something only a naive romantic would bother with.

"We went to Cabo on our honeymoon." Anne snapped her tote bag shut. "My only mistake was not leaving my husband there."

"Oh, for Chrissake—"

"There he goes again, did you hear that?"

"Snowball," said Josh.

Suzanne cast desperately around for something, any-thing to get the Marshalls out of Josh's hospital room. She turned to Rock and batted her eyelashes. "Rock, do you know what Josh was telling me right before you came in? He was saying that what he'd really like is a taste of home. Some real Texas barbecue maybe, or some..." What did people eat in Texas? She couldn't come up with anything. "Other Texas stuff."

"Tequila," muttered Josh. "A six-pack of Lone Star. Or maybe a twelve-pack."

Suzanne ignored that as being unhelpful. "Even a hunk of Texas beef," she continued. "But I've never even been to Texas, and if anyone knows what Josh likes to eat, it's you and Anne, right? I bet one of you can come up with the per-fect taste of home for our poor invalid here."

She patted him on the shoulder while he did his best to look pathetic. Even though he had that morphine-induced haziness around the eyes, Josh still exuded that sun-browned, sun-streaked, healthy male look. He made post-surgery look good.

"You shouldn't be asking him," Anne sniffed. "I'm the one who knows her way around the kitchen." As the parent standing closest to the door, she was in prime position to get a head-start on the barbecue hunt. She took a half-step in that direction.

"Since the grill is my domain, you came to the right guy, Suzanne." Rock edged toward the door, almost as if he thought no one would notice.

"Where do you think you're going?" Anne asked as she placed her body firmly in front of the exit.

"Can't a man get barbecue sauce for his son? What's wrong with you, woman?"

"Name-calling, again!"

"Since when is the word 'woman' an insult?"

"I can read behind the lines."

"*Between* the lines, woman."

And they were off down the corridor, the sound of their bickering voices trailing behind them. Suzanne ran to the door and closed it, then leaned against it. She heaved in a long breath of air, smelling the leftover traces of rose petal. "Oh. My. God."

"You thought I was exaggerating, didn't you?" Josh beckoned to her with a wave of his hand. "Come here."

She came to his side so he could take her hand. He raised it to his lips and pressed a kiss on her fingers. "You are a goddess. How did you do that?"

"You said they turn everything into a contest, right?" She shrugged. "It was disturbingly easy, to tell you the truth. If my kid was in the hospital, you couldn't tear me away."

"They know I'm not dying. I think if I was in dire shape, they'd put the battle on pause. Maybe."

"They like fighting, don't they?"

"Yeah. They fought nonstop the last few years they were married. They fought after the divorce process started. My brothers and I kind of hoped they'd stop once they weren't living together anymore, but nothing really changed. What you see is what you get with my parents."

"Wow." She whooshed out another long breath of air. "It's enough to convince you never to get married."

"You think?" He grinned at her ruefully. "Now you see where I'm coming from. I figure it's probably genetic, so I'm sparing the world from any more Fucked-Up Fighting Marshalls."

"I can see what you mean, for sure." It was all falling into place now. Of course Josh avoided commitments and relationships, if that was the example he'd grown up with. "You know, I meet a lot of newlyweds in my line of work. I see a lot of relationships. And I can tell you one thing for sure."

"They're all doomed?"

"Funny. No. I can tell you that they're all different. I guess your parents like their relationship the way it is, divorced or not." She shook her head in wonder. "To each their own. Anyway, the barbecue sauce ploy is only going to work for so long. What's our next move?"

"What do you mean?" The look of desperate hope on Josh's face made her laugh—he looked as if she was offering him a double scoop of ice cream after a month of dieting. "Are you going to get me out of here?"

"You certainly can't stay here. It's inhumane."

"I think I love you, woman."

Even though he said it lightly, the words skipped through her heart like sprinkles of fairy dust. "Did you just call me a name?"

"If the word 'woman' is wrong, I don't want to be right. Now what's the plan?"

"Let me talk to the doctor. If I explain that you're coming home with me, and that you don't need the morphine drip now that your parents are gone, and that I'll make sure you do all your PT and whatever else—"

She broke off when he took her hand again, using the other one to hoist himself into a sitting position. "Why are you doing this? It's a lot to take on. You have your own life."

"I'm your fiancée," she said lightly. "Please don't tell me you've forgotten."

"I haven't forgotten." The odd intense look in his eyes gave her a quick thrill. "I also haven't forgotten that it's not—"

"If it were real, this is what I'd be doing," she said firmly. "So this is what I'm going to do. There's no argument, unless you really don't want to stay with me. If you'd rather go to the base, that's fine. I'll drive you there."

"No." He was still watching her steadily. "If you're willing, I'd be grateful. You know the best part?"

"What?"

"They can find the hotshots base pretty easy. I think I'll be safer at your condo. It's got that security system." He laughed, looking revived and invigorated. "Go find the doctor. Tell him I'm going to break their morphine budget if I stay here any longer."

"On it."

An hour later, she was wheeling him out of the hospital into the baking-hot parking lot. She had a thick sheaf of aftercare instructions tucked into her tote bag and a prescription for serious painkillers. Not that he'd need them—he seemed like his old self now that they were heading toward freedom.

"How did you do that?" he marveled. "That doctor didn't listen to a thing I said, and I'm the patient!"

"Well, Josh, I might not have a lot of good qualities. I'm stubborn and willful and can definitely be a little selfish. Evie will tell you. But I am really, really good at planning things and talking people into following the plan. Besides, I found out the doctor's a little crabby because his wife's been bugging him about their anniversary. I set him up with a Stars in Your Eyes sunset cruise—on the house."

He twisted his head around to meet her eyes. "Don't downplay yourself, Suzanne. You're an amazing person. Not even Sean could convince them to spring me, and he's used to telling people what to do."

"Maybe he should dye his hair blond and smile more." She batted her eyelashes at him.

He squinted at her. "Nah. Not buying it. You're a fighter, is what you are. You're loyal as fuck. You didn't even have to come out here, let alone rescue me from a fate worse than death."

She slowed the wheelchair as they reached her Miata. "Speaking of which...you promised."

"Right. Hand me my phone."

As irritating as his parents were, she still didn't feel right about kidnapping Josh away from them. She'd refused to take him anywhere until he called them.

He dialed a number and spoke quickly into the phone. "It's Josh. I checked out of the hospital and they said I'm good to go. Yeah, I'm going back to Jupiter Point. I appreciate you coming out. Really. ... Well yeah, it is hard when you and Dad...I'm sorry, about that... What do you want me to say? I can't be around it. Especially now. It doesn't mean I don't love you both. ... Of course I do, you're my parents.

Yes, I love him too. He *is* my father...I gotta go. My ride's leaving. Bye, Mom. I'll call you soon. Yes, I'm in good hands."

When he was finished, he dropped the phone to the pavement.

"Will you please drive over that thing so they can never find me again?"

Laughing, Suzanne bent to pick it up. "You're such a drama queen."

"You saw them. You heard them."

"Hey, no getting your blood pressure up. Think nice re-laxing thoughts. I'll tell you what. Let's get you into my car and then I'll put some Enya on and maybe spray some rose petal fragrance and—" She broke into laughter at his out-raged glare.

"I see what's happening now. Now that you've learned how to torture me, you're kidnapping me so you can try all those same things at home."

"Bwhahahaha. You're on to me." She let fly her best evil laugh as she opened the door of the Miata. "My car's kind of small. You might have to stick your cast out the window."

"At this point, I'd gnaw my leg off to get out of here. Come on, let's make this happen. Wheel me next to the door."

Following his instructions, she got him close enough so he was able to maneuver himself inside using the sheer strength of his arm and chest muscles. His command over his body was truly impressive, not to mention sexy. Every time she looked at his cast, her heart twisted. But still—he was here. Alive.

What was it going to be like when he was in her condo all the time? Where was he going to sleep? She really hadn't thought this through very well, she realized as she hit the highway back to Jupiter Point.

He sat in the passenger seat, which was pushed all the way back to make room for his cast. The effort of getting into the car had worn him out, and he closed his eyes. In stillness, his face had a different appearance. When he was conscious, he was always laughing or talking, exuding life and playfulness. Now, she could see the laugh lines around his mouth, the creases fanning from his eyes, a scar next to his nose. He was still extremely good-looking, but different—as if another person lay behind the jokester version of Josh.

She wondered what that hidden part of Josh was like, and if she'd like him as much as she liked the one she knew. Or maybe she'd already seen that other Josh. He was the one willing to step in when Logan bailed. He was the one who got awkward kids at a party to join in on a game. The one who'd gone after Tim and saved his life.

More and more, she couldn't believe how easily she'd dismissed him as nothing more than a cute, funny guy not worth taking seriously.

Maybe she was the arrogant one. Maybe she'd gotten everything all wrong.

CHAPTER 17

Suzanne kicked off Josh's rehab stay by reciting a list of rules as she made up the futon couch in her living room. "My bedroom is off-limits unless you're *specifically* invited."

Josh smothered a smile. As long as there was a clause in the rules that involved him entering her bedroom, he figured there was a chance. "Got it. Here's hoping the invitation is pink and smells like roses."

She made a face at him. He propped himself against the wall and watched her. Ever since she'd shown up in his hospital room, his feelings for her had shifted to something he didn't recognize. Desire, yes. But something else, too. He felt...touched, even honored, that she was there for him.

Suzanne continued her lecture. "Rule number two. I have sensitive skin and require frequent facial masks. No laughing should you witness anything unusual on my face."

"Fair enough. No laughing. Can I scream in horror?"

"No. Rule number three. I have the right to make up any rule I want at any moment."

"Then why bother to have the first two rules?"

With a scathing glance that kind of turned him on, she continued. "Rule number four. I don't have time to cook. I usually microwave something or order takeout. If you want anything beyond that, you're going to have to do it yourself."

He raised his hand from his position against the wall. "What about hiring a cook to move in with us? I'll chip in."

"No. Also, no interrupting during the announcement of the rules."

"Are you done?"

She snapped the top sheet into place and tucked it in. "For now." With a sassy smile, she tossed her long blond hair over her shoulder. "Your bed awaits, hotshot."

She was so sexy, he couldn't resist her another moment. "Thank you. I might need some help, though. Can you come give me a hand?"

As soon as she got close enough, he reached for her hand and tugged her against him. Her light scent, which had been driving him crazy in the car, now surrounded him. He bent his head closer and breathed her in. "Thank you. I'll never forget this."

She swayed toward him ever so gently, and more than anything he wanted to take her head between his hands and claim her mouth in a deep and passionate kiss. The moment drew out as he sorted through all the feelings cascading through him. Her eyes grew large and her breath hitched. He read desire on her face, along with hesitation.

He bent his head closer, electrified by the proximity of her soft skin and wide eyes. Despite the persistent ache in his leg, his cock stirred. Maybe being close to Suzanne had healing powers.

"Rule number five," she whispered, a warning filtering into her deep blue gaze.

"Don't say it. I'll behave." He dropped his hands. "I shouldn't have done that. I don't want to put you in an awkward position. I take it back."

"Rule number five," she repeated, still pressed against him. "Before I was so rudely interrupted, I was going to say that rule number five is that you do nothing to interfere with your recovery. I'd feel terrible if I made you worse."

"You think you're making me worse?" He shifted his hips so she could feel his growing erection. "I'm feeling about five hundred percent better right now."

Color flooded her cheeks. Instead of moving away from the hard cock against her thigh, she rubbed her center against him. Her warmth penetrated through the sweatpants she'd bought for him in the hospital gift shop. God, he wanted to be inside her, feeling her wet, silky flesh against his. Nestling his crutches under his armpits, he planted his hands on her ass and amplified the grinding motion of her hips. Her breath came faster, her eyelids drooped, cheeks got more and more pink.

"You know what would really make me feel better?" he growled. "If you came against my thigh right now."

"But...it might hurt you..."

"Honey, I'm alive. I could have died. Watching you come would be like coming back from the dead. Please, for me. Because you feel sorry for me. Because it will make me feel like I'm not half-dead still. Because you're gorgeous and sexy and I want you so badly I could scream, except it's against the rules. Come on, baby. Come for me." As he poured hot murmurs into her ear, he manipulated her sex against his thigh, his hipbone, any part of his body he could bring into play.

Even though his injured leg was throbbing, it was nothing compared to the ache in his cock as she slid her lithe body against him. "Are you wearing that underwear you wore at the party?" he murmured. "Do you have any idea how many times I've dreamed about those panties?"

"No," she gasped. "Not those. I think they're...pink...maybe...oh my God...harder Josh...right there...faster...ahhhhh!"

She erupted into an explosive orgasm that made her entire body shake against his. He held his arms tightly around her, loving the tremors that ran through her slim frame. She didn't hold back her cries of fulfillment. He loved that too. A girl who knew what she liked and wasn't afraid to show it—yeah, he loved that a lot.

When they finally separated, she pushed her tumbled hair away from her flushed face. "Um...I didn't intend...I'm pretty sure the rules..."

"We weren't in your bedroom, I didn't laugh or scream, and you didn't have to cook. I think we're good." He grinned at her. It took some effort to look casual, considering the extreme state of his arousal.

"I'm definitely good. But what about you? It doesn't seem fair." She slid her hand between his legs to touch the hard shaft forming a tent in his sweatpants.

"As much as I would love every second of that, better not," he said regretfully. "I should really get off my feet now."

"Yes, of course. Oh my God, I'm so sorry."

"I'm fine. Just tired. Can we come back to this later, maybe? After I've slept for about a week?"

"Yes. Okay." She tucked a long strand of blond hair behind her ear. Really, it was amazing how rattled she looked. Maybe she wasn't used to coming like that—against the thigh of a man who happened to be on crutches.

If he had his way, it would be the first of many times she came, in any number of ways.

*

He slept solid for the next two days. The aftereffects of the disaster in the forest and then the surgery took a heavy toll. Also, the painkillers made him groggy as a rock star on a bender. He hated taking the stuff, but did as Suzanne said the first couple of days. Those were the rules. Besides, he owed her.

She'd rescued him. Okay, maybe not from a life-or-death situation like a fire. But something almost as painful.

No surprise, Suzanne turned out to be a very organized caretaker. She filled the coffee table with everything he might possibly need while she was at work. Water, medication, snacks, books, TV remote. She programmed meds reminders into his phone before she left for work, or for Pilates class, or her volunteer shifts at the Y, or margaritas with her friends, or... Suzanne had a very busy life.

He was a little bit in awe of her at this point.

When he wasn't sleeping, he soaked in the comforting, cheerful ambiance of Suzanne's condo. She had a real sense of order. Everything was tidy and well arranged, with no extra clutter. She liked a classic style, with a few bold splashes of color, such as the red upholstery of the couch. Framed photos decorated the walls.

He spent a lot of time looking at one shot in particular, which showed Suzanne and Evie playing on the beach as kids. Suzanne was about to dump a pail of sand on Evie's legs, while Evie laughed and egged her on. Corkscrew curls bounced on Suzanne's head like little blond springs, and she wore an expression of manic mischief.

She was so adorable it hurt.

Other photos showed her parents—he assumed. An older man gazing adoringly at a much younger, fragile-looking blonde. He could see Suzanne's physical resemblance to her mother, but he would never use the word "fragile" for Suzanne. She must have gotten her strength and sass from somewhere else. Wherever it came from, he liked it. A lot.

At first he worried that it would be awkward staying at her place with her. In the past, he'd rarely spent more than one night in a woman's space. It wasn't his style. That sort of thing might lead in a direction he didn't want, so he avoided it. He kept telling himself that staying at Suzanne's was different. It was more like...roommates. Roommates, with a dash of post-surgery recovery. Definitely nothing romantic. Hell, they weren't even sleeping together.

Just because he looked forward to the moment when Suzanne's key turned in the lock, just because the sound of her zapping dinner in the microwave made him smile, just because the connection between them still sizzled with heat, none of that added up to romance.

Did it?

Neither of them mentioned the moment he'd brought her to orgasm. First of all, he slept a lot the first few days. Second, he wanted to follow her lead. After all, she'd just broken things off with her fiancé and now she had an injured firefighter on her couch. He didn't want to push her into anything.

Also—go figure—he had fun just hanging out with her during those few hours when she was home. She liked to make sweet and salty popcorn with coconut oil and cayenne pepper. She set up Monopoly on the coffee table and they battled it out over the course of days. They talked about all sort of things as they played. Favorite movies...the kid who used to bully Josh in third grade until he took Tae Kwando...the time Suzanne saved someone from drowning at

Stargazer Beach, the time she'd gotten stung by a jellyfish, the time Josh accidentally asked two girls to junior prom.

He still wanted her, more than ever. But he liked this, too.

*

The next time the hotshots were home, Sean stopped by with news about Tim.

"Apparently there was an incident in Afghanistan that he suppressed. Like it never happened. A chopper nearly clipped him. He got knocked out and when he woke up, he didn't remember what happened. I guess being out with those C-130s triggered a flashback."

"I figured it was something like that. How's he doing?"

"He's getting a psych evaluation. He broke a couple of ribs too."

"Man, I'm sorry, Magneto. The crew's down two guys now, must be pretty tough."

"Hey, don't worry about any of that. Worry about getting yourself healed up." He fiddled with a glass dish of pebbles that sat on Suzanne's end table. "Why do girls like to keep bowls of rocks around?" he asked, puzzling over it.

Josh settled his leg back onto its pillow. "It's called decor, you barbarian."

"Huh." Sean shrugged and left the pebbles alone. "We miss you, man. It's not the same without you."

"Yeah." Josh poured a glass of water from the pitcher Suzanne had left him. "I miss the action, but I have it pretty good here. There's a beautiful girl leaving me snacks and doling out meds. And I think she's letting me win at Monopoly. Can't complain."

Sean eyed the game board still set up on the coffee table. "Speaking of real estate, is Suzanne okay about losing the house?"

Josh frowned at the crew leader. "What are you talking about? She got the house."

Sean made a face, as if he wished he hadn't said anything. "Sorry, I figured you would know. She cancelled the signing so she could get to the hospital. Someone else weaseled in and made an offer."

"Mother..." Josh bit back a stream of swear words. The thought that he'd been responsible for her losing the house didn't sit right at all. "I'm going to call Mrs. Chu. She put Suzanne through more hoops than a hula contest. This is total crap. Hand me the phone, Sean."

"Hell no. You're supposed to be relaxing and recovering. Forget it, it's done. If Suzanne hasn't said anything, maybe she's fine with it. Maybe she doesn't want a monster mortgage after all. Evie thinks it's for the best."

"Well, that just goes to show that Evie doesn't know as much about Suzanne as she thinks."

Sean looked at him strangely. "What, and you do?"

"Yeah. I do. Some things, anyway. She deserved that house."

He brooded over the injustice for a moment, then forced himself to let it go. "Did you bring my laptop?"

"Yup.

Sean reached into the knapsack he'd brought with him and pulled out Josh's laptop, which was encased in a hard rubber shell because he carted the thing everywhere. He set it on the couch. "Are you getting bored? Lying around waiting for a beautiful girl to come home isn't all it's cracked up to be?"

"That part's just fine. But I'm the worst couch potato in the world," Josh agreed gloomily. "I hate TV. If I'm going to be flat on my back, it ought to be at a beach."

"Just take it easy, bro. The worst thing you can do is push yourself too hard."

Josh lay back, ready for a nap. "Thanks for coming by, Magneto."

After a last fist bump, Sean took off. Josh was still trying to decide what to say to Suzanne about losing the house, when the door opened and a furry meteorite flew in. Snowball jumped onto the couch and began licking him with wet thoroughness.

"Snowball! Gentle." Suzanne tried to grab her collar, but she squirmed away. Josh didn't mind the tsunami of affection that came his way from the dog. When she was done licking his face and sniffing various parts of his body, the pooch curled up next on him on the couch and started storing.

"I was wondering what ol' Snowball was up to," Josh said, delighted to have the dog's warm body curled up next to him. "How did she behave for Evie?"

"Just fine. And actually, my aunt Molly really likes her, so Evie's been leaving her over there while she's at the gallery."

"Look at you, Snowball. Miss Popular." He scratched the dog's head. "Everyone in town wants a piece of you. Which reminds me." He shifted his attention to Suzanne. "Why didn't you tell me about Casa di Stella?"

She got up and cleared away the dishes on his coffee table. She looked cool and crisp in a cobalt-blue tunic style top and white leggings. "Because I'm over it. We gave her every single bit of information she wanted. I jumped through every possible hoop and even some she didn't ask for. Then I miss *one* meeting and suddenly it's all off. It's ridiculous! So when Lisa told me another offer had come in, I told her I was out. They can have it. I don't care anymore."

"You did care. A lot."

She shrugged and whisked the dishes toward the kitchen. "I also used to care about who would get the rose each week. Doesn't mean I care now."

"The rose? What are you talking about?"

"God, you and your freakish ban on TV."

"It's not a ban. I just don't like it."

"Well, if you watched you would know what I'm talking about. On *The Bachelor*, you get a rose if he wants you to stay."

"I still have no idea what you're talking about." He swung his leg over the side of the couch and propelled himself into a standing position. He stumped after her.

"Forget it! Forget the rose and *The Bachelor*. My point was that just because I used to care doesn't mean I have to care forever. I made a choice. I missed the meeting. I called her and told her I was going to miss it. It shouldn't have been such a big deal. That just proved to me that I'm not meant to have Casa di Stella."

Her voice quivered at the end of that sentence. So...she wasn't as nonchalant about the situation as she wanted him to think.

"I'm going to call the Realtor and explain that it was my fault, because I got injured and you missed the meeting. They shouldn't play games like this. We did everything she wanted. We were totally straight up with her."

"Josh." She whirled on him. "We lied to her. We pretended we were engaged, remember?"

"But—you *were* engaged."

"Not to you!"

The fierceness of her tone shut him up right away. She sniffed, as if holding back tears, then brushed past him and fled into her bedroom, the door clicking shut behind her. The forbidden zone.

He felt like crap. First he made her lose her dream house, then he made her so upset she might be crying behind that closed door. And there was nothing he could do about it. He couldn't get her house back. Or her family. Was there anything he could do for her?

"Hey, I'll give you Park Place for free," he called through the crack. "That would give you three monopolies."

He was pretty sure he heard her laugh.

CHAPTER 18

If Suzanne had known that hosting Josh was going to bring a constant stream of firefighters through her door...well, she might have done it even sooner. Whenever the Jupiter Point Hotshots were in town, at least one of them came to visit Josh. Most often it was Rollo. He helped Josh with his exercises. Then he and Josh—still on crutches—would walk the half-mile from her condo into the historic downtown area and wreak havoc on all the local businesses.

The good kind of havoc—shopping.

Josh stocked up on reading material at Fifth Book from the Sun. Rollo bought rounds of coffee for the old geezers who hung out at the Milky Way Ice Cream Parlor. They brought her take-out from Don Pedro's and the new sushi place that had just opened. She got used to having the big, bearded Rollo around; he was the kind of guy whose sheer size might be intimidating except that his eyes were so kind.

One afternoon, she came back to find them scanning through video on Josh's laptop and laughing their asses off.

"What are we watching?" she asked as she dropped next to Josh on the couch, nudging him over with her hip. She ignored the goose bumps that rose on her arm from that simple contact. She'd been trying really hard to keep things simple with Josh. Just because she was wildly attracted to him didn't mean they should get involved.

Even though she thought about it nonstop.

"Marsh has all this crazy video from the fires we've worked. He has some awesome shit in here."

"They let you take a camera with you?"

"It's easy with an iPhone. I have about ten battery packs I take with me." Josh spoke absently, totally focused on the laptop screen. "This was from Big Canyon. Day before the burnover. Remember that, Rollo?"

Suzanne watched a strange-looking green truck roll into view. It had a boxy shape, almost like a big ice cream truck. A man rolled down a window and stuck his head out like a wild man, eyes manic, mouth fixed in a scream. If not for his crazy expression, he'd be extremely good-looking, like an Italian prince.

"Who's that?"

"Finn. He's in LA now."

Neither hotshot seemed to want to say more about Finn. The shot switched to Josh, who was holding the camera on himself while pretending his own glove was attacking him. It was hilarious to watch, and in the background firefighters were howling with laughter.

"Always joking around." She elbowed Josh in the ribs. "Why am I not surprised?"

Rollo was wiping tears from his eyes. "You'd better get your ass back to work soon, Marsh. Things are getting too serious."

Josh grinned. "Maybe I'll come out and harass you guys soon."

"Yeah, baby."

*

But now that Josh was living on her couch, Suzanne knew that he didn't joke *all* the time. Sometimes he had nightmares. She tiptoed into the living room one night and caught him thrashing on the couch, muttering words like, "stop," and clamping his hands over his ears.

In the morning, when she asked what he'd been dreaming about, he told her it was the burnover.

"You dream about it a lot?"

He shrugged. "Sometimes. Not too often."

"I heard you say 'stop.' Were you telling the fire to stop?" She smiled, expecting him to joke about it, but he just looked uncomfortable and changed the subject.

He did the same thing whenever she asked about his parents and their nutso divorce. He did *not* want to talk about it. His brothers called every couple of days but he kept those conversations short too. Yup, she was definitely seeing layers of Josh Marshall that she never would have if he hadn't been crashing on her couch.

None of them made her less attracted to him. The more time she spent with Josh, the more she liked him. She liked the way he played so patiently with Snowball. She liked the way she sometimes caught him scowling at his laptop in concentration. She liked the way he teased her, the way he listened to her.

The way he looked at her with raw appreciation.

But he didn't kiss her again. He didn't touch her beyond a friendly hand on her arm as she reached for the dice in Monopoly. It was driving her crazy. She hadn't forgotten one second of how it had felt to be pressed against him, with his big hands driving her to orgasm. She still remembered how his body had felt, the way his voice had sounded as he'd urged her to come. Even the way he'd smelled—a little smoke, a little antiseptic, a little sweaty.

How could she break through the "friend" barrier between them? *Should* she break through it? Or was that just asking for trouble?

Sweaty, manly men were not her type. She liked sophisticated, ambitious men who wore suits to work and used sculpting product in their hair. Men who were serious about their futures. Josh wasn't that kind at all. He wasn't a stick-to-it type of guy. And honestly, she completely understood why not. Now that she'd seen his parents in action, she didn't blame him one bit for wanting to avoid marriage.

She was lucky; she saw the bright side of marriage all the time in the starry-eyed newlyweds who came through her door. Even though her parents had skipped the country, they still loved each other. She believed in marriage, although she had to question her "logical" approach to it, given the fiasco with Logan.

But Josh...Josh seemed to see marriage as something to avoid, like a hot stove or measles. She wasn't naive enough to think she could change that. So as much as she wanted him, as much as she yearned to go out there and straddle him, ride that perfect ripped body until he screamed for mercy...

She knew better. If only she could convince her impractical side. The rebellious, fun-craving, reckless side that wanted one man only: Josh.

*

About two weeks after she learned that she'd lost Casa di Stella, Suzanne came home to find her condo empty. Josh must have taken Snowball for a walk; he claimed it was part of his rehab. She'd been in a terrible mood all day—restless, antsy, irritable. She'd even snapped at a honeymoon couple, causing the new bride to burst into tears.

She knew exactly what the problem was. The problem was six feet tall and sexy as sin. The problem had sun-streaked hair he liked to push back from his face, gray eyes, a playful grin, and *no interest in putting his hands on her.*

Damn him.

When someone knocked on the door, she figured it was Josh, forgetting his key again. But when she opened the door, she saw the last person she expected—or wanted—to see. "Logan?"

He gave her a smile, which she didn't return. She was too much in shock. In his open-collared shirt and dark trousers, he looked...smooth. That was the best way she could put it. Maybe her eyes were too used to Josh now. She wanted to tousle Logan's hair, maybe force him to grow a little more stubble on his chin. Lose that smug, cocky smile. Allow his clothes to wrinkle once in a while.

"Can I come in?"

She shook herself out of her paralysis. No, she really wasn't ready for him to come inside. "Um...what are you doing here?"

"I wanted to tell you I finished my finals. And I got a job."

"Congratulations. That's great." Still she didn't open the door any farther than a crack.

"And I have a surprise for you. I really think you're going to like it, so why don't you just let me in? Jesus, Suzanne."

"Sorry. Sure, come on in." Forcing a more gracious expression onto her face, she opened the door for him. He breezed in, all smiles again. Logan always felt entitled to whatever he wanted, whenever he wanted it.

That was the key to his whole character, she realized suddenly.

"Is someone staying here?" He surveyed the living room, which was littered with evidence of Josh. His laptop sat open on the coffee table, a copy of the *Mercury News-Gazette* lay scattered in sections, some on the floor, some on the table.

"Yeah, it's...a friend of Evie's fiancé. One of the hotshots broke his leg during a fire and he needed a place to stay."

Ugh, why did she sound so defensive? She and Logan were through, she didn't have to explain anything to him.

"You didn't fly all the way here from Palo Alto to tell me you got a job, did you?"

"No." A look of barely suppressed triumph simmered in his eyes. "I said I have a surprise for you." He held up a manila envelope. "You're going to love me for this. I mean, I think you already love me. I believe that. We were good together and I know I messed it up. I'm here to make up for all that."

"Logan—"

"No, listen. As soon as I got that last exam out of the way, it was like a weight lifted off me. As if a *house* had landed on me and now it's gone."

He looked at her expectantly, as if she ought to know what he was talking about.

"Well, I'm glad you got through your exams okay. But there's more to it than that."

He groaned. "Please don't mention the free pass again. We talked that shit to death already. I'm ready to move on. You will be too when you see this."

He teased open the flap of the envelope. She stopped him with a hand on his, then snatched it away. She didn't want to touch him.

"Logan, you really shouldn't be here. Our relationship wasn't right, I can see that now. I'm sorry I didn't see it earlier, but I definitely see it now. It wasn't based on anything real and lasting. It was based on...I don't know. Mutual self-interest, I suppose."

He cocked his head with a puzzled frown. "Of course it was. That's why it worked. There's nothing wrong with mutual self-interest. Everything is about mutual self-interest. You find me the lowest scum of the earth, and I can make a deal with him once I know what he wants. Mutual self-interest makes the whole world go around. It's just the way it is. Face the facts, babe."

Her face twisted in revulsion. His point of view sounded so logical, and maybe she'd believed the same thing when they'd gotten engaged. And yet it didn't feel right anymore. It didn't cover everything.

For one thing, it didn't take *love* into account.

"Some people say that love makes the world go around."

"People say all kinds of things. Are you willing to risk your future on something you can't touch or see or...*live in?*" He raised his eyebrows meaningfully.

"*What* are you talking about?"

"Take it." He handed her the manila envelope. The weight of it felt ominous in her hand. "Open it," he told her.

Carefully, she pried open the flap and peeked at the documents inside. On top was a title of ownership.

The property in question—Casa di Stella.

The buyer: Logan Rossi.

"I got my dad to pony up for the down payment," he said smugly. "Kind of a graduation gift."

She was still staring at the evidence before her. "*You* made the other offer. You're the reason she didn't reschedule my signing."

"Yes, isn't it awesome?"

"*You* own my house now."

"See, that's the beauty of it. Once we get our wedding back on track, you'll own it too."

For a moment, the future shimmered before her just as she'd planned it. Married to Logan Rossi and living in Casa di Stella.

Then he kept talking. "I looked at the pictures of it on Zillow. I have a plan to turn it into vacation rentals. We can make bank."

Vacation rentals? She shuddered. Logan didn't understand anything about what made the house so special. "Why didn't you just let me buy it? Why'd you have to get in the middle of it?"

"It's a *gesture*, Suz." He gave her an annoyed frown. "A romantic fucking gesture."

A romantic gesture...was it? She shook her head, trying to make sense of this. She'd get the house, but only if they got married. Wasn't that more like bribery? "If it was really romantic, you would have put it in my name."

"Yeah, right." He snorted. "Nice try. Not until we're married."

She stared at him, speechless for a long moment. Was she crazy, or was he? "Sell it to me, then. That'll prove you're being romantic."

His face darkened. "I don't like your attitude. I was trying to do a nice thing for you. You act like I did something wrong by shelling out a hundred thousand dollars."

"You mean asking your daddy for it."

"You didn't used to have a problem with my family's money."

"Well, I still don't. The money isn't the problem. *You're* the problem."

"Because I bought you a house?"

"You keep saying you bought it for me, but in case you're wondering, I *hate* the idea of vacation rentals. That's the opposite of what that house is supposed to be. It should be a home, someplace where people are happy together. An oasis in a world of crap. A place to come home to where everything is calm and safe and beautiful and..." Her breath caught in something close to a sob. Sure, it was a fantasy. But it was *her* fantasy.

"Are you hormonal, babe? You're crying when you should be kissing my ass."

"Are you going to sell me the house?" she demanded.

"Not unless you start acting a lot nicer to me."

And that was it. Suddenly she couldn't bear to have him in her house another second. "Just get out. Forget the house. I don't want it anymore."

"Babe. Babe, come on."

"You heard me! Go! Get out!" She manhandled him across the living room. The door opened before they reached it, and Snowball bounded inside. Josh appeared right behind her, a messenger bag slung over his chest.

"What's going on?" His slate-gray eyes scanned the two of them. Even on crutches, his muscular physique and alertness made an impact, especially on Logan, who took a quick step away from Josh. "We heard yelling."

"I bought her a house and this is what I get for it." Logan ducked past Josh and stormed down the sidewalk. "Forget about trying to buy it from me. If you want to stay in it, you can rent it like anyone else."

Fighting tears, she dragged her gaze to meet Josh's. His expression mirrored exactly what she felt inside—disgust, fury, incredulity. "Was he talking about Casa di Stella?"

Unable to speak, the breath catching in her throat, she nodded.

Not long ago, marriage to Logan and Casa di Stella were the sum total of her dreams.

Now both were gone.

CHAPTER 19

Josh stepped carefully over the threshold, following in Suzanne's wake. He took off the messenger bag Evie had given him at the gallery and set it on the coffee table. This wasn't the right time to give Suzanne the gift he'd gotten her. She could have been a walking storm front. Emotions poured off of her.

He settled on something neutral.

"Want a beer?"

Then he winced at how cavalier that sounded. *Hey, you just lost your dream house to your weasel fiancé—want a beer?*

But luckily, Suzanne wasn't the kind of girl to take offense at something like that. "Yeah, I could probably use a beer right about now. But I'll get it. You're on cru—"

He threw up a hand. "I got it. The day a guy can't walk on crutches and get a beer out of the fridge is the day he turns in his man card."

Humor lit her deep blue eyes. "Someday I hope I get to see this mythical man card I've heard about." She flung herself onto the couch. Josh gave a quick glance to make sure he'd left it in an acceptable state. Not too bad, although he'd left his laptop on the coffee table. He stumped to the kitchen and snagged a longneck bottle, which he held between his index and middle fingers as he crutched back to the living room. He handed it to her, which earned him a questioning glance.

"Nothing for you?"

"I still occasionally pop a pain pill at night. Not a good mix."

She put down the bottle. "Never mind, then. I have a rule against drinking alone. I might end up sloshed and sobbing my heart out, and no one wants to see that."

"Honey, this is your place. You do what you need to do. I'll stand guard. I'll be your designated...not driver. Something else."

"Designated   keeper-from-making-a-fool-out-of-myself? Keeper for short?"

He snorted and lowered himself onto the couch next to her. "I'm no one's keeper. Can't barely keep myself." With both hands, he lifted his cast onto the coffee table to rest.

"That makes both of us." She twisted her long hair into a rope, which she settled over one shoulder. The soft, lustrous strands slid across her skin, too slippery to stay put. "What did I ever see in him?"

"It wasn't love?"

"No." She answered quickly, like an exclamation point. "Definitely not that. Unless you call mutual self-interest love."

"If you're asking for a definition of love, you're asking the wrong guy. Are you okay?" He brushed her cheek with his knuckle.

"Oh sure. Don't worry about me. I'm always okay." But her lips didn't curve in any kind of a smile, and her eyes stayed fixed on her knees.

"You're one tough chick, is that it?" Somehow he thought there was more going on under her dry-eyed exterior. "Nothing fazes you."

"I suppose you want me to burst into tears?" she snapped. "Is that what a girl is supposed to do when she finds out the man she was engaged to is a selfish, shallow dick, and it was her own fault for ignoring every single red flag out of a million?"

Josh laughed. If Suzanne had been born in a different time, she would have been one of those tough-talking dames in a fifties rom-com, played by Lauren Bacall or Barbara Stanwyck. "Please don't. Unless you want to. I like you feisty and sassy. Gets me going."

She shot him a sidelong glance from under her lashes. Whether she intended it or not, that look was hot. His cock responded with definite interest.

"Is that a come-on? You really know how to pick your moment."

He threw up his hands in surrender. "I promise, I'm really not coming on to you at your most weak and vulnerable moment. Actually, I got you a present." He gestured at the bag on the coffee table. "A 'thank you' for putting me up. And putting up with me.'"

Her expression shifted. "You didn't have to do that."

"Too late. I already did. You can return it if you don't like it. No biggie." Except that it kind of was. He'd spotted it in Evie's gallery while he walked Snowball and known instantly that it should belong to Suzanne.

She reached for the messenger bag and pulled out a flat object wrapped in plain brown paper.

"A book?" she asked as she slid a finger under the tape to open it.

"Not saying a word."

She pushed the brown wrapper aside and stared down at the framed photograph that had captivated him at the Sky View Gallery. It was a time-lapse shot of a meteor shower—bright streaks of light streaming across a dark sky, with a low outline of hills underneath. She said nothing.

"It made me think of your shooting stars. The meteor shower you watched on the roof at Casa di Stella. And I noticed all your other photos here, and figured you liked—"

"Yes." It sounded like a sob, and when she looked up, tears stood in her eyes. "I like it. I love it. I love it so much."

"You aren't crying, are you?" he asked, alarmed.

She put the photo onto the coffee table, then scrambled off the couch and stood between his legs. He gazed up at her, so slim and tall and lovely, and lost all his words.

"Not crying," she murmured. "I'm done crying."

It was starting to sink in that she was up to something real here. The lump in his pants swelled a little bigger. She noticed; how could she not? She was looking straight down at him. He decided to let her take control of this situation.

She touched the hem of her blue sundress and inched it upwards. He swallowed hard. Suzanne was in such a strange mood—edgy, tearful, unpredictable. It probably wasn't a good idea to take this any further when she was still reeling from Logan's treachery. But with each inch of creamy skin that she revealed, his willpower lessened. His gaze traveled up the long lines of her sleek thighs. The lower edge of her panties peeked out from under her dress, beckoning to him. Not boy shorts this time. Just regular panties. Except they were bright yellow, and they said "My Happy Place" on them.

He made a strangled sound in his throat, part laughter and part lust.

"Are you laughing?" she demanded.

He couldn't answer or he might completely lose it. He reached between her legs and traced the writing across her panties. He felt the soft, downy curls underneath, and clenched his teeth against the need to delve deeper. "Sorry, there's just no way I can *not* laugh at these."

She glanced down, pulled her dress up so she could peer around it. "Oh my God. I forgot I was wearing these. I swear, they're my last-resort, haven't-done-laundry-in-forever underwear." She tried to drop her dress, but he was having none of it. He blocked the fall of her dress by bunching it in one hand.

"I have a better solution." With the other hand, he grasped the top edge of her undies and dragged them downwards. Soft blond hair peeked over the top. His mouth watered. He reached out an exploratory finger and touched secret wetness. Her thighs trembled. He looked up at her face and saw that she'd drawn her lower lip between her teeth and a wash of pink burned across her cheekbones. "Let's get these off," he ordered in a gruff voice.

She bent down and shimmied off her panties. "Fair's fair, Josh. Unzip your shorts."

"Yes, ma'am." He took his cast off the coffee table and settled it onto the floor, which seemed like a safer position for any potential shenanigans. He unsnapped his khaki shorts and pushed them down his thighs. Underneath, his swelling cock was trying to burst free of his boxers.

Suzanne let out a long sigh. "What about your leg?"

"Don't worry about my leg." He beckoned her to come closer. "Besides, I'd happily break it again for a chance to get naked with you."

She giggled, the heady color coming and going in her cheeks. She placed her knees on the couch, on either side of his hips. Slowly, she settled her soft heat right over his engorged shaft, still covered by his boxers. He laid his head back against the couch and groaned deeply.

"Oh sweet Happy Place. I'm in heaven right now."

"Really? And here I thought you might want to...get a little more intimate." She rotated her hips in a taunting motion that made his blood pound.

"Such a tease." He gripped her hips to stop her movements, afraid he might come embarrassingly fast. *Would* come. She'd been keeping him in a constant low-level state of arousal forever, it seemed. But he was operating with a handicap, and he didn't want to crash and burn. "I want this to be good for you, Suzanne. But I've never had sex with my leg in a cast before."

"So I'll be your first." She drew down his boxers and took him between her hands, stroking softly. God, it felt good. Out-of-this-world good. Once-in-a-lifetime good. "Besides, things seem to be working just fine."

"That part's not the problem," he managed.

"What about your hands? Your mouth? All good?"

"All good. But I'm a little worried about my blood pressure."

She smiled mysteriously. "You rescued a man from a wildfire. I'm not worried. Do you have any condoms?"

"My wallet. In that messenger bag." After she found the condom, she tore it open. For a long moment, she gazed at his erect cock. He had no idea what she was thinking. If she was having second thoughts, he might explode out of sheer frustration.

"Everything okay?"

"I've just...it's a little embarrassing, but I've been thinking about this for a while."

"Me too. And I'm not embarrassed at all."

"Good. Then you won't mind if I do this first."

She kneeled between his knees and bent her head toward his cock. Delicately, she swirled her tongue around the head. Pleasure exploded through him.

"Oh my God," he breathed, as she lavished his penis with sweet, wet attention. He closed his eyes and let the kaleidoscope of light and color take over. Every stroke of her tongue sent reverberations through his system. His hips pushed up, wanting more, more. What made it so intoxicating was the fact that this was *Suzanne*, with her sassy words and her attitude and her tough outer shell and generous heart, not to mention the face and body that haunted his dreams. Suzanne, her mouth wrapped around his shaft, her hair sifting over his belly, making the muscles under his skin twitch.

The drumbeat of pleasure marched down his spine. He felt his balls tighten, his cock harden even further. He gritted his teeth to stop the inevitable. "Suzanne, you're incredible, and I wish we could just do this forever, but if you want to do anything with that condom, now would be a good moment."

She lifted her head, those ocean-deep eyes dark with desire. "I love how you feel in my mouth."

"Oh, *shit*. Don't say anything more." He slapped one hand across his eyes. "Stop looking so fucking gorgeous, stop saying things guaranteed to make me come. Just get on it. Get on that thing."

Laughing, she slid the condom onto his shaft, then straightened up. He gripped his cock with one hand and held her hip with the other to help guide her down. The moment her sweet flesh gave way to the thrust of his arousal, he thought his head might explode. Panting, he held on to his control by the skin of his teeth. She leaned forward and put her hands on the back of the couch. That changed the angle so her clit slid across his cock. As her body embraced him, inch by slick, hot inch, he corkscrewed his hips, pushing in, looking for a reaction. Where did it feel good to her? Where was that sweet spot? Where was her happy place?

When she moaned and rocked her hips, he knew he'd found it. He gripped her hips tight and powered into her. He used long, merciless strokes and a pounding rhythm. She picked up on it right away, and they moved together, increasing the pace, the intensity. He felt her skin heat under the tight grip of his fingers, her muscles tighten and shiver.

Oh God. There was only so much a man could take. "I'm coming," he warned, just as he felt the first flutter of her orgasm approach. He slid his hand between them, to the hot kernel pulsing between her legs. She arched, her body going rigid, a cry ripping from her throat.

And he exploded into an orgasm that was hot and wild and filled with shooting stars.

CHAPTER 20

Suzanne wasn't sure what made her finally give in to her lust for Josh Marshall, but once she did, there was no holding back. They spent the next week inventing creative ways to work around his cast. Lying side by side on her bed worked pretty well—very well, to be honest. She was able to feel his strength in every flex of his hips and imagine what it would be like when he had full use of both legs.

It would be mind-blowing, just like every time they made love.

They also spent a lot of time laughing. That was thanks to Josh, who had to be the most playful person she'd ever known. Being with him was more fun than she'd ever had with a man—not even close.

Fun...but not serious. It couldn't be between them. He wasn't a "serious" type of guy. And she had goals. Ambitions. Needs. Okay, so her life plan had gone off-script. No house, no engagement. She just had to find another way. Suzanne Finnegan wasn't about to admit defeat so easily.

"I have a new idea about the house," she told Josh as they sprawled naked in her bed one night. This time, she'd held on to the headboard and straddled his face while he did outrageous things with his tongue and fingers. Even now, she shivered as she remembered the orgasm that had overwhelmed her senses.

"I knew you would." Josh opened one eye and peered at her lazily. "You can't keep Suzanne Finnegan down."

"No, you can't. Or at least not until I've tried everything."

"So what's the next step?" His hand rested on her upper thigh, a pleasant, arousing weight. He wasn't even trying, and he was turning her on. And that was after she'd just experienced the biggest O a girl could have. The man was out of this world.

"Have I ever mentioned that I'm a whiz when it comes to PowerPoint?"

He moved his thumb in small circles. "I'm not even sure what that is. Sounds wizardly. Like a wand you point at stuff that needs fixing."

She smiled even as her sex pulsed with warmth—as if her body knew to expect pleasure whenever Josh laid his hands on her. "Do you actually use your laptop for anything? Or is it just to look like a sexy nerd?"

"Fantasy football. Firefighting forums. My Tumblr," he murmured.

"You have a Tumblr?"

"What do you think I've been working on? Everything you ever wanted to know about life on the fire lines, baby."

Wow. That was unexpected. Every time she turned around she stumbled across another new aspect of Josh that surprised her. "I want to see it."

He shrugged uncomfortably, the movement highlighting the taut definition of his shoulder muscles. "Maybe later. What's your idea about the house?"

Clearly he didn't want to talk about his Tumblr, but she made a mental note to hunt it down herself as soon as possible. "Logan is driven by money. He's going to find out that turning Casa di Stella into vacation rentals is a very spendy proposition. So I'm going to present him with my plan about the shelter. I'd raise the money for the renovations. All he has to do is donate the use of the house. It could be a big tax deduction for him. The downside is that I have to meet with him."

"I'll be backup. I'll retrofit my crutches with peashooters."

She giggled. He was so darn cute. "I already have backup. Some of the other volunteers at the Y are going with me. They can tell their stories, and if Logan has any heart at all, how can he resist?"

He reached over with one long arm and rolled her on top of him, so her breasts pressed against the solid, warm structure of his chest. "I don't know how anyone can resist you."

"Strange, isn't it?"

"Incomprehensible."

He rolled over so she lay under him, and for the first time, they made love that way. His deep gray eyes bore into hers as he moved within her. She inhaled the clean, masculine scent of him, licked the smooth skin of his neck. She wanted to gobble him up, devour him, scream with him.

Even with his sexual powers temporarily handicapped, Josh made her happier than she'd ever been.

For now, she reminded herself.

*

Suzanne, her PowerPoint presentation, and her posse of three former runaways sat in the Realtor's office for half an hour before Lisa came out and broke the news that Logan had cancelled the meeting.

"He's going forward with his rental plan," she explained.

"Ugh, that jerk. I really wish I'd known he was the one who'd made that offer. *Anyone* but him." Suzanne zipped up her briefcase with a snap.

"I feel so bad, Suzanne." Lisa groaned and sat next to her. "He told me it was a romantic gesture. He said you were getting back together and that you'd love it."

Suzanne shouldered her bag and stood up. "Maybe I would have, before. I don't know."

"Listen, I've been thinking. Casa di Stella is a very unique property, of course. But we do have other locations in Jupiter Point that might be even better for what you guys are planning."

"Better?" It felt disloyal to say that anything could be better than Casa di Stella.

"I've heard rumors that Sean Marcus might be willing to sell the old airstrip at the beach. Should I look into that? On my own time, because I feel awful about how this played out."

Suzanne forced herself to nod and smile. How could a ratty old airstrip take the place of whimsical, charming, enchanting Casa di Stella? It couldn't. But she didn't have a choice.

After that meeting, they stopped in for a quick espresso at the Sky View Gallery. They brainstormed ideas for the shelter, and decided to set up a Kickstarter account. Suzanne pulled out her laptop and started taking notes. Everyone's enthusiasm was so inspiring. They were all talking a mile a minute, throwing ideas out, making lists, claiming tasks. They decided to meet once every other week to keep track of their progress.

They left in a flurry of hugs and "squees."

After the girls left, she sat at the counter and input all the notes into her newest Dream File.

Speaking of "dreams"...and dream lovers...she did a search for Josh Marshall and "tumblr" and got a quick thrill when a page popped up. Its background showed an incredible close-up shot of a spruce tree so consumed by flames, it looked like a torch.

Completely captivated by the photo, she jumped when someone slid onto the stool next to her. A glimpse of vivid ginger hair out of the corner of her eye told her it was Brianna.

"Those girls who just left don't look like your usual sort of friends," Brianna said in her usual blunt way. "They have at least twenty times the normal number of piercings and tattoos."

"What kind of a snap judgement is that? They *are* my friends, and we're working on a great project together, and who cares what they look like?"

"I wasn't criticizing. I like tattoos. I've been considering getting an onion tattooed on my lower back. Like a tramp stamp, except mine would be a "ramp stamp." Brianna settled her elbows on the counter. Suzanne noticed the dirt under her fingernails and the bits of dry grass clinging to her forearms. As a landscape artist, Brianna seemed to spend much of her time rolling in the dirt.

"A ramp stamp? What does that even mean?"

"You know, a ramp. It's a wild onion, kind of like a leek."

When Suzanne kept staring at her blankly, she rolled her eyes. "Why does no one else in my life know anything about plants?"

"Sorry, I'm still trying to picture an onion tattooed on your back. It's disrupting my brain waves." She picked up her espresso cup, but the smell of the coffee no longer appealed to her. She set it back on its little saucer.

Brianna leaned closer and peered at her laptop. "So what's the big project you're working on? Ooh."

Obviously she'd caught sight of the shot of Josh in his firefighting gear, bandanna draped under his helmet, a wild grin on his face. Suzanne tried to close her laptop, but Brianna prevented it.

"Is this project Josh-Marshall related?"

"No, that's something different. My project is about finding a piece of property with plenty of space..." She trailed off, since Brianna had stopped paying attention and was scanning the first post.

She read aloud. "*Accountability. Here's a tip. If you see a group of hotshots standing in a circle after a fire, that's not a group hug. That's breaking it down, saying what went wrong and who fucked up. We're brutally honest because it could be life or death next time. If you can't take a hard look at yourself and what you might have done better, you shouldn't be a hotshot. This is why I have mad respect for my guys. Nothing is harder than admitting you fucked up. But better to say it than leave it unsaid, like a smoking time-bomb.*"

She paused. They looked at the shot that accompanied the post. It was a black-and-white, documentary-style photo that showed the Jupiter Point crew in tight formation, heads together. Their expressions—seen only from profile or in snatches—were serious, even grim. Sean's eyebrows were drawn together, Rollo's mouth unsmiling, an unfamiliar dark-haired man's handsome head bent.

"Wow," said Brianna softly. "Did he write that? It's kind of powerful. I thought he just joked around all the time."

"There's a lot more to him than that," Suzanne told her, slamming shut the laptop.

"Oh really? Do tell..." Brianna grinned. "Wasn't it you...yes, I'm totally sure it was you...who said you never went for the sweaty types?"

Suzanne drew herself into her most dignified posture. "Everyone sweats. It's called sweat glands."

"I know everyone sweats. I've been pro-sweating for years. I'm just glad you're finally onboard with the concept. Seriously, you and Josh? What gives?"

"He's staying with me while he recovers from his broken leg, that's all."

When Brianna just waited, obviously expecting more of an explanation, she gave in. Why not, after all? Brianna could keep a secret. She might be tactless, but she wasn't a gossip.

"Okay, we might be doing our best to enjoy ourselves while he's laid up."

Brianna dissolved into a half-laughing, half-coughing fit. "Are you telling me he's getting laid while he's laid up?"

"Ha. Ha." Suzanne pounded her on the back as she tried to recover. "You're hilarious." And then she caught sight of the woman who'd just pulled up a camp chair next to them. Mrs. Murphy plopped into it. It must be children's story hour, because she wore a Shrek-inspired green face mask and wig. Suzanne wondered if she'd ever get that image out of her head.

"That's old news, Brianna," Mrs. Murphy announced. "Some of us saw this coming way back in the spring, when they first came to town. How's Josh doing, Suzanne? I talked to Tim Peavy's wife, and she just can't say enough good things about what Josh did. She's wondering if...well...you know. She has a few single friends. I said I'd ask you."

"Why me?"

"Well, he's staying with you, and you were looking at houses together. Some are saying you have a secret engagement. I thought it best to check."

Suzanne slid her laptop into her bag and planted her feet on the floor. "Josh and I aren't engaged."

Mrs. Murphy made a sympathetic noise. "Another broken engagement? Oh dear."

"No, no...we never were, that was just a rumor."

One she'd started, and was now fueling by hosting him at her condo. And if people knew they were now sleeping in her bed and getting very little sleep...

"Just...let Rosario know that he's still recovering from his injuries. He's in no shape to date anyone."

"Thanks for clearing that up, Suz," Brianna said. "We'll let the waiting list know."

"The *waiting list?*" When she realized Bri was joking, she made a face and headed for the door. Those other girls could just keep on waiting. She was nowhere near ready to walk away from Josh yet. Not even close.

CHAPTER 21

When she got back to her apartment, Josh was standing on his crutches, glaring at his laptop, which was propped on a pile of books on one of her high stools. He wore a dark blue Dallas Cowboys t-shirt and his shoulders looked about half a mile wide. Snowball was curled on the floor next to his cast. At the sight of Suzanne, she heaved herself up and trotted to greet her. She bent down to rub between the dog's ears.

"Hi." For a moment, she felt almost awkward. It was one thing to have a temporary roommate, another to have wild uninhibited sex with him. Did that make them roommates with benefits?

"Hi." He closed his laptop.

She wondered if she should mention that she'd seen his Tumblr. But she had something more important on her mind. "I should warn you that we're the talk of the town. Sorry about that."

His gaze flashed to hers, their slate-gray color darker than normal. "So?" He shrugged. "Talkers gonna talk."

"You don't mind being the subject of gossip?" She came farther into the living room, dropped her bag on the floor and flopped onto the couch. He crutched over to her.

"Depends on what they're saying, I guess. How did it go with the Realtor?"

She'd nearly forgotten about that meeting. It felt like ancient history now that she and the girls were taking things into their own hands. "No go." She rolled her shoulders, just now realizing her muscles were bunched with tension. "He's going forward with his plans. Nothing we can do."

"I bet there's something I can do. Take off your jacket."

The husky tone in his voice made her body immediately respond. She slid off her blazer, pleasant fantasies of afternoon sex skittering through her brain. But instead he put his warm hands on her shoulders and pressed his thumbs between her shoulder blades. It felt so good, she moaned out loud.

"Josh, you are a prince among firemen."

"So that's the way to your heart? A shoulder rub?"

"Mmmm." Pleasure flooded her body. "What do you mean, the way to my heart?" she murmured. "Aren't you more concerned about the way into my pants?"

He paused, and she immediately regretted the flippant comment. "Sorry. I didn't mean it like that."

Resuming the magical thing he was doing with his thumbs, he spoke again. "It's just that I've been thinking about something. About you. About us."

"Us?" His unusually serious tone gave her a thrill. "How do you mean?"

"I..." He ran his thumbs along her spine, forcing it to unfurl from its hunched position. "I like this. I like being with you. I like what we have going on here."

The words dripped into her consciousness like honey. So sweet, so honest. So...non-specific. "I do too. I have no idea what it is, but I like it."

"Right?" He chuckled. "Do we have to know? Can't it just be what it is? Same old story you've heard a million times. Boy meets girl. Boy pretends to be engaged to girl so girl can buy house. Girl rescues boy from crazy parents. Girl allows boy to stay in her house while they fuck each other senseless."

"And boy gives girl amazing back rubs," she added dreamily.

"And girl gives boy amazing blow—"

"Hey, don't ruin the mood," she interrupted, laughing.

"If blow jobs are wrong, I don't want to be right."

He smoothed his thumbs along the tendons between her neck and her shoulders. Every movement of his big hands was divine. "I'm so glad we're on the same page with all of this."

"All of this?"

"Our...relationship. Or non-relationship. Whatever you want to call it."

Did his hands hesitate just a tiny bit? Maybe. "Yup, same page," he murmured. "And it's a good page."

"Yes, it has all the sex and none of the expectations that get brutally crushed at the end."

"Right. Speaking of sex..." His hands left her shoulders and slid down her front, inside her blouse. He unbuttoned it enough to expose her bra. She arched her back, feeling herself slide effortlessly into the sensual haze she always felt with Josh.

The pads of his fingers skimmed across her skin. Her breath kept pace with his movements, speeding up as he slipped his hands under her bra, to her nipples. She jumped as he reached the tender, tightening skin of her areola. Amazing how she kept getting more and more responsive to Josh's touch. Or maybe her period was going to start soon...often she got more sensitive then. When was her last period, come to think of it?

She tried to calculate, but Josh's fingers were now closing around the tips of her breasts and her entire body was arching off the couch. "How do you do that?" she moaned.

"We're on the same page, right?" He lightly squeezed her nipple until she gasped. "The page where you strip all your clothes off?"

"This isn't *Penthouse*," she gasped. "I'm not stripping unless you do."

"No problem. Except I'm on crutches and you're going to have to help. Come over here. And don't button your blouse up. Leave it how it is."

The I'm-in-charge note in his voice made her shiver. Funny how she normally didn't like anyone telling her what to do. With Josh, it was different, because it always ended in a mind-altering orgasm. She got to her feet, noticing that she was already a little unsteady on her legs. She came around to the other side of the couch, Josh tracking her every move. He scanned her up and down with hot appreciation and whistled.

"Woman, you make my heart sing," he said in a low growl. "Now undo my pants."

"Excuse me?"

"I'm injured thanks to risking my life in a fire. Is it so much to ask?" He raised one eyebrow as if daring her to disagree.

"You're not helpless. Weren't you just rubbing my back two minutes ago?"

"Yes, which is another reason you should be nice to me. Come on. Unzip me. You can go ahead and do it on your knees if that makes it easier."

She burst out laughing; he was so outrageous. And the way he was devouring her with his eyes made her feel beautiful and sexy and powerful. So she did drop to her knees, and she did unzip his pants and close her lips around the big, beautiful erection that greeted her. She closed her eyes as she took him into her mouth, losing herself in the deep sensuality of the moment.

No more words after that, just the harsh rasps of his breath, the soft suckling of her lips around his shaft, the distant ticking of the kitchen clock. Then he stopped her with a trembling hand.

"You forgot to strip," he told her in a voice so deep and dark he could have been a blues singer.

Still kneeling, she took off her blouse and bra. "Happy now?" God, her voice sounded just as breathless as his did.

"I will be." Balancing on his crutches, he used one hand to draw her closer, bent his head to her breasts and swirled his tongue across her nipples. "The second I get inside you."

Her sex clenched with hot excitement. He turned her so she faced the back of the couch, then put his hand on her back. "Grab the back of the couch, honey."

She loved it when he called her honey, especially when passion edged his voice. She bent at the waist and put her hands on the frame of the couch. "Like that?"

"Just like that." His crutches clattered to the floor as he planted his hands on her hips. "Perfect."

She felt her skirt being drawn up the back of her thighs, felt cool air brush her sex as he brought her panties down. She was already wet, just from his voice and his commands and the time she'd spent with her mouth on him. He dragged his fingers through her folds, lingering on the swollen nub of her clit. A sharp jolt of pleasure ripped through her. She tried to chase his hand with her hips, wanting more friction from those long, skilled fingers. But he refused to give her control. He kept teasing and taunting, fingering and massaging, until she thought she might lose her mind.

Then his hand vanished, and she heard the sound of a plastic package ripping open. A condom.

It occurred to her that she and Josh had used a condom every single time they'd had sex, whereas she and Logan had stopped once they'd gotten engaged.

She wanted to feel Josh inside her in his raw, unshielded state. Someday. Maybe. If they were still doing this non-relationship whatever-it-was.

In the meantime, she'd take this. She'd take the slow slide of his thickness pushing against her inner walls. His hard palm against her clit, the way he pinned her between his hips and his hand, the way he thrust deep and pinched just right, the way he stoked the fire inside her until it burned so bright, the entire world went white and she cried out in perfect ecstasy.

She came down in slow stages. First she became conscious of the ripples of his orgasm, the grind of his body between her thighs. Then she realized she was hanging on to her couch frame as if she might fly off into the atmosphere. Finally she became aware of a sensation of lightness, as if she was swimming in bliss, floating in a feeling of endless safety and happiness.

Her happy place. She never would have guessed her happy place would be in bed with a hotshot.

CHAPTER 22

Something was changing between him and Suzanne. Josh knew it, but he couldn't put his finger on it. Usually, at this point in his involvement with a woman, he'd be itching for the exit. He kept waiting for that moment to come—the moment when he started making travel plans, or booking tickets, or writing the "it's been fun, but..." speech.

It didn't come. He didn't want to say goodbye to Suzanne—the opposite. He wanted to spend *more* time with her. More, and more, and more. It wasn't just the wildly intense sexual connection between them, or the fun they had just talking and hanging out. The suspicion was growing inside him that this was something completely different from anything else he'd ever shared with a woman. Sure, they'd both agreed they were "on the same page"—a page that didn't mention emotions.

But that really wasn't how it felt. He missed her when she was gone at work. Missed her like crazy.

And she inspired him with her persistence over the shelter idea. She was all fired up about it, always dragging out her laptop, researching and emailing and networking.

Partly to pass the time before he could go back to the base, partly because of Suzanne's example, he hauled out his own laptop and read through some of his Tumblr posts and the comments and shares. To his surprise, some had gotten a lot of attention. He remembered when he'd first started the blog, right after the burnover. That experience had been so intense. It had burned away a lot of the silly crap in his head. It was like a big fiery wakeup call. *You don't have forever. You might not even have tomorrow.*

So he'd gone through some of the many hours of footage he'd been taking from all the fires he'd been on. Not just the fires themselves, but the fire line operations, the Incident Command Centers, the choppers, the medic tents, the catering trucks. Footage, photos, whatever. And he'd started writing. He didn't have a lot of time between fire assignments, so he liked the shorter format of the micro-blog. Once the off-season started, he fleshed it out even more. He'd even written longer pieces. They probably weren't very good. But maybe they were. He'd always been pretty good in English class. He hadn't had the patience for college, but he'd audited several writing classes in the off-season.

He loved fighting wildfires. He loved being a hotshot. He never wanted to stop. But he also wanted something else. He wanted a voice.

Maybe a documentary. Maybe articles for a newspaper. He wasn't sure exactly how he wanted to do it. But it was a desire that had been growing in him for a long time.

On impulse, he called Finn Abrams, whose father was a Hollywood producer who was making a movie about the burnover. Finn was the one guy who hadn't stayed with the crew during the flash. He'd panicked and run, but luckily he'd made it to a gravel stream bed, where he'd waited out the fire, which roared on all sides. He hadn't returned to the crew; word had it he'd suffered pretty substantial burns, but no one had yet seen him.

"Dude," he said as soon as Finn came on the line. "What's shaking?"

"Josh? Hey, man, how are you? I heard about Yellowstone. You still laid up?" Every time Josh had spoken to Finn since the burnover, he'd noticed the change in his voice. He sounded older, less of the wild-eyed cocky rookie, more like a survivor.

"On crutches for a few more weeks. That's it. Could have been a lot worse. So anyway, I'm lying around here with a lot of time on my hands and nothing to do. I started going through some of my old footage. You know how I always used to shoot anything anyone let me? I've been thinking I should do something with it."

"Like what?"

"Not sure. I was hoping you might have some ideas. You're the Hollywood guy."

"That's me, huh? The Hollywood guy." The faint bitterness in his tone made Josh regret the phrase. "Tell you what. You come up with something—anything. A script. A rough cut. A proposal. Anything. I'll look at it and see what I can do. But just for the record, my father's the Hollywood guy. I'm the firefighting guy. At least I was." He abruptly ended the call, leaving Josh feeling like an ass.

Finn hadn't always been this touchy, had he?

But still, the guy had a point. He needed to come up with something to show Finn. This was on him, no one else. He lay back on the couch and settled his cast on a pillow. Propping his laptop on his belly, he pulled up his library of footage.

What would Suzanne do? She'd roll up her sleeves. She'd come up with Plan A. And Plan B. She'd make a damn PowerPoint. Whatever that was.

He opened up a file to take notes in, and started scanning through footage.

*

When Suzanne came back after work, a delicious fragrance filtered through her apartment. Tomato sauce, garlic, a hint of oregano. She found Josh propped on his crutches over the stove. He was bobbing his head in time to whatever was on his headphones. His t-shirt strained over his wide shoulders, and his cotton sweats clung to the muscles of his rear end. His shaggy blond hair swung down to his jaw, maybe even a little farther. He probably hadn't cut it in a while. With a long wooden spoon, he stirred the sauce to the same rhythm that must be pumping through his headphones.

Honestly, she was surprised her panties didn't just drop off her body at the mere sight of him. Whoever was in charge of handing out sexy had gone completely overboard when it came to Josh Marshall.

For a moment, she stood blinking in the doorway, just taking him in. Finally he looked over his shoulder and gave her a wink, a quick flash of gray that sent a shiver over her skin. "Honey, you're home," he teased, slipping the headphones off his ears.

"You're cooking."

"Yup. Trying to earn my way around here. I've got decent kitchen skills, you know. I was a cook on a fishing trawler one winter." He blew on the wooden spoon, then offered it to her. "See for yourself."

She came closer, stomach growling. She sampled the tomato sauce, which had an odd taste to it. But maybe it was just her. Her stomach was doing some strange things lately. "You really didn't have to do this."

"Hey, it gave me a break from all the hard work I put in today."

At first she thought he was joking, but then she noticed the self-conscious look on his face. "I assume you don't mean couch-warming?"

"Nope." He had a wild, fired-up look about him. "I had a breakthrough today. You know when all of a sudden everything is clear and you realize you're exactly where you're supposed to be and you know exactly what you're supposed to do?"

She flashed on that moment on the stargazing platform, when she'd watched the meteor shower burn so bright. "I guess so."

He pointed the spoon at her. "My broken leg has a bright side. I came up with a plan today. I want to bring attention to the wild world of wildfire fighters. YouTube channel, Tumblr, blog posts. The life of a wildfire fighter, in video, in his own words. The real thing, unfiltered and totally authentic."

"Wow." She had to hand it to him, it sounded pretty impressive. "That sounds amazing, Josh."

"It's especially important right now because we have more wildfires than ever. And I'm the guy to do this. Did you know that I won a writing contest in fifth grade? I bet you didn't." He grinned, looking so handsome, her heart clenched. "I've been shooting video ever since I got an iPhone. I have tons of footage. Just have to get everyone's permission. Clear things with the USFS, the BLM, the CFS, the D of I, the blah blah blah. Should be no problem. I'll just make myself a PowerPoint."

She laughed. His enthusiasm was absolutely infectious and so endearing. "PowerPoints are the answer to all life's little problems."

He put down the spoon and snagged his crutches from their position leaning against the wall. He stumped toward her, his sun-bleached hair swinging along with his movements. When he was directly in front of her, he balanced on the crutches while he cupped her face in his hands. "I owe you a huge thanks for this."

"Me?"

"Yeah, you. You inspired me with all your energy and ideas and dedication."

"And my PowerPoint skills."

"Skills, yes. Maybe not those skills." He lowered his voice to a sexy rumble. "I can think of a few other very inspiring skills belonging to Suzanne Finnegan."

He rested his forehead against hers. She shivered, thinking of all the skills *he* had to offer. Her stomach growled again. He laughed, then released her so he could get back to stirring the sauce. "You can inform your stomach that this will be ready in two minutes. I nearly forgot to ask, how did it go with the property search today? I heard Sean has other plans for the airstrip."

She lit up, remembering the huge news she'd gotten earlier in the day. "Yes, he's talking to some Air Force guys who want to buy it. That's off the table. But that's okay— Brianna has a lead. She does gardening work for an old man who can't keep up with his farm anymore, and he's looking for people to help him. It could be perfect!"

He turned to her, his smile so big and genuine it made her heart sing. "That's great news. Big day all-around, huh? Way to rock it, Suzanne. Want to grab some plates and we can celebrate with a big old plate of carbs?"

Smiling, she crossed to the cupboard. "You're going to make such a good wife someday."

"Since I'll never be a husband, maybe I should aim for wife instead," he quipped back.

On autopilot, she took out two of her favorite plates, the ones with a bright sunflower design around the edges.

Never be a husband? It was the same thing he always said, but for some reason, this time it bugged her. But why? She had no interest in him as a permanent life partner. Josh was someone to have fun with. Like a playmate. A grown-up sexual playmate, someone who made every moment more enjoyable. In bed, on the couch, in the kitchen...

Something funny happened to her heart just then. Like a twang. Like a guitar string someone had plucked. Its reverberations traveled through her entire being, with one clear note.

Josh.

Josh was...special. No one else was like him. Even after he went back to his regular life, no one else would ever quite take his place. He would leave a hole that would never really be filled. Someone else might come along—a husband, for instance. A man who wanted the life she wanted. But he wouldn't be Josh.

Oh, hell and damn and sweet mother of insanity—she'd fallen in love with Josh.

With *Josh.*

The man who wanted nothing to do with any of the things she wanted the most.

"Everything okay?" She jumped when his voice sounded in her ear. The plates she was holding clattered against each other.

"Yes, sorry. I was just...um...imagining how amazing it would be if we got that farm. Brianna says it's beautiful and has all these outbuildings where farmworkers used to live. They're kind of rundown, but I think if we spread the word about our Kickstarter or something, or maybe I'll plan a fundraising event so we can renovate the living quarters, because I don't have quite enough in the bank to cover the purchase and fixing the place up—"

He turned her so she faced him and gazed at her steadily. It felt as if her heart did a full end-over-end rotation during that endless moment. She didn't want him to see the truth, but didn't know how to hide it either.

But even though it felt as if he had X-ray vision, he didn't say anything about the emotions somersaulting through her. A slow smile spread across his face. "I like seeing you so excited."

"Well, it's, um, yeah. Of course I'm excited. It could be great, and I guess I'm getting a little carried away." Oh Lord. She was going to make a fool of herself, wasn't she? She cleared her throat. "Actually, we should eat quickly because I have a meeting later with the girls."

She didn't have a meeting scheduled, but she wasn't sure she could spend the evening alone with Josh. She needed to figure out how to handle this situation.

She needed to be practical and think this through. Make a plan.

His smile dropped. "Oh, really? I had some other ideas about tonight." He dropped his face to the crook of her neck and nuzzled her there.

Her resolve weakened, along with her knees. He smelled so good, the fresh, clean scent of his skin mingling with the aroma of tomato sauce. And the way he touched her was just so perfect. Sometimes light, sometimes firm, always as if she were the most beautiful thing he'd ever seen. It was irresistible. Maybe she should do this just one more time...what harm would it do?

Just more amazing sex with the man who wouldn't stick around. That was all.

She put down the plates and threw her arms around him. He was so strong that even with a broken leg, balancing on crutches, he caught her against him without wavering. "You always have really good ideas."

"Only when I'm inspired. And you definitely inspire me. Over and over and over again." He punctuated each word with a kiss until her face tingled everywhere he touched. Then he was kissing her on the lips, deep and thorough and utterly intoxicating. When he finally drew away, she felt lightheaded and clung to his broad shoulders.

He was just as affected as she was; his breath came fast, his pupils dilated.

"Damn, Suzanne," he muttered. "Sometimes I think I'll never get enough of you."

She ran her hands down the rippling muscles of his chest. "Never is a long time. We don't have to think like that."

"Right. Live for the moment." He nipped at her lower lip, using his teeth with just the right amount of pressure, so she felt the frisson all the way down her spine. "That's what I do best."

Of course it was. She didn't need to hear it all over again. She got it. "Shut up and make love to me."

"Yes, ma'am."

*

Whatever had gotten into Suzanne, Josh wanted more of it. She was on fire that night. "Maybe I should make spaghetti sauce more often," he whispered to her as they lay, spent and panting, on her big bed. Their sexual marathon had been interrupted by a break for pasta, but only briefly. Priorities...

"Anytime, hotshot. Anytime. A low-calorie option might be good too."

"Nope. Won't do it. Know how many calories I eat when I'm on a fire? Over four thousand a day."

"You're not on a fire," she pointed out. She rested on her side, the long lines of her curves begging to be caressed.

"You sure about that?" He stroked her hip, enjoying the graceful turn of her hipbone, and the way her skin pebbled at his touch. "I think we just burned off that entire dinner. Hey, darlin', want to burn up some calories with me?"

"Nice line. Does that work with the ladies?"

"What ladies? There's only one as far as I'm concerned."

She went quiet, and he wondered if he'd taken his flirting too far. It was hard not to. She brought out his flirtatious side more than anyone he'd ever known.

His cell phone rang from the living room. "Ring of Fire," his tribute to his favorite singer and his profession.

"I'll get it." She scrambled out of bed so quickly that he wondered if she was looking for an excuse. He watched her disappear out the door, captivated by the sight of her perfect heart-shaped ass. He settled deeper into the sheets. Obviously, he wasn't a settler-downer type, but if he were, it would be hard to imagine anyone more perfect for him than Suzanne.

She came back wearing the top he'd practically ripped off her body in the kitchen. Now it hung open, allowing the inner curves of her breasts and her trim little waist to peek through. She was a wet dream walking through the door, and his cock reacted accordingly.

She handed him the phone and mouthed, "Your brother."

And that was the end of fun for the night. His parents and his brothers had been calling on a regular basis since he'd made his great escape from the hospital. He didn't like ignoring their calls, even though they were probably bad for his stress level.

"Hey, Andy. Before you even ask, I'm doing good."

"Glad to know, but that's now why I'm calling. Mom and Pop are headed your way."

"What?" Josh sat bolt upright in bed, then winced as his leg protested. "Why? When?"

"Mom has been talking about it the last couple of days. Dad got wind of it and decided to beat her to the punch. He left this morning. I tried to talk him out of it, but he wouldn't listen. He's in the Caddy. Mom is flying, I think. She threw a fit when she found out."

Josh clenched the phone, all his Suzanne-induced contentment evaporating. "I want to join the Witness Protection Program. That's my only hope."

Suzanne giggled, then put a hand over her mouth. He wished she wouldn't. He loved hearing her laugh. Right now, he *needed* to hear her laugh.

"Isn't there some mission to Mars I can stow away on? I'll be that robot they send out to take soil samples."

Over her hand, Suzanne's face was turning pink with mirth.

"They're worried about you. Give them a break."

"Yeah, they should be worried about me. It's hard to run for the hills with one leg in a cast."

"Ha ha."

"Anyway, thanks for the heads-up, bro. I appreciate it." He ended the call and turned to Suzanne. "You're enjoying this, aren't you?"

She nodded gleefully, then shook her head. "Not at all."

"Ohhh, you're going to pay, young woman." He snagged her arm and spun her around so he could give her a little whack on the ass.

She gave him a saucy look over her shoulder. "What kind of payment did you have in mind?"

"I was thinking maybe you could be my sex slave. That seems fair, right?" He stroked the smooth skin of her ass, soothing the sting he must have left.

Her eyes darkened to the shade he thought of as "fuck-me blue."

"You'd like that, wouldn't you? Actually, I was thinking of something a little different."

"You want me to be *your* sex slave? That works too."

"No." She spoke as if explaining herself to a small child. "I was thinking I'd help you out with your parents. I think I know how to handle them."

"Keep going." He entwined his hand with hers and brought it to his lips. "This might be even better than making you cater to my every sexual whim. Jury's still out."

"The agency where I work, Stars in Your Eyes, has a special package aimed at couples who are at a turning point in their lives. It's for older couples, or those who are going through a tough time. We call it the 'Rekindle Your Fire' package. How about if I take your parents on one? I'll comp them. And I won't tell them what it is. I'll just say it's a tour of Jupiter Point."

He gazed up at her, feeling like a puppy dog in the presence of a goddess. "You would do that?"

"Sure."

"But they're...you saw what they're like."

"Yes. They bicker. A lot. A lot of people do that." She cocked her head at him with a curious look? "Why is it so awful for you?"

A flash of memory gripped him—crawling under his bed to escape the horrible shouting. The way it would follow him anyway, no matter how many pillows he stuffed around his ears.

Why was it so awful? Because it tore him apart. It shredded him.

"I don't know," he said hoarsely. Then he caught himself, and deflected with a joke. "Maybe I'm allergic."

She waited for him to say more, but when he didn't, she pulled away from him. "Well, I don't want you to suffer any medical setbacks, so I'm stepping up. Otherwise, you might be stuck on my couch forever." She stuck her tongue out at him and whisked herself into the bathroom.

Stuck on her couch forever...oddly, that didn't sound as bad as it ought to. Though he might replace "couch" with "bed."

He lay back and contemplated the amazing fact that Suzanne was willing to spend time with his parents. He'd never asked a girl to do that. It had never even come up before. But here was Suzanne, offering up her time and a tour package that must cost a fair amount. She was such a standup girl, always ready to throw herself feet first into whatever her friends needed. He remembered Sean telling him that Suzanne used to confront other kids who were talking trash about him. Having Suzanne in your corner...well, it felt good, that was all. It made him want to do something equally heroic for her.

He realized she was taking a long time in the bathroom. "Suzanne? You okay in there?"

"Yes," came her muffled reply. He heard the toilet flush and shortly afterward she emerged back into the room. He thought she looked a bit pale, and hoped it wasn't his pasta's fault. She turned out the light and crawled under the covers with him.

When she cuddled against his body, all warm and soft and silky, his heart swelled. He adjusted their positions so her head rested on the divot between his shoulder and his chest. She fit there perfectly.

For the moment.

CHAPTER 23

Ohmigod, ohmigod, ohmigod...

That refrain had been going on a nonstop loop ever since she'd nearly thrown up in the bathroom.

It was the pasta. It had to be. She'd eaten too fast. It had too much oregano. Something. It couldn't be anything else. She and Josh always used condoms, every single time. There had never been a rip, or a premature disposal, or a lapse. They'd been absolutely meticulous.

Calendar, calendar...how long had it been since her last period? She'd been keeping track pretty carefully when she was with Logan. They'd stopped using condoms, so knowing where she was in her cycle was pretty important. But his schedule had been so sporadic toward the end. He'd been wrapped up with his finals and barely made it to Jupiter Point at all. They'd had sex maybe once in the last couple of months of their engagement.

But one is all it takes.

No. Impossible. She and Logan were through. This couldn't be happening. Okay, okay, think. When exactly was that one time they'd had sex?

Sadly, there wasn't much to remember. It was over quickly, she hadn't enjoyed it, and she'd lain awake fuming to herself about what a selfish lover he was. But that hadn't happened during the danger time. Had it?

She tried to count the days and weeks, but kept losing track. She was probably just late. It happened, especially when she was under stress. Yup, that was it. She was late, and she'd eaten too fast, and her breasts looked bigger because...late growth spurt? Maybe?

This couldn't be happening. It just couldn't. Not when she and Logan were completely done. Not when she loved another man. A man who didn't even know she loved him. A man who would probably run screaming if he did know. This wasn't the plan.

No. No no no. Not possible.

*

Yes, it definitely was possible. Not just possible, but "holy shit this is real." The news was delivered via a drug store pregnancy test that she'd driven all the way to nearby Benson to purchase. In fact, she'd bought five tests, which added up to quite a bit of money.

If you think that's a lot of money, imagine having a kid. By yourself.

She stopped at a gas station and barricaded herself into the bathroom. Now she was on test number three, and so far the results were unanimous.

Ohmigod. OMIGOD.

Not only that, but she'd pored over the calendar and counted the days and there was simply no doubt about it. The father was Logan.

In a dingy gas station bathroom off of Route 5, she buried her head in her hands and sobbed.

A month ago, getting pregnant with Logan's baby would have meant just moving things up a bit. Get married a little earlier, start their family right away instead of in a few years. But everything had changed. She didn't love Logan. She didn't want a life with Logan. And despite his "romantic gesture," he didn't really want her either. And he really wouldn't want to have a baby.

Someone pounded on the door. "Are you almost done?" a girl yelled. "I'm like a water balloon out here."

"Do you mind? I'm in the middle of something."

"What kind of something? You got some kind of craft project going on in there?"

"Yes. I'm crocheting my own toilet paper," Suzanne snapped. "It takes time."

The girl outside started cracking up. "That's funny. So funny you're making me pee my pants, for real. Come on!"

"Hang on," Suzanne grumbled, although the exchange had actually lifted her mood from despairing to battle-ready. She gathered together all the tests, wrapped them in a wad of toilet paper and stuffed them in her bag. Maybe it was a little gross, but she was not going to leave the first official evidence of her pregnancy in the trash can in a random rest stop.

Outside, she took a moment to glare at the girl outside, who was hopping from one foot to the other. "Sorry for the delay," she said, sweeping past her.

"It's all right, you made me laugh."

Great. At least her life crisis was making strangers at rest stops laugh.

In her car, she rifled through her mental rolodex. She didn't want to dump this situation on Evie. She was too happy these days. Brianna—she loved Brianna, but she could be kind of blunt and outspoken. She would have strong opinions about the situation and she wouldn't mind sharing them. She needed to talk this through with someone she could trust, someone who cared about her, who wouldn't be too judgmental.

If only she could tell Josh. Josh would be the perfect person. He never judged. He would be comforting, irreverent. He'd make her laugh. He'd make her worries seem less daunting. Yes, he'd be the perfect person to tell—if she weren't in love with him. And sleeping with him.

But he could never, ever know.

Silly. Of course he'll know. Eventually everyone in Jupiter Point would know.

She thought about calling her mother, but she wasn't ready for that conversation yet. She had to sort out how she was going to handle this. She needed support and common sense, two things Desiree Finnegan knew nothing about.

In the end, she called Merry, who promised to meet her at Stargazer Beach. On her way to the beach, Suzanne stopped at her condo and picked up Snowball. Josh had left her a note on the coffee table. At the base hanging out with the crew.

She breathed a sigh of relief that she didn't have to pretend everything was normal in front of Josh. He had a way of sneaking behind her defenses and she might end up spilling everything before she was ready. As soon as she told him, they'd be through. She could already picture that conversation.

"So, yeah, just thought you should know there's going to be a baby here in a few months, and...relax, it's not yours, and...okay, bye! It's been great. See you around."

At Stargazer Beach, she let Snowball off the leash so she could bark at the waves and told Merry what was going on. The reporter listened in that attentive way she had. No wonder she was such a good journalist. She really knew how to hold back and let someone tell their story.

"So basically what you're telling me is, you don't want Logan, but you do want his baby—"

"Not because it's his," Suzanne added hastily. "Because it's mine."

Merry continued. "And you do want Josh, but you think he doesn't want you."

"He wants me, but not me-with-a-baby me."

"Are you sure about that?"

A seagull swooped past them on its way to a sandwich someone had unwisely left on their picnic blanket.

"Have you met Josh? What do you think?"

"I think you know him better than I do. But he sure seems to like you a lot."

Suzanne bent down to pick up a stone shaped like a heart. It was perfect for her collection of pebbles from this beach. "He likes me fine. But he doesn't want a family. I've heard him say it about a million times. It's not even a question in his mind. And I can't blame him. His parents are crazy. They fight all the time. I don't know how he came out as nice as he did. Anyway, Josh isn't the point here. What should I do about Logan?"

Merry pushed a chunk of curly hair from her face. "Lay it out for me. What are the options?"

"I knew you'd be the right person to tell. You're always so logical. Okay, I've thought a lot about this part. Here are the options. A. Don't tell Logan. B. Get back together with Logan. C. Inform Logan, but tell him I don't want child support and I don't want him in the baby's life. D. Inform him, and ask for child support and let him be part of the baby's life. E. Join the Witness Protection Program. Am I leaving anything out?"

Merry burst out laughing. "Please tell me you have all this in a PowerPoint somewhere."

Suzanne actually found herself smiling, something she hadn't done much since the fateful moment in the rest stop bathroom. "Haven't had time. It's a good idea, though. PowerPoints are so soothing. So what should I do?"

"You want my take?"

"Yes. I do."

"A is off the table. You gotta tell the dude he's having a child. It's only fair. In my opinion, B is off the table, too. But that's just me. You might want to think about that one a little more. E might be nice, but you have to actually be a witness to a major crime committed by someone who wants you dead. So you have C and you have D. As for which one is better, you're going to have to work it out with Logan. If he wants to co-parent with you, then he kind of has that right. And he is a lawyer. They know their rights."

Suzanne stopped in her tracks as fear shot through her. "Do you mean he might have the right to take the baby?"

"No, of course not. Not unless you do drugs or some other heinous thing. But here's something to think about, Suzanne. Every kid wants to know who their parents are. It's just natural. So if he wants to know his child, that might be the best thing. No matter what, you gotta tell him."

Suzanne kicked at a log that had washed up on the beach. Maybe she should have called Brianna after all. Merry was entirely too intelligent and cool-headed. Maybe logic wasn't everything it was cracked up to be. The last thing she wanted to do was call Logan.

And damn it all, she couldn't even have a margarita first.

*

Suzanne believed in getting unpleasant tasks out of the way first, so she called Logan as soon as she got back to her condo. The conversation was even more awful than she'd expected.

"If this is about Casa di Stella, you can forget it. I already have a contractor over there working up a bid for the renovations. You missed your chance, babe."

"It's not about that," she said through gritted teeth. "This is more important. But it's better if I tell you in person. I can get a flight out tomorrow morning if you're available."

"Suz, if you're thinking about getting back together, I've moved on." He lowered his voice, as if he didn't want someone to hear. "And she wouldn't like you showing up here. Just tell me what it is. And make it quick, we're late for tapas."

"Moved on? Weren't you buying a house for me a few weeks ago?"

"If you're calling to dig up ancient history, I'm hanging up."

Pain throbbed in her temples. What was the point of even telling him? Logan had moved on. He already had a new girlfriend. This news would just interfere with his plans.

But this wasn't about him—or her. This was about a baby who deserved to come into the world with a clean slate. No secrets. No bullshit. "Okay, Logan, you forced me into doing this on the phone. I hope you're sitting down."

Uncomfortable silence on his end. Maybe he was starting to guess what she was going to say.

"I'm pregnant."

Was that a gulp she heard from his end of the line? A choke? A shout of joy?

"And I suppose you're going to claim it's mine?"

Oh. My. God. The weasel. "I'm not claiming anything. There's no doubt."

After another drawn-out silence, he gave a snide laugh. "I always knew you'd change your mind and beg me to take you back. I didn't think you'd go this far."

She stomped across the room, brandishing her phone in the air with a silent primal scream. Snowball watched her, ears perking up. Logan Rossi. Was. Such. A. Dick. And she was an idiot for not seeing the full extent of his dick-ness before now.

"Let's be honest, you jerk. Do you want to help raise this baby?"

"Suz, I have a new girlfriend. Come on, don't do this to me."

Again, she held herself back from screaming into the phone. Keep it logical. Option D was evaporating. Option C was looking better and better. She would raise the baby on her own. So be it.

"So...just a crazy thought, Logan. If I send you something that says I'll never ask you for child support—"

"Child support? I'm warning you, babe—"

"Never ask you for child support," she continued relentlessly. "If I sign that, will you sign something that says you give up all custody rights?"

"Sign?" She heard doubt in his voice. She got it; signing was such a permanent thing. Then again, so were babies.

"I just want things to be clear, Logan. It's only fair. But if you want a different arrangement—"

"No, no. I don't. Fine, whatever."

Suzanne's stomach cratered as the full reality of Logan's response sank in. Her baby was going to grow up without a father.

"Logan, think about this," she said, deadly serious now. "Think hard. I'm not trying to get back together with you. You've moved on, I've moved on. We were never right for each other. But there's a baby, and that changes things. I'm willing to work things out so you can see him or her. I wouldn't want to stand in the way of my baby having a father."

In the background, a door opened and a lightly accented female voice called out, "Logan, caro, I need you, darling! I've been counting the minutes. Where are you, mi amore?"

"Wait." A horrible realization struck Suzanne. "Is that Monica? Your cousin from Italy?"

"Second cousin," he muttered. "Actually, more like third cousin."

"The one you've known forever. The one your parents always wanted you to marry. She was your free pass, wasn't she?"

Uncomfortable silence. Suzanne felt as if she was in a boat pushing away from shore, as everything familiar got smaller and smaller. She'd never really known Logan, had she?

"I'll draw up the agreement," he said, and hung up.

Now she was truly on her own.

CHAPTER 24

Since Josh couldn't participate in the crew's PT, he volunteered to lead—Josh-style. Bullhorn in hand, he patrolled up and down the line of hotshots doing pushups. "Faster," he yelled, voice booming. "Call that a pushup? I've seen better pushups on a bra!"

Jessica, one of the female crew members, cracked up and nearly lost her rhythm.

Josh kept crutching up and down the line of firefighters. "Get it together, people. This is serious business. Fires don't wait for you to finish your pushups, do they? They don't say, 'Oh, are you feeling okay today? Are your muscles sore? Would you like some tiger balm for that? Maybe a bubble bath?'"

Other crew members were starting to snicker, even Rollo, who took his pushups very seriously. His bulging deltoids twitched as he lowered himself rapidly up and down. Josh grinned to himself. He'd missed this. Missed the camaraderie and brotherly bonds. Sorting through footage was fun, and he was finding lots of great stuff and already had several videos edited. But this—this was what he loved.

"No, we gotta be ready for that fire. Feel that burn. Cop that feel. Burn that bra."

Jessica collapsed onto her front, laughing too hard to keep her pushups going. She propped her elbows on the ground and rested her chin in her hands. "Would you get out of here, Marsh? I call interference."

"I'm not interfering. I'm inspiring. Right, guys?"

A chorus of boos answered that. Josh caught Sean's eye. The leader of the hotshots was standing with his arms folded across his chest, clearly trying to keep a straight face. "You heard them, Josh. Take a hike."

"Take a hike. Is that an appropriate thing to say to a man on crutches?" He put a hand over his heart. "I'm wounded. Inside and out."

A new arrival caught his eye, someone strolling from the parking lot toward the crew assembled on the grass.

Tim Peavy. Looking shaky as hell.

Josh immediately stopped his joking around. Sean followed his glance and went to greet the newcomer. Josh watched them share a chest bump, a forearm grip, and a low-voiced conversation. Finally Sean looked his way and gestured him over.

He stumped toward the two of them. Peavy seemed embarrassed and kept his gaze fixed on the ground. Sean put a hand on the rookie's shoulder as Josh approached.

"Peavy here has been wanting to talk to you, Marsh. I'm going to leave you two alone now. Gotta get this PT back on track."

Josh nodded, then turned his attention to Peavy. "Good to see you, dude."

Tim's Adam's apple worked up and down. "Listen, man. I just gotta say this. When I first got back from overseas, I had a few flashbacks. Then they stopped. I thought it was over. I didn't know it was going to come back like that. I'm real sorry. I wouldn't have—"

"Hey." Josh put a hand on his shoulder and squeezed. "You went over there and put your life on the line. You still have the scars from that. You don't need to say one word of apology."

"But I should have told you guys it might happen. Rosario told me I should, but I thought I could handle it. I thought it was over. I was wrong and I could have died. *You* could have died."

"We didn't. It ain't exactly a risk-free profession, bro. We're always taking that chance. Let me ask you this, though. Are you getting some help now? You shouldn't be in this alone."

"Yeah." He lowered his head. "Rosario made me. She said she'd have the baby by herself if I didn't work on this. It's good. It helps. I wish I didn't need it, but I guess sometimes you just do."

"True. Look, you're a good man, Peavy. I hope we both get back out there soon. Sitting at home is for the birds, you know?"

Finally Tim's expression lifted. "You said it. Rosario has me working through a to-do list a mile long. Makes cutting chain look easy. You ever put together an Ikea bookcase?"

"Nope. It's on my bucket list though."

At Peavy's skeptical expression, he laughed. "Not hardly. I'll leave that sort of thing to you married guys. How Rosario?"

"Well, she's only got a few weeks to go and she's getting antsy. She's hungry all the time, but then she gets full right away. We go to the Milky Way just about every night because all she wants is those Big Dipper sundaes with extra pralines. Can't be walnuts. Has to be pralines. And God forbid they put a maraschino cherry on there. She will *flip out.* She says even the smell of those little red toxic bombs makes her lose it."

"Okay then."

Tim shoved his hands in his pockets. "I bet you're wondering why I'm telling you all this."

"Well..." Sort of, yes. Wasn't exactly a typical firefighter convo, that was for sure.

"We want to name the baby after you. Because you saved me."

Josh's jaw dropped open. A baby named after him...honestly, he wasn't sure how he felt about that. "You guys don't have to do that."

"It was Rosario's idea, and she's eight months pregnant and hormonal as fuck, so you try talking her out of it."

Josh stopped his flow of words with an uplifted hand. "Say no more. I'm honored."

"Her first choice was Edgerton, so believe me, Josh is a big step up."

"Edgerton?" Josh grinned. "Damn, bro. No wonder you freaked out at that wildfire. It was all about the baby names, wasn't it?"

After a moment of astonished silence, during which Josh wondered if he'd gone too far, Tim burst into laughter. It was a rusty, out-of-practice laugh, but better than nothing.

A baby. Named after him. Josh couldn't wait to tell Suzanne. She'd probably get a huge laugh out of that one.

*

But Suzanne didn't seem to find it as funny as he did.

"See, it's perfect," he explained. "Tim does all the actual work of being a parent, and I don't have to lift a finger but I get a kid named after me."

"Do you ever get tired of making a joke about every single thing?" she snapped as she thrust a water bottle into a small backpack. She was preparing for the Rekindle Your Fire trip with his parents. They were both excited about Suzanne's offer, which he'd presented as more of a group tour than a relationship-builder.

"It's a coping mechanism. Tried and true. You may find yourself turning to it frequently when you're with my parents."

"Maybe. Or maybe I'll just enjoy the ocean and the sunshine like a normal person." She jammed a sun visor on her head and pulled her ponytail through the gap in the back. From her movements, he could tell she was irritated, though he had no idea why. She'd been acting very strange the past couple of days. Distracted, jumpy, edgy. No interest in sex.

But every time he asked if something was wrong, she said no.

"Are you sure you don't want to come with us?" she asked. "The weather's perfect."

"If we capsized, I'd sink like a stone." He indicated his heavy cast. "And if we didn't capsize, I might have to jump. Same outcome."

"You're kind of ridiculous, you know that? Your parents are just people."

Josh kept his mouth shut about that one. Of course they were just people. People who drove him crazy.

At that moment, someone knocked on the door. When Suzanne opened it, his parents came bolting through like racehorses out of a gate.

"Josh! You look so much better!" cried his mother, fluttering toward him in a floppy sunhat and dark glasses.

"Of course he does. He's got my constitution," said Rock. He wore a baseball cap from the local feed store and a vintage Houston Oilers shirt.

"Nonsense, he looks much more like me. Everyone says so. I'm sure it's the same genetically for the rest of him, all his inner systems and so forth."

"Mom, can you please not talk about my systems right in front of me? It's embarrassing." He returned his mother's hug, wishing he could squeeze all her hostility right out of her.

"Don't embarrass your son, Anne, if you can help it."

Right on time, Suzanne stepped in. She really had a knack for handling them, Josh had to admit. She offered them each a tube of sunscreen.

"Why don't you two get lathered up on our way out to the car? The sun can really sneak up on you."

"Josh, you aren't coming?" His mother pulled a sad face as she took the sunscreen.

"Sorry, crutches and sailboats are not a good mix. But we'll have dinner when you get back."

"Just you and me, or you and..."

"Big group dinner. The more the merrier." He'd drag the hotshots into town if he had to. Maybe Peavy would come. He'd saved the dude's life, after all.

Suzanne shepherded his parents out the door. At the last second, she looked over her shoulder at Josh and gave him a wink. "Bye, Josh, I hope you and all your systems have fun while we're gone."

He gave her a "touché" salute and watched her slip out the door behind his parents. The fresh, breezy image of Suzanne in her hip-hugging pants, blue canvas sneakers, and blue-striped halter top stayed with him. Not to mention that sassy wink she left him with. Suzanne had a way of being...perfect. There really was no other word for it.

The most amazing part was that even though being trapped on a sailboat with his parents sounded like a literal nightmare—he actually wished he'd gone with them. Just so he could watch the wind flirt with Suzanne's ponytail and the sun scatter golden freckles across her nose.

Time to face facts. He was kind of a goner for Suzanne. And he had no idea what to do about that.

*

Suzanne kept a constant stream of directions and chatter going until she and Josh's parents were safely settled into the romantic two-masted sloop, *That's Amore*. She pointed out the sights as they pulled away from the harbor and cruised past Stargazer Beach. The observatory perched on the hill overlooking the ocean, the imposing bulk of Jupiter Point, the rundown airstrip not far from Stargazer Beach.

Jonas, the captain and owner of *That's Amore*, offered them chilled peach Bellinis, then turned his focus to steering them toward the pretty islands that lay offshore. He was an expert at ignoring what was said on these sailing expeditions.

"Now, Mr. and Mrs. Marshall," Suzanne began.

"Oh no, sweetie," Anne interrupted. "Please start over without using his name."

Rock scowled, but before he could respond, Suzanne held up a hand. "Sure, let's start over. At Stars in Your Eyes, we like every excursion to include an *extended* moment of silence."

Anne and Rock exchanged looks of alarm, as if they'd never heard of the concept of silence before.

"It's a way to let the ambiance really take hold," she explained. "The sound of the ocean, the salty wind on your face, the slap of the water against the hull of the sailboat, these are all very soothing sounds."

Rock curled a lip in Anne's direction and spoke in a hoarse whisper. "She means compared to your yapping."

"What part of 'moment of silence' don't you understand?" she snapped back.

Lord, this was going to be a long trip. Suzanne heard a choking sound coming from Jonas's direction as he tightened the jib. The boat heeled as they headed closer into the wind.

Nausea grabbed her by the throat. Seasickness? Pregnancy symptom?

She never got seasick.

Crap.

"Back to that moment of silence," she managed through the queasiness. "I think you would both find it a valuable experience. So let's give it a try, okay?"

She closed her eyes, pretending to listen to the water while she fought against the queasiness. She hadn't had any pregnancy symptoms yet—unless you counted "foggy brain." Ever since the phone call with Logan, she'd felt paralyzed and confused. She hadn't gone to a doctor yet. She hadn't told anyone besides Merry and Logan. She hadn't called her parents. She'd ignored Josh. Neglected Snowball.

All she'd done was lie in bed and spin worry after worry into impossible scenarios.

She'd always been a decisive person. She knew what she wanted and wasn't shy about going after it. But now she was having the opposite experience. She couldn't decide anything. All she wanted to do was curl up in bed and sleep and let someone else figure everything out. But there was no one else. That was the problem. There was just her.

For the first time she could remember, she had no idea what to do.

The moment of silence dragged on. She peeked under her eyelashes at Josh's parents just in time to see Anne step on Rock's foot, and Rock lift one eyelid to glare at her.

Sigh. So much for harmony on the high seas.

They hit a higher-than-normal wave, and the sailboat lurched awkwardly through a head of spray. Suzanne's stomach clenched and nausea crawled up her throat. The entire contents of her stomach were clamoring to be released. She couldn't hold it back.

This was going to be ugly.

She scrambled for the side of the sailboat, nearly losing her footing on the slick deck. She bumped her hip against a cleat—ow. She was going to have a wicked bruise from that. She grabbed the railing and leaned as far as she could over the side. And then it came, all the vomit in the free world, apparently. Everything she'd eaten today, yesterday, and probably last month. And it kept coming. Long, deep heaves. Endless spasms of food rejection.

When she was done, she stayed in that same position, weak and spent, letting the mist churned up by the sloop cool her face.

Behind her, she heard Anne and Rock exclaiming in concern.

"Poor child. Was it something she ate?" Anne asked in a low voice.

"Maybe just seasick."

She turned around. This was so embarrassing and un-professional—so unlike her.

"Yes. I'm so sorry. I don't usually get seasick, but there's always a first time." She staggered back to her backpack and dug out a bottle of water. A long swallow made her feel a bit better. One hand on her belly, she slumped back to her seat.

Anne was watching her closely out of eyes as gray as Josh's. "Are you sure it's just seasickness? The only time I ever threw up that much was, well..."

Rock chimed in. "All three boys did that to her." He was watching her a little too closely, too. God, was it that obvious? She really didn't want Josh's parents getting in the middle of this.

At least they weren't quarreling.

"I'd like to point out the island to your left, which is a popular spot for—" She gagged as another twist of nausea hit her.

"Are you okay?" Anne leaned forward and put a hand on her knee.

"Yes. Perfectly fine—" *Oh no.* She jumped up and made it to the side just in time for a convulsion of dry heaves. When it was over, she could barely manage to straighten up. She felt dizzy, drained, half-dead. She wanted to lie draped over the side of the boat forever.

"Suzanne—honey!" The alarm in Anne's voice dragged her from her stupor. "You're bleeding."

Oh crap, that cleat must have gouged her as well as bruising her. She glanced down at her hip and saw no trace of blood.

Anne came next to her, lurching as the boat hit a wave. She put an arm around her and spoke in a low voice. "Honey, is your period starting?"

Suzanne stared at her in horror. *That* kind of bleeding? "No. *No.* Oh my God, I have to...get—" Here it came again. She gagged over the side, leaning over so far it was a miracle she didn't fall in.

Anne grabbed her by the shoulders and held tight. The boat rocked from side to side, sending ocean spray in cold droplets against Suzanne's face. She felt as if the entire world was churning around her, with only Anne's grip keeping her safe.

"Rock?" Anne called over Suzanne's head. "Tell that sailor-man we have to turn around. We have to get her to a doctor."

Rock roared, "Ahoy, man. You heard my wife. Gotta turn the boat around." Then he added, in a lower voice, "I meant ex-wife. Don't get your panties in a bunch."

Suzanne wanted to laugh, or cry, or throw up some more, she didn't know which. After Jonas had reversed course, Anne helped her stagger to her seat. The older woman pulled a jacket around her and hugged her against her side. Suzanne didn't object. She huddled against Josh's mother, grateful for the warmth, the human kindness.

To keep from crying, she kept her gaze fixed on the rocky promontory that jutted into the ocean, the majestic rise of Jupiter Point, the twinkles of light reflecting off glass surfaces at the observatory. All the familiar, beloved landmarks of her childhood.

And she silently begged, and pleaded, and promised, and bargained. To the heavens and all the stars above—*please, let my baby be okay.*

CHAPTER 25

Josh could make no sense of the frantic message from his mother, but he did make out the word "emergency room." Had something gone wrong out on the water? Maybe one of his parents had pushed the other overboard? He called a cab and got himself across town to the urgent care clinic in record time.

Inside the clinic, he found his parents sitting together in the lobby, but no sign of Suzanne. For the first time, it occurred to him that she might be the one in trouble. He swung forward on his crutches. "Mom, Pop. What's going on?"

"Josh!" His mother jumped to her feet and came hurrying toward him. "Suzanne's going to be so glad you came."

"Of course I came. What happened? Is she okay?"

"She will be, now that you're here. At a time like this, a girl needs support."

A time like what? Josh had no idea what was going on, and the fact that his parents weren't fighting added to his confusion. He felt as if he'd stepped into some alternate reality. It made him nervous, actually.

"Where is Suzanne?"

"She's resting comfortably now. Of course, that's a ridiculous euphemism, as I can tell you based on my own personal experience. There's nothing comfortable about it. Luckily it was a false alarm. The heartbeat is still good."

"Heartbeat?" He glanced from one parent to another, his alarm skyrocketing. "Is something wrong with her heart?"

"I'd say her heart got her into this mess. Along with a few other parts of her." Rock crossed his ankle over his knee and jiggled the change in his pocket.

"Rock," his mother scolded. "That's so indelicate." She turned to Josh. "Just ignore him and focus on what's important."

Josh shook his head from side to side, with the sense he was knocking cobwebs out of his brain. What would it take to get a clear answer out of his mother? "I'm. Trying. To. It would help if someone would tell me what's going on."

"Haven't I been doing exactly that? Honestly, I really wish you'd told me, Josh. I don't know why you feel the need to be so secretive. The poor girl is all alone. Her own mother virtually abandoned her, did you know that? They're off traveling the world while poor Suzanne has no one to turn to. Of all times in a woman's life, this is when she needs the most support."

A horrible suspicion popped into his brain. Was Suzanne—no, she couldn't be. He always used a condom, every single time—

"Excuse me, are you Suzanne Finnegan's fiancé?" The cool female voice made him jump.

"I...uh..." Was he supposed to be? He'd honestly lost track of their fictional relationship at this point.

"He is," Anne jumped in quickly. "This is my son, Josh."

"Nice to meet you, Josh. I'm Betsy Johannsen, nurse midwife." Numbly, Josh shook the woman's hand. The nurse's hand. No, the nurse *midwife's* hand. The—?

He couldn't summon a single word of response.

The nurse continued. "I'm happy to report that your baby is going to be fine. Early spotting like this isn't uncommon. Suzanne got dehydrated and disoriented, but she's going to be just fine and the pregnancy is in good shape."

The *preg*—

He reeled backwards, nearly toppling over on his crutches. So it was true. Suzanne was pregnant. And everyone apparently thought that he was the father.

A sort of panic came over him. As if a wildfire was chasing him down...cornering him...

"No," he blurted. "I'm not part of this."

The nurse's smile vanished. "Excuse me?"

"I'm not the father." He turned to his parents. "It's not me. We've been very careful. And Suzanne and I haven't even been having sex long enough—"

Okay, talking to his parents about his sex life—awkward.

"It's not me," he finished, certainty ringing through his voice. "Did Suzanne say it was?"

"Well, no, we just assumed. She didn't say anything, she was too sick." Anne's bottom lip was starting to quiver. She dabbed at her eyes. "It's not you?"

"Of course it's not me. Haven't you heard me say a million times that I'm not continuing the damn Marshall line? I'm not father material. I'm not husband material."

"That's absurd, Josh. You'll adjust to the idea. Just give it some time to sink in."

Rock stood up, his tall, bulky form dwarfing that of his former wife. "Take it from me, son. It's terrifying at first, but you'll settle down. Just like I did."

Settle down.

The words rattled around in his head like bullets trying to end him.

No. He wasn't going to settle down. He wasn't going to end up like his parents.

He backed away, using his crutches to swing toward the front desk. "You both need to stay out of this." He heard the harsh edge in his own voice. "My life is not your business."

"You're our *son*. How can you say that?" Anne cried.

"I'm going to see Suzanne and straighten this out."

The nurse stepped into his path. "I don't think so, buddy. I'm starting to doubt you're even her fiancé. She'll be checking out soon and then you can talk to her on your own time."

"Fine." He spun around on his crutches and stumped for the exit. "Tell Suzanne I hope she feels better and I really, really look forward to finding out exactly what's up. Everyone else, stay away."

"Are you implying that she's making this all up?" Suddenly Rock was in his path. He glared at his father. "Son, we were out in that sailboat with her. She was throwing up and bleeding. It's lucky we were there because she wasn't thinking clearly. Something terrible could have happened to your baby."

"*Stop saying that.* This has *nothing to do with me.* It has nothing to do with you, either. Now let me out of here. Goddamn."

With a shake of his head, his father fell back to let him pass. He stormed out, the rubber tips of the crutches making loud squeaks on the linoleum floor.

But he still wasn't in the clear. He stalked to the sidewalk, toward the taxi stand where the cab had left him. And there was his mother, angrier than he'd ever seen her.

"Josh Marshall, you stop right there."

He stopped. Even though he wanted to flee, with every fiber of his body, this was his mother, after all. He stared at her stonily while she planted her hands on her hips.

"I know what's going on here. You're afraid. You love that girl."

"I'm not afraid. But it's not my baby." He tried to pass her, but she blocked his path again.

"You're *afraid*." She gave him a little shove in the chest. "You're afraid of getting ripped apart the way you were by all our fighting. The way you still are."

His jaw went so tight he couldn't have spoken if he'd tried.

"That's why you're afraid to love anyone again. Because let me tell you something, Joshua James Marshall. You were the sweetest, most loving little boy that was ever born. You loved us, you loved your brothers, you loved every single animal on the ranch. And you're still that loving boy, underneath that carefree, footloose act you try to pull. I understand why you're afraid. I know how much we hurt you with all our fighting. And I'm sorry. I'm sorry for it. But this is your life, buckaroo. You're the only one who can fix it."

He couldn't move, couldn't react, couldn't speak. His mother refused to look away, refused to let him pass.

When a taxi pulled up at the curb next to him, it might as well have been a rescue chopper. He dove into it and shut the door behind him.

Where now? Run...hide...what?

In a hoarse voice, he told the driver to head to the hotshot base.

CHAPTER 26

Suzanne wasn't generally a crier, but tears had started rolling down her cheeks as soon as she heard Josh say the words, "I'm not part of this." And then he kept going, and it got worse and worse. *I really look forward to finding out exactly what's up. I'm not father material...did Suzanne say it was? This has nothing to do with me.* Each sentence left scorch marks across her heart.

As she lay in the narrow hospital bed, an IV doling fluids into her system, she made herself repeat each of those lines to make sure she didn't forget.

Believe it, Suzanne. Remember it and believe it. He doesn't want any part of this. Why would he? It's not his baby and he knows it. He doesn't want his own baby, let alone someone else's.

The IV must be working, because the more she stewed over the things he'd said, the angrier she got. It was energizing, really. She felt rejuvenated and not at all foggy-brained anymore. Josh had run out of the clinic so fast, his crutches must have left skid marks. She didn't need that kind of attitude in her life. Screw Josh. Just because she was in love with him—yes, still, she had to admit it—didn't mean she was going to let him insult her.

The truth was, part of her had been fantasizing about a crazy scenario in which Josh loved her and wanted a life with her. One in which he embraced the idea of a baby and a family.

Well, now that fantasy had a giant crutch-sized stake through its heart. She'd heard every word Josh had said to his parents, and she'd also heard the panic in his voice. *Panic.* As if she was going to march out of the exam room and get her settling-down cooties all over him.

Yes, screw Josh Marshall. She didn't need him *or* Logan. She had her friends. She had the McGraws. She had the entire town of Jupiter Point. They'd helped her after her parents left town. They'd help her now too; that was what people here were like. She had her parents, who would probably kick in some savings bonds or something equally useless but well-intentioned. And she had her own savings. It was a good thing she hadn't bought Casa di Stella after all. Now she could use that money for a smaller, more manageable house.

Everything had worked out the way it was supposed to after all.

*

The clinic released her around dinnertime. Josh's parents reluctantly put her in a cab after she insisted she was fine. Ten minutes after she got back to her condo, all of Josh's stuff was packed into his duffel and sitting on her front stoop.

Snowball watched her with ears perked into full alert mode. "I'm sorry, Snowball, I know you love Josh. But you're going to have to stay with me. Josh has no business adopting a dog. I promise he can visit you, and you can visit him on the base. We'll work it out."

When she was done ejecting his stuff from her place, she scrawled a note and pinned it to the canvas material of his bag.

Saved you the trouble of packing. And yes, I did let you win at Monopoly.

Pretty childish, she had to admit. But, then again, she wasn't a full-fledged mother yet. Might as well get her juvenile behavior out of the way now, before a baby had to suffer from it.

She plopped onto the floor next to Snowball, who cocked her head and fixed bright, dark eyes on her. "The nurse said it's official, Snowball. Ten weeks. Ten whole weeks of a baby is living inside me. Can you believe it? I'm going to be a mother, and I'm going to do the best job I possibly can. Whatever it takes."

She scratched Snowball's head, thinking through all the things she needed to plan over the next seven months. PowerPoint city. So many details, so many plans...

But first—she swallowed hard. First, she needed to call her parents.

She dialed her mother's number, vaguely surprised when she got an answer. Generally she left a message and got a call back days later.

"Hi, Desiree. It's Suzanne. I...uh...have big news." She raced through her announcement, hoping her mother wouldn't notice the lack of a husband in her story.

"A *baby*. My little girl, with a baby." Desiree's dreamy tone didn't hold any judgment. "I think this is wonderful, Suzie."

"You do?"

"Of course I do." Suzanne heard rustling on the other end of the phone, and someone speaking in Spanish. "You'll be the *best* mother. Such a wonderful time in a woman's life."

"Do you think...I mean..." Suzanne screwed up every bit of her courage. "Any chance you could come back...you know, just for a bit, when...?" She couldn't finish the thought. Every time she suggested that her mom come back, the idea got shot down, right along with her heart.

"Oh honey, I'm not sure if that's a good idea—"

"You're right. Bad idea. Never mind. Anyway, I just wanted you to know. I'll send you belly pics as soon as I have some!" As chipper and cheerful as she could manage, she hung up.

So, not even a new baby would get her mother back to the States. She truly, truly was all alone. With a sob, she closed her eyes, a thousand images from her childhood cascading through her memory. She wanted to be back there in the sweet lost past having tea parties with her mother at Casa di Stella.

Casa di Stella.

One more part of her childhood about to be lost forever.

She opened her eyes and dashed her tears away. She was *not* a crier, goddamn it. Never had been, not about to start now. "Snowball, there's something I have to do before I never get another chance."

Snowball gave a little yip.

"Exactly right. How did you know? I need to do some stargazing at you-know-where. Sorry I can't take you, girl. I'm going to be trespassing, and I can't drag an innocent dog along while I commit a crime."

She grabbed a sweater and a flashlight, then stuffed her phone in her bag too, even thought it was practically dead after all the day's drama.

All she needed was one more night on the roof of Casa di Stella. She needed to say goodbye. And then the rest of her life would begin.

*

The fire and fescue compound was a ghost town except for a light on at the forest ranger's office. The two crew buggies were gone, as was one of the Ford Super Duty's. The other was parked in its usual spot, but somehow its presence made the lot seem all the more empty.

Josh roamed the hotshot's wing for a while—the mess hall, the kitchen, the barracks. It all looked so...small. As if it had shrunk while he'd been recuperating at Suzanne's. But of course it was small. It was a temporary way station between fires, not a home. And it felt so deserted.

He should do something. Occupy himself. He stumped into the storage cache and did a quick inventory. Nothing was out of place, nothing needed organizing. No new deliveries were waiting to be unloaded. Nothing to do, no one to talk to.

Damn, the quiet was getting to him. Thoughts kept crowding in. His father's words. *She was throwing up and bleeding. Something terrible could have happened.* The nurse's words. *Suzanne got dehydrated and disoriented.* Most of all, his mother's astonishing statements. *I'm sorry.... Most loving little boy in the world...You love that girl.*

Stop it. Damn. He needed a fucking distraction. Someone had to be on duty at the forest ranger's dispatch. They were staffed on a twenty-four hour basis during the summer.

He crutched out to the pavement and down to the squat concrete outbuilding where the forest ranger was located. It was a beautiful evening, the air as soft as velvet. He glanced up at the first brilliant points of light peppering the magnificent canvas of the night sky. For a moment, he simply stood and watched in wonder. This happened every night, this magical drama unfurling overhead. He usually ignored it. Too caught up in his own life.

You're afraid of getting ripped apart...this is your life, buckaroo.

Damn, here came those thoughts again. He shook himself and stumped into the forest ranger's office. The dispatcher, a fifty-ish woman named Lou, huddled over the receiver, which was turned up to full volume.

"Heya, Marsh," she greeted him. "You got here just in time."

"What's going on?"

The radio squawked and she held up a hand for him to be silent. Josh recognized the voice of one of the local Jupiter Point firefighters—Rabbit. "The eagle has landed! Got her through the door in the nick of time. All hands on deck can relax."

"What'd I miss?" Josh asked Lou.

"Rosario Peavy got trapped in an elevator at City Hall. The firefighters came to get her out, then she went into labor, and things got a little crazy. Sounds like they got her to the hospital just in time."

"Holy shit. Where's Tim?"

"Tim's been going nuts. He was at City Hall the whole time, talking her through it. Luckily she had her cell with her. They're both at the birthing center now."

"Is he okay?"

"She's a trooper. Never lost her cool once." Lou grinned. "Can't say the same for the menfolk. I didn't know Tim Peavy could swear that creatively."

She held up her hand as the radio began emitting the staticky sound that meant more information was coming.

"Quick update before we free up this channel." It was Chief Littleton. "The Peavys have a new baby. A little girl named Jocelyn. Everyone is healthy and passes along their thanks for all the help. We might have to scrape Tim off the floor, but he'll recover. Thanks for the good work, everyone. Now back to work." He clicked off the emergency channel.

A lump formed in Josh's throat. He had a namesake. A little girl named in honor of him. Jocelyn Peavy. Tim must be a nervous wreck. Imagine your wife being trapped inside an elevator with a baby coming. If that was Suzanne...

A horrifying series of images flashed through his mind, all his parents' words rushing back to him. Suzanne, throwing up and bleeding...dehydrated...*something terrible could have happened*... Suzanne falling overboard...tripping over a rope and hitting her head. Suzanne, unconscious. Hurt. Lost. Her bright spirit gone forever.

He stumped outside, nearly stumbling on the threshold with his crutches. The evening air embraced him, but it didn't feel comforting this time. It held a chill, like a warning, from the ocean. All the twilight color had disappeared from the night sky and the stars shone with icy brilliance.

Suzanne could have been in serious trouble out there on the water. If anything had happened to her...

God.

Suzanne. He loved her.

He *loved her.*

And he'd screwed everything up.

CHAPTER 27

Suzanne saw no signs of construction at Casa di Stella yet. That was a relief—it meant she didn't have to worry about a security guard stopping by or workers putting in overtime. She parked in the courtyard and jogged to the front door, which was locked.

Not a problem. She knew every nook and cranny of Casa di Stella, including the kitchen window that never quite closed properly. She climbed onto a garbage can and slipped inside. The infusion of fluids had done its job and she felt no sign of the exhaustion and lightheadedness she'd experienced on the *That's Amore*.

In fact, she felt crystal clear. About everything.

She practically ran up the spiral staircase to the third floor and pushed open the trapdoor that led to the attic. A ladder was built into the door; all you had to do was pull it out once the door was open. She climbed into the attic, just as she had a thousand times as a little girl. In the attic, another hidden door led to a tiny balcony. From there, it was just a few steps up an old fire escape to the stargazing platform.

Mrs. Chu had closed off the platform, most likely as a safety issue. She was probably too much of a rule-follower to enjoy a platform that wasn't built to code. But Suzanne had no problem shoving aside the barrier the former owner had installed.

Suzanne pulled herself onto the platform and lay back with a satisfied sigh. The vast array of brilliant heavenly bodies seemed to smile down on her. "Hello, old friends," she whispered. "Long time, no gaze."

The stars shimmered and sparkled. She kept talking, almost as if the stars were listening. They seemed so close, so friendly. As if they really wanted to hear what she had to say. Even though she knew it was slightly ridiculous, she didn't care. "I wanted my baby to experience this place, because there most likely won't be another chance. I tried to buy this house, I tried really hard. It just wasn't meant to be. But I promise that my baby and I will do plenty of stargazing. Also beachcombing, and hunting for sea glass. Playing make-believe. Building fairy houses in the woods. Picking apples, carving pumpkins."

She fell silent, all the wonderful memories of her childhood swarming in. The childhood from before the market crash that led to the collapse of everything else. So many of her happy memories took place here in this whimsical old castle. Maybe she'd wanted Casa di Stella so much as a way of recreating what she'd lost. But did she need a building for that?

Maybe what she needed already existed in her own heart—and belly.

"I'm going to stick with my baby no matter what," she told the stars. "I will never leave him or her behind. I promise you that, stars as my witness."

The constellations twinkled back at her. She spotted a satellite in orbit.

"Know what else? Even though none of this is happening the way I planned, that's okay. I'm fine with that. Actually, I love it. Because I'm going to have a baby and that's...really great." The night breeze swept over her skin, giving her a little chill. She hugged her arms around her front, glad she'd brought a sweater.

She fell silent and listened to the rustle of the wind in the treetops, such a familiar sound from when she used to sleep in the turret bedroom. The cypresses had grown so tall since she'd been gone. They reached almost as high as the platform.

Then an odd noise caught her attention. She went still, listening hard.

There it came again. Furtive footsteps across the cobblestones of the courtyard.

Something about the sound put her on guard. Maybe it was the slow pace, as if the person was stopping every few minutes to make sure they were alone. The step had a deliberate lightness, as if the intruder was trying not to make any noise.

She opened her mouth to call down to the stranger, then thought better of it. After all, she was trespassing. And she was alone here. What if it was a burglar who didn't know the house wasn't empty? What if they decided to climb up to the platform and take her purse? Shivering, she dug into her bag and pulled out her phone. She'd turned it off to preserve the battery, and saw that she'd missed several calls. Josh's father, his mother, and Josh had all called.

Even though she was mad at Josh, she wouldn't mind getting his help right now. She pressed redial, but before the call could go through, her phone died. Great.

She sucked in a long breath. What next? She crawled on her belly to the edge of the platform and peered in the direction of the footsteps. Three stories down, she spotted a dark blob next to the house. Was that a person or a rose bush? Or a person *in* the rose bush? What was he doing? Looking for a key? Stopping to smell the roses?

And what was that weird smell?

She sniffed, her nostrils prickling. It smelled like a gas station.

Then several things happened at once. A flame flared to life, then another. The dry vines of ivy caught fire. The dark figure rose to his feet and jogged across the cobblestones toward the pillared entrance of the drive.

And Suzanne realized she was completely screwed.

*

Josh had called Suzanne, but gotten no answer. He was about to call a cab when his phone rang. Not Suzanne, though—it was his father. "Son, just wanted to tell you we're heading out of town. We're at Suzanne's place right now. Wanted to check on her and say goodbye. You might want to get over here."

His gut clenched. "Why? Is she okay?"

"She's not here, and your stuff's sitting outside. But there's a dog in here barking its head off. Sounds like something's wrong. We tried calling Suzanne's cell but didn't get an answer."

"Okay, Pop. I'll take care of it." Josh hesitated. His parents had taken care of Suzanne in her moment of need. They'd gotten her to the clinic, and he hadn't even thanked them. In fact, he'd been a dick. As maddening as they were—as crazy-making, as frustrating—they had very possibly saved Suzanne and her baby. "Listen, uh...I was a little thrown back there at the clinic. Never thanked you guys for taking care of Suzanne. So, uh...thanks."

Rock paused before answering. "It was our pleasure, Josh. Kind of brought us together, in a way. Your mother was a champ out there. I'm not saying we're getting back together, so don't get your hopes up. But we're going to drive back in the old Caddy together and try to figure out a way to show a little more respect to each other."

Would a "hallelujah" offend his dad? "That...uh...sounds like a good plan, Pop. Good luck and drive safe. If things get heated, pull over."

"Roger that. See ya next time, son."

For the first time, that prospect didn't fill Josh with terror.

But right now, he had a bigger worry. It would take a cab at least half an hour to get out here. Snowball wasn't a dog who barked at nothing. If she was upset, there must be a really good reason why. He stumped back to the hotshot area and grabbed the Super Duty keys from the pegboard. The Super Duty was an automatic shift, so he ought to be able to handle it.

It was too awkward trying to switch his good foot back and forth between the pedals, but he worked out a two-footed method that was jerky as hell. With his left foot hovering over the brake, he used his cast to press the accelerator. He tried not to think about the potential damage being done to his healing bone. Pressing down was one of those motions he was supposed to avoid.

But bones could heal. If Suzanne was in trouble, it was worth the risk.

By the time he reached the city limits, he had the technique down pretty well, though his leg was sending him a constant dull message of protest. It was a good thing he'd spent big chunks of his life doing PT. He knew how to manage pain.

At Suzanne's condo, he found exactly what his father had described. His duffel sat outside, with a note pinned to it. When he read it, he had to laugh—and wince. As he'd feared, Suzanne had overheard his rant at the clinic. And she'd responded in a perfectly Suzanne way. He had to find her and apologize...no, he had to grovel. Beg her to give him another chance. Tell her how much he loved her.

He stuffed the note in his pocket and unlocked the condo. Snowball came hurtling toward him.

"Hey girl, hey there, what's the matter? Do you need a little pee break? Come on out here on the grass. Come on, that's a good girl."

But she had no interest in peeing. She danced around him, giving little nips and barks.

"Are you hungry?" He peered through the door toward the kitchen. Her food bowl was overflowing. Definitely not hungry.

"Something's obviously bugging you, girl, but I have no idea what."

He pulled out his phone and dialed Suzanne's number again. No answer. He shot her a text, but got no response.

When he looked up from his phone, he saw Snowball was gone.

He looked around in bewilderment, finally locating her next to the Super Duty. Waiting for him, alert and ready as a soldier.

He stumped to the truck and opened the passenger-side door. She jumped into the seat and cocked her head at him. Grumbling, he went around to the driver's side. "It would help if I had any clue where to go. You want me to just randomly drive around Jupiter Point looking for her?"

Snowball gave a little bark.

"I know, I know, I'm talking to a dog like you can understand." He thought for a moment. "She's probably with a friend."

He called Evie, only to get the news that Evie was with Brianna, and neither of them had seen Suzanne. He called the *Mercury News-Gazette*, figuring Merry would be working late. She was, of course, but she hadn't seen Suzanne either.

A persistent sense of dread grew in his heart. Was she with her friends from the Y, the ones who were helping her with the shelter project? He didn't have their phone numbers, but his gut told him that Suzanne probably wasn't with them. In the course of one day, she'd been violently sick on a sailboat, gotten rushed to a clinic, and dumped all his stuff on her doorstep. She probably wasn't following that up with a shelter-planning session.

Where would Suzanne go to seek comfort?

The answer was so fucking obvious he slammed his hand into the steering wheel, causing Snowball to startle.

Casa di Stella, of course. Her childhood home, the place she'd spent years dreaming about. The place she was about to lose forever.

He jammed the key in the ignition and slammed his throbbing foot into the accelerator.

Snowball seemed to get more and more agitated the closer they got to the beautiful rolling hills of the subdivision where Casa di Stella was located. Something was definitely wrong. The back of his neck was prickling, goose bumps were rising on his arms. It was the same feeling he got at the first hint of smoke from a wildfire. He rolled down the window and sniffed.

Yup. Smoke. And it was coming from the direction of Casa di Stella.

He drove like a madman the rest of the way, which was only a few more turns. Finally, there it was, like a grand old lady at a Victorian tea party. Except now the lady was wearing a skirt of fire.

Flames surrounded the entire base of the quirky old structure. And at the very top, just behind the turrets, a figure jumped up and down, waving her arms and yelling over the crackling of the blaze.

Suzanne.

CHAPTER 28

Suzanne recognized the hotshots' big Ford truck right away as it drove into the cobblestone courtyard. Was it Josh? Had to be! She jumped up and down on the platform and waved her arms and yelled.

The door flew open and Josh tumbled out of the vehicle, practically flying on his crutches. Snowball leaped out after him.

He stopped and shooed Snowball back into the truck. Good call—it would be hard to keep her out of harm's way. It would be hard to keep Josh out of harm's way too, but he was a trained firefighter.

On crutches.

With no firefighting gear.

Wait. He was doing something in the back of the Super Duty. When he emerged again, he wore a bulky padded jacket and a helmet.

At least it was something. He closed the door, enclosing Snowball inside, then swung toward the house at a rapid pace, phone to his ear. Probably calling 9-1-1. Thank God. She prayed the fire department would come quickly. The fire was building so fast, it was crazy. The flames were gobbling up the dry ivy and old shingles.

Fear tightened her throat. There were only two ways down from this platform. She could go back into the attic and down the stairs or she could try to climb down the outside. She went to the edge and peered over. What if she tried to jump to one of the trees? What if she missed? Even if she didn't miss, how hard would it be to climb all the way down a tall cypress tree? What if it caught fire while she was making her way down?

Oh God.

Josh yelled something, but she couldn't hear him over the roar of the flames. She shrugged her shoulders in a gesture as exaggerated as she could make it, and shook her head from side to side. He came closer and yelled again.

"Say you're a car!"

Say you're a car? That made no sense. Oh—of course. Stay where you are.

"Are you sure?" She yelled back.

He returned her shrugging gesture from before. It was probably even harder for him to hear her, with the wind snatching her words away. Then she remembered something—the sound-traveling effect she and her friends used to play with. The whole house was riddled with speaking vents, including a gutter that ran along the edge of the roof and acted as a sort of megaphone, broadcasting sound over the lawn. She crawled to the corner of the gutter and lay on her belly.

"Hi, Josh. Can you hear me?"

Josh gave a little jump of response. He made a megaphone of his own hands and yelled up to her. "Yes. Can you hear me?"

She nodded vigorously. "Did you call the fire department?"

"Yes. Don't go anywhere. Rescue chopper coming."

"How long?"

"Soon." His voice was rough and strained as he shouted over the sound of the flames. "Just stay calm."

Stay calm. Right. Her gaze clung to his tall, wide-shouldered frame. It was totally selfish of her, but it helped that he was here. But what if he got hurt? She couldn't bear that. "Be careful," she yelled through the gutter. "You're too close to the flames."

"I'm okay. Don't worry about me. I do this for a living."

"You won't leave?"

"I won't leave until that chopper comes. But I might take a step back." There, a hint of the usual Josh playfulness. It took the edge off her fear.

"You won't leave?" She heard the pleading note in her voice, like a childlike sob, but couldn't help it. She hated being left behind.

"Pinkie promise." He grinned, and at that moment, she loved Josh so much she thought she might burst. "Even if you kicked me out, I wouldn't leave."

"I'm sorry." She choked up at the thought of how she'd ejected his things from her condo. "I'm sorry about the note."

"I deserved it. I was an ass." He yelled that word with extra-loud emphasis. "Do me a favor, Suzanne."

"What?"

"I can't kneel because of my broken leg. Can you use your imagination?"

Kneel? What was he talking about?

"Can you picture me kneeling?" he repeated.

"Okay, but Josh, this house is about to burn down and I really don't have time for make-believe right now and—"

The wind swirled a flame in Josh's direction. He took a big step backwards and nearly stumbled over a garden gnome.

"Josh!" she screamed, horror sweeping through her. What if he hit his head? What if he got knocked out and burned alive?

But Josh regained his balance in a matter of seconds. "Humor me," he yelled. "Please. Just keep your eyes on me. Don't think about the flames. I only have a short window before the chopper gets here."

"Okay, okay." Tears were running down her face. Plan B, Plan B...if Josh got knocked out, she'd run down the stairs and take her chances with the fire. She'd drag him out to his truck. She'd—

"Suzanne, can you hear me?"

"Yes!"

"I love you! I love you with all my heart and soul and I want to marry you."

She let out a strange mutant sound somewhere between a sob and a laugh.

He cupped his hands around his mouth again and yelled it more loudly. "Did you hear me? I want to be with you. Together. You, me and your baby."

"You're crazy!" she yelled into the gutter. "You don't want that stuff. You said so."

"I was wrong. Everything's different now. I love you!"

This was insane. Maybe she was having delusions because of dehydration or pregnancy hormones or smoke. This couldn't be happening. Josh couldn't actually be here yelling up at her like some kind of Romeo on crutches.

But, if it wasn't real, what harm could there be in telling him how she felt?

"I love you too," she called into the gutter. "I'm crazy head over heels in love with you!"

He must have heard, because his face lit up. The effect was amplified by the vivid orange glow from the leaping flames.

"Is that a yes?" he hollered.

Before she could answer, a low whirring drowned her out. A wicked wind whipped her clothes against her body. She looked up to see the belly of a helicopter hovering overhead, a blur of blades pinning it against the dark sky. A man in some kind of harness dropped toward her. She started to get up, but he gestured at her to stay where she was.

She looked back down at Josh, who was watching the whole process with close attention. He seemed oblivious to any danger he might be in. He kept his gaze fixed on her, his crutches planted on the grass, unmoved by the crazy chaos of flames between him and her. Out on the street, she saw lights flashing from two big fire engines zooming into view. Even over the *thump-thump* of the helicopter's blades, she heard the reassuring sound of the trucks' sirens.

Her eyes stung from the smoke saturating the air. Tears sprang into her eyes. She blinked and coughed, eyes stinging. With the smoke and the chopper and the sirens, it felt like the end of the world. In a way, it was—her childhood home was burning down, her former dreams along with it. The past was evaporating in a vortex of smelly smoke.

Firefighters in full bunker gear jogged from the fire engines. One of them came up to Josh, clearly trying to get him out of there. He shook his head firmly, but he did step back, well out of the reach of the flames.

A sob racked her body. Even though rescue was here, firefighters with engines and hoses and a helicopter to snatch her away, Josh wasn't leaving. He was keeping his promise to stay with her to the end.

The man from the helicopter landed next to her and crouched at her side. "I'm going to fasten this harness around you," he shouted over the din. "Then we'll get you out of here. You ready?"

She looked back at Josh. Leaning on his crutches, he gave her a big thumb's up. Then he flapped his wings like a bird. Funny guy.

When she looked back at her rescuer, she was smiling. "I'm ready."

"Is anyone inside the house?"

"No." The man who had set the fire was long gone, and the house had been empty when she got there. The fire-fighter relayed that information into his helmet mic, then set to work.

He wrapped the harness around her and clipped it into place. He attached the carabiner to the same cable he was using. Then he made a hand gesture to the chopper up above. Slowly, the helicopter rose higher above the plat-form. With a jerk, Suzanne felt herself being lifted up. She clung to the firefighter as they swooped through the smoky air. Wind pummeled her face, making her eyes water.

She looked down at Casa di Stella, shocked to see that the back gazebo was already collapsing. A long ladder ex-tended from one of the fire engines. A firefighter perched on a platform at its tip and aimed a stream of water at the flames, but it seemed so hopeless. The entire structure was disintegrating before her eyes.

Goodbye, dear sweet home. Goodbye. Tears streaming down her face, she watched her beloved building recede beneath her.

And then she looked again for Josh. Craning her neck, she spotted him off to the side, gaze still fixed on her. He blew her a kiss with a wide swing of his arm.

Wait...she hadn't answered his question!

CHAPTER 29

The Jupiter Point firefighters told Josh they were taking Suzanne to the clinic to get checked for smoke inhalation. Exhaustion—an adrenaline crash—dragged at him as he steered the Super Duty across town. For the entire drive, Snowball bounced up and down in the seat next to him.

"I don't even know how you knew Suzanne was in trouble," he told her. "You are by far the best dog in the world. You probably saved Suzanne's life."

He shuddered at the thought of what could have happened if he hadn't called in the chopper. Or if his parents hadn't called to let him know Snowball was barking like crazy. "You, my friend, are getting doggie treats for the rest of your life." He scratched between her ears until she wriggled with joy.

For the second time that day, he walked into the clinic looking for Suzanne. As he passed the spot where he'd heard the news about Suzanne's baby—and had acted like an idiot—he gave himself a mental reminder. *Don't be an ass, Marsh. Don't let Mom and Pop's fucked-up relationship ruin everything. It's your life, buckaroo.*

Amazingly, the same nurse midwife was on duty. Ms. Johannsen scowled at him. "You again?"

"Yes. But this time I really do have a right to be here."

"So now you really are Suzanne's fiancé?"

Well, he'd proposed on imaginary bended knee. She'd said she loved him. Crazy head over heels in love, were her exact words. But she hadn't ever said yes. "Um...maybe?"

She raised a skeptical eyebrow. "You're going to have to do better than that."

"I love her. I want to marry her. She says she loves me. I proposed to her and she was just about to say yes when some other man dropped from the sky and took her away in a helicopter. Does that count?"

Her mouth twitched. "I'll ask if she wants to see you."

It was a big relief when she came back with a "follow me."

Inside the curtained space, Suzanne was sitting on the edge of a hospital bed talking to a pair of investigators. Her eyes had dark shadows under them; she looked just as exhausted as he felt. She beckoned him to her side and took his hand, urging him onto the bed next to her. He sat down gratefully. His leg was one solid ache by now. As she interlaced her fingers with his, a knot of tension dissolved inside him. She was okay. She was right here. Next to him. He wasn't going to let anything mess with that, ever again.

He recognized Police Chief Becker, who had tangled with Sean Marcus back in the day. Since that time, they'd grown to be good friends. The tall, imposing African-American nodded hello, then gestured for Suzanne to continue.

"I couldn't see who it was, just someone dressed all in black. Tall, though. Definitely a man. He seemed like he knew what he was doing."

"And you smelled gas?" the other investigator, who wore a Jupiter Point Fire Department t-shirt, was taking notes. "You're sure about that?"

"Pretty sure. Yes. It made my nose prickle, and the same thing always happens to me at the gas station."

"Wait a minute," Josh broke in. "You're saying someone deliberately set that house on fire?"

"We're not saying anything yet," Becker answered. "We're just asking questions."

He looked at Suzanne, then at the investigators, then back at Suzanne. "You told them who owns it now?"

She gave a small, miserable nod, and wiped a tear away from the corner of her eye. "They'll figure out who did it. I bet I know what happened. He realized it would cost a fortune to renovate it into vacation rentals and that he'd have to get permits and all that. He must have decided to cut his losses and get the insurance money."

Becker unfolded himself from the chair and rose to his full six-foot-seven-inch height. "No need to speculate, Ms. Finnegan. We'll find out what happened. I think we have what we need. Thanks for your time." He glanced at Josh. "How about you, Marshall? You okay?"

"Sure," he managed. A jolt of excruciating pain flashed through his leg. He hid his wince behind a wry smile. "Long night."

As soon as the officers were gone, Suzanne threw her arms around Josh and burst into tears. "I can't believe I was with someone who would do such a thing! He knew how much I loved that house."

He held her close and murmured into her hair, "I'm just glad you're okay. Do you know what it was like watching you up on that roof? Worst moments of my life."

She sobbed against his chest for a while. He stayed with her, inhaling the smoky scent clinging to her hair, and the fresh, *alive* fragrance underneath that. He wanted to take her home and put her in the bathtub. Cover her in soapsuds and massage her sore muscles until she moaned. The image gave him so much pleasure that he drifted into a half-waking, half-sleeping fantasy.

He and Suzanne, hiding under the covers, skin against naked skin, whispering secrets, with nothing to hide, nothing to fear, together forever...

He was pulled out of his trance by the sound of her voice. "Josh! Didn't you hear what I just said?"

"Oh. No. Sorry, I think I fell asleep for a second." He rolled his neck, trying to wake himself up. "What did you say?"

She poked him in the ribs. "Remember how you proposed to me? On imaginary bended knee?"

"Yeah, I remember."

"I was trying to answer you. Then I heard you snoring."

"Snoring? No way. This is the most important moment of my life, how could I possibly snore? Go on. Answer the question."

She turned to face him fully, her eyes deep and serious. He couldn't read her expression, couldn't predict how she'd answer. "What about everything you said before? You didn't want marriage and family and children. You didn't even want a home address."

He marshaled his thoughts, hoping they'd make sense once he laid them at her mercy. "I was running. Fooling myself. I thought all I needed was freedom and a fun time. And then I fell in love with you, Suzanne. Everything's different now. I want you, I want a life with you. I want a family with you."

Tears misted her beautiful blue eyes. "Are you sure?"

"I'm so sure. And I'm also sure that you need me, because who else is going to be the fun parent? I hate to say this, but PowerPoints aren't any fun for kids."

She burst out laughing and blotted a tear from her cheek. "I see what you mean, and that's a really good point. So I guess the answer is—"

The curtain whipped open and Nurse Johannsen strode in.

"Oh for Pete's sake, I'm fine!" Suzanne rolled her eyes. "And I'm in the middle of something. Can you give us a second?"

The nurse shook her head firmly and headed for Josh. "Chief Becker says Josh here looks like he's hurting and ought to be checked out. You have a broken leg, right?"

"Yes, but that doesn't matter right now—"

Ignoring him, she picked up his wrist to check his pulse. "Your pupils are dilated, your pulse thready. How's your pain on a scale of one to ten?"

"About a twelve and a half," he admitted. The nurse shook her head and pulled out her pager. "We need to X-ray your leg."

"But—"

Suzanne gasped and slid off the hospital bed. "Josh Marshall, I can't believe you didn't tell me you were in pain while I'm babbling on."

"I want you to babble. I want you to answer."

"You're crazy. You can't just go around proposing to people when you're having a medical crisis."

Two medical types in scrubs came into the room. They seemed to know what they were doing—which was to take charge of him and drag him away from Suzanne.

"Just say yes!" he called as they helped him onto a gurney. "I don't want to lose consciousness until I hear a yes."

Suzanne skipped alongside the gurney as they wheeled it out of the exam room and down the hall. "Shouldn't we talk it over a little more? We should talk about the baby. Are you really ready to have a baby?"

"Honey, I'm just getting an X-ray," he told her. "I'm not having a baby."

He heard a few laughs from the orderlies pushing the gurney. Suzanne rolled her eyes. "Only you could make jokes at a time like this."

They approached the double doors that led to the operating room. "Wait. We're not finished. Answer the question," he called to her as she stopped outside the doors and the gurney kept going.

The last thing he heard was, "Yes! The answer is yes!" before the doors slid shut.

For a guy who'd never planned on proposing, he'd totally aced it.

CHAPTER 30

The first work party to turn the old Turner farm into the Star Bright Shelter for Teens took place in November, By then, Josh was off his crutches but still using a cane. That didn't stop him from acting like he was in charge, Suzanne noticed. iPad in hand, he hustled around the property. She'd set him up with a multitude of PowerPoints—a volunteer schedule, a task list, fundraising target goals. Since she was five months along in her pregnancy and just starting to show, he wanted to do everything he could to make things easier on her.

As a good husband should.

"I still haven't forgiven you," Brianna murmured in her ear. Dressed in her usual work uniform of grubby overalls and straw hat, she was directing a crew of girls putting in a vegetable garden. "I had the flowers all picked out for your wedding. Stargazer lilies and Blaze of Fire salvia."

"I'm sorry to break your garden-nerd heart, but we were in a hurry. We aren't even doing a honeymoon. And I spent years planning other people's. It's funny how things turn out."

"It's all right," Evie smiled as she joined them. "I'm going to give you free rein at our wedding, Bri." She put an arm around Suzanne and gave her a little hug. "In return, I call first godmother."

"First godmother? Is that a thing?"

"I don't see why not. You have a few contenders."

Suzanne grinned at her friends. That was true. All of her friends were excited about the baby coming—and about the Star Bright Shelter. Merry was interviewing the volunteers for an article in the newspaper. Cindy and the others from the Y had been working their butts off all day. But Brianna—Brianna probably deserved more thanks than anyone.

"None of this would be happening without you, Bri." Suzanne smiled affectionately at her redheaded friend. "I can't believe you managed to talk that old farmer into selling. He's the biggest grouch in the world."

"I have hidden powers of persuasion." Brianna mimed brushing lint off her overalls. "It's because I'm so diplomatic and such a smooth talker." They all had to laugh at that one. Of all the ways Bri could be described, diplomatic wasn't one of them. "Speaking of smooth talkers, what's the latest on Logan?"

"Well, police arrested the guy who set the fire and the police found a wire transfer to him from Logan. Logan's facing criminal charges, which means his law career is in jeopardy. But the Rossi family has deep pockets, so who knows."

"He should pay for what he did!" Bri bristled with indignation.

"Of course he should. But you know what, I'm going to focus on the good things about Logan." He was her baby's biological father, after all. "Maybe he'll learn from this whole stupid thing."

Evie smiled kindly at her, but Brianna rolled her eyes. "You're a lot nicer than I am. If he ever comes back to Jupiter Point, I have a few garden tools I'm not afraid to use." She glanced around at the crowds. "So where are the rest of the hotshots?"

Suzanne exchanged an amused glance with Evie. "Why do you ask? Is there one in particular you're wondering about?"

"No." Brianna flushed a deep beet red.

"Maybe...Rollo? The big, hunky bear with a trust fund, who you're always hanging out with?" She had a soft spot for Rollo because he was the one who had rescued Josh in Yellowstone. Only someone of his caliber would be worthy of Brianna.

"What? No! You know we're just really great friends." A mischievous expression crossed her freckled face. "Actually, I'm pretty sure Rollo has his eye on Merry. I've seen him watching her."

"Ooooh." Suzanne hadn't noticed *that* undercurrent. But she wouldn't be surprised. Merry was beautiful and intelligent and a little mysterious, too. But she was very focused on her job and had never seemed impressed by the whole hero-firefighter thing.

She changed the subject before Brianna got too uncomfortable.

"Well, back to your question about where they all are to-day, there's big news, as a matter of fact."

"Big news?" Merry joined them, notepad already in hand. "Something I can share with the *Mercury News-Gazette?* We're desperate for news these days."

"It's about that movie, *Miracle in Big Canyon*. The hotshots who were in the burnover are being interviewed by the movie studio right now. And guess what? Finn Abrams is in town."

"Finn? The one who ran away from the others?" Merry jotted that down. "He's pretty controversial. I'm surprised he's even here."

"Apparently he was burned pretty badly," Evie said. "Part of his face, I heard?"

"It's not that bad," Brianna burst out.

Everyone turned to look at her.

"You've met Finn?" Suzanne asked in surprise.

That same beet-red color spread across Brianna's cheeks. "It's a long story."

"We have time," Merry said promptly.

"Nothing but time," agreed Evie.

"I just think people should be more thoughtful about someone who nearly died in a fire, and people shouldn't jump to conclusions and think they know what really happened when there's a lot more to the story, and—"

In the middle of Brianna's intriguing explanation, Suzanne caught sight of Josh gesturing to her. He had a playful grin on his face, and the fact was, she could never resist his smile.

"Sorry, girls, gotta go check in with my husband," she told her friends. "And yes, I do love saying that."

The other women laughed. She waved and headed for the wildly attractive fireman she'd married two weeks ago.

"Hey, babe," Josh said, yanking her close as soon as she was within range. "I'm doing all this hard work for free, the least you could do is throw me a kiss now and then."

She rose up on tiptoe and peppered kisses along his stubbly jawline. His hair brushed against her face and his laughing gray eyes gazed into hers.

"That's more like it," he murmured. He put his hand to her lower back, which had been bothering her lately, and smoothed out the tight muscles. "You hanging in there?"

"Better now." She snuggled against him. Being with him always made her feel better. "Where's Snowball?"

"Doing that thing she does. Shepherding people where she wants them to go."

"She knows best." They shared a smile. "Josh, there's something I've been wanting to say to you."

"If you want to take back your 'yes,' it's a little too late."

She swatted him on the arm. "Of course not. I nabbed you fair and square, and I'm not letting you go."

"Fair and square? You call scaring the life out of me fair and square? Your tactics were pretty low, if you ask me."

"Whatever it takes, hotshot. Results don't lie." She pressed another kiss onto the corner of his mouth, then got down to business. "But seriously. Josh, I know this is all a huge change for you. I don't want you to feel...you know, trapped." She cringed as she said the word that brought back so many bad memories. "If you need to take some time for yourself, maybe a trip to Fiji or New Zealand, or whatever...safari...hike Mount Everest...we have four months before the baby comes. I don't want you to feel stuck here in Jupiter Point."

His smiled dropped as he studied her face. "You're serious."

"Yes. Very serious. Your whole life has changed in a very short time. You probably have whiplash."

"Well," he said slowly. "Here's the thing. I didn't plan to meet you. I didn't plan to fall in love. I didn't plan any of this. But I've never been much of a planner. It's like in firefighting. No matter how much you work things out ahead of time, no matter how hard you train, you have to work the fire you're in. Well, Mrs. Josh Marshall, you're the fire. And I'm in. All in."

She hugged him, tears stinging her eyes. God, her hormones were out of control. How did women get through nine months without crying nonstop? "I really love you, Josh. It's crazy how much. I never thought I could love someone the way I love you." She sniffed. "I seriously thought my biggest passion in life was going to be Casa di Stella."

They shared a moment of sadness for her childhood home, which had burned nearly to the ground. The ivy was already growing over the remains of the foundation in a tumbling, romantic way.

"I'm sorry you didn't get your dream," Josh murmured in her ear. "I'm really sorry. But you can just forget about me going anywhere right now. I have no intention of missing a single minute of the next four months. Or the next lifetime, for that matter. There isn't a single tropical island, back-country trek, or surf break out there that could tempt me away from you."

Her sorrow over the fire evaporated in the face of his heartfelt words. This man was her future, her days and nights, her sunshine and starlight. Her life shimmered before her, wide open and filled with joy. She smiled up at Josh, feeling as if stars were bursting inside her, turning the whole world bright as dawn. "I have news for you, my love. I did get my dream. This is it."

She waved at the wonderful scene around her, then put her hand on his chest, feeling the steady beat of his heart.

"My dream is right here, right now, with you. Just the way I didn't exactly plan it."

ABOUT THE AUTHOR

Jennifer Bernard is a *USA Today* bestselling author of contemporary romance. Her books have been called "an irresistible reading experience" full of "quick wit and sizzling love scenes." A graduate of Harvard and former news promo producer, she left big city life in Los Angeles for true love in Alaska, where she now lives with her husband and stepdaughters. She still hasn't adjusted to the cold, so most often she can be found cuddling with her laptop and a cup of tea. No stranger to book success, she also writes erotic novellas under a naughty secret name that she's happy to share with the curious. You can learn more about Jennifer and her books at JenniferBernard.net.

Drive You Wild
Crushing It

34758030R00222

Made in the USA
San Bernardino, CA
04 May 2019